# ONION STREET

## a Moe Prager Mystery

# REED FARREL COLEMAN

TYRUS
BOOKS

F+W Media, Inc.

Published by
TYRUS BOOKS
an imprint of F+W Media, Inc.
10151 Carver Road, Suite 200
Blue Ash, Ohio 45242 U.S.A.
www.tyrusbooks.com

Hardcover ISBN 10: 1-4405-3945-6
Hardcover ISBN 13: 978-1-4405-3945-9
Trade Paperback ISBN 10: 1-4405-3946-4
Trade Paperback ISBN 13: 978-1-4405-3946-6
eISBN 10: 1-4405-6117-6
eISBN 13: 978-1-4405-6117-7

Printed in the United States of America.

10   9   8   7   6   5   4   3   2   1

*This book is available at quantity discounts for bulk purchases.*
*For information, please call 1-800-289-0963.*

# ALSO BY REED FARREL COLEMAN

*Gun Church*

*Tower* with Ken Bruen

Dylan Klein:
*Life Goes Sleeping*
*Little Easter*
*They Don't Play Stickball in Milwaukee*

Joe Serpe:
*Hose Monkey*
*The Fourth Victim*

Moe Prager:
*Walking the Perfect Square*
*Redemption Street*
*The James Deans*
*Soul Patch*
*Empty Ever After*
*Innocent Monster*
*Hurt Machine*

Gulliver Dowd:
*Dirty Work*

Detective John Roe (ret):
*Bronx Requiem*

*For Ben LeRoy*

# ACKNOWLEDGMENTS

I would like to thank Ben LeRoy, David Hale Smith, and the late David Thompson for their faith in me.

A nod to Sara J. Henry, Ellen W. Schare, and Peter Spiegelman. As always, thanks to Judy B. But mostly to Rosanne, Kaitlin, and Dylan. Without them, none of this would be worth it.

"Look around the table. If you don't see a sucker, get up, because you're the sucker."

—"Amarillo Slim" Preston, poker champ

# PROLOGUE –
# DECEMBER 2012, BROOKLYN

Some men are born to die. Some, like Bobby Friedman, are just so full of life that you can't imagine death will ever touch them. Even as I sat in front of his coffin and his rabbi told story after story of Bobby's mischievous spirit and seemingly boundless generosity, I couldn't quite accept the fact of his death. Like any of us who knew Bobby, I assumed he would be eighteen forever. During the worst of my treatments, when all I wanted to do was surrender to death, I'd sometimes amuse myself by thinking of the eulogy Bobby would have delivered at my funeral. Now here I was at his.

"What are you smiling at, Dad?" Sarah leaned over and whispered.

Although death had been so much on my mind over the months since my diagnosis, I wasn't sure I could explain my smile in a way she'd have understood it. I wasn't sure I understood it completely. Instead of answering, I winked and put my finger across my lips. *Shhhhh!*

I was done with my treatments for the time being, but the surgery and the chemo had left me a frail shell of my old self: ashen and skeletal. I tired easily and I was still too weak to be trusted behind the wheel of a car, so Sarah had come down from Vermont to take me to the funeral. She said she wanted to come visit anyway. We had things to discuss, she said. I didn't like the sound of that.

I dreaded the day she would ask me to move up to Vermont with Paul and her.

"Surely," said the rabbi, "it is no wonder to any of us who loved Robert that, of all things, it was his heart to finally succumb. There is only so much in a man to give, but how many of us truly give everything we have? Even the most charitable among us hold back a little in reserve. Not our Robert. Wherever his journey takes him now, he will go there having held nothing back. God will look Robert in the eyes and be proud of his creation. I will miss him, I think, more than I could have imagined. I already do."

Of course, only a few guys from our days at Brooklyn College had any notion of the genesis of Bobby's generosity, and now I was the only one left. Crowded as the chapel was, there weren't many faces familiar to me. None of the old gang was there: some already dead, most just gone. Dead or not, gone is gone. It's what happens to friends: they fall away. Time erodes them into fine grains of powder carried by the wind to alien places to teach or to start up a business or to settle down or to just run away. Me, I'd never strayed too far from Coney Island, but I suppose we all had to kill time somewhere before, in the end, time killed us. In the scheme of things, it didn't much matter where that time was spent.

I can't say I was pleased with feeling as weak as I did. There aren't a basketful of joys that come with stomach cancer—even when your oncologist says you seem free of it. At least my condition gave me an excuse not to get up and eulogize my old friend. For that I was grateful. Had I the strength to speak, I might have been tempted to reveal what it was that had driven Bobby's generosity. The depth of Bobby's guilt might have forced the rabbi to reassess his vision of Bobby's meeting with the Almighty. But his secret was safe with me. Secrets were always safe with me. When *I* died, I wondered, would the weight of all those secrets hold me down, or would they vaporize in the flames with the rest of me? Surely fire would remove the burden of my secrets and sins. I hoped they would, but where had hoping ever gotten me? Where had hoping ever gotten anyone?

It was a brutal December afternoon—raw, misting, gray—the kind of New York winter's day that inspired the suicidal soundtrack years of the Paul Simon songbook. Like shrapnel, the jagged-edged wind gouged holes through the exposed patches of my pale, papery skin, and rattled my bones before passing out the other side of me. Since the chemo, my body's thermostat had been on the fritz. There were days I could not cool down. On others I could not get warm. Cancer had gotten me in touch with my reptilian ancestry. Soon I'd have to sun myself on rocks in the morning like an iguana. Better to be a live iguana on a rock in the sun, I thought, than to be as cold and dead as Bobby Friedman. When you get as close up to death as I had been, as I likely still was, you'll do practically anything to keep yourself on the other side of the coffin lid . . . even pray.

One step outside the funeral home, and Sarah balked at our going to the cemetery. She wouldn't let me go, and I let her not let me.

"New Carmens for onion rings and thick shakes?" she asked. "My treat."

My hair had started growing back. A sign of recovery, some said, but my appetite hadn't gotten the memo. Just the thought of onion rings and thick shakes in the same zip code made me gag. It didn't stop me from saying yes to Sarah's offer. New Carmens was a restaurant—a diner, really—at the bent elbow of Sheepshead Bay Road in Brooklyn. New Carmens had been our special place, Sarah's and mine: a place where a father could go to celebrate his little girl's perfect report card or to discuss her broken teenage heart. It was also the place where, a few years back, we'd taken our first tentative steps toward reconciliation in the wake of her mother's death.

She ate. I watched her eat. It was all I could do not to turn green at the smells in the place, but at least it was warm and the holes the wind had cut through me were healing nicely. Sarah was unusually quiet, and that scared me some. I could see she was building up her nerve to have that little talk with me. Then she looked up at me.

"Dad . . ."

*Oy gevalt*, I thought, *here it comes*. I had rehearsed my reaction in my head a hundred times over the last twenty-four hours and now the moment of truth was at hand. *No, kiddo, I'm not ready to give up the business with Uncle Aaron and move to Vermont with you guys. I'm still getting my legs back under me and all my doctors are here. Besides, Pam has been coming down a lot and we're in a good place.*

"Dad," she repeated. "I've been thinking a lot about us lately."

My body clenched. "What about us?"

"You know, I don't think you ever told me why you became a cop in the first place."

I nearly keeled over with relief. "Is that what you wanted to talk to me about, why I quit college and became a cop?"

"To start with, yeah, Dad. And why are you smiling like that? That's the same goofy smile you had on your face when the rabbi was talking."

"It's because, in his way, Bobby Friedman was responsible for changing the course of my life. Without him, I don't suppose I would have become a cop, or met your mother and we wouldn't have had you."

"How's that?"

"You really want to know?"

Her face went utterly serious. "I asked, didn't I?"

"Okay, kiddo. Take me back to my condo and we'll talk. It's gonna take a while."

◆

When we got back to my place, I poured myself a glass of an excellent Rhone. Sarah stared out the window as the skies fully darkened over Sheepshead Bay.

"Should you be drinking?" she asked, looking back at me.

I shrugged my shoulders. "No, but living through cancer, chemo, and surgery gives you a different perspective on shoulds and shouldn'ts. You want a glass?"

"No, thanks."

"Are you sure? It's a 1990 Châteauneuf-du-Pape."

"Not today. I don't feel like it."

"Did my daughter just turn down a glass of one of the best red wines of the twentieth century? I already survived cancer, don't gimme a heart attack."

"That's not funny, Dad."

"Sorry." I stood next to her and put my arm across her shoulders. "So, what's up? You seem so serious today. You miss the old neighborhood?"

"It's not that," she said.

The gray mist that had dominated the day evolved into a pelting, icy rain. Gusting winds bent the trees over like cranky old men forced to touch their toes. The ferocity of the storm destroyed the reflective oily sheen that usually floated on the surface of the bay, making the water seem particularly cold and lifeless.

"Then what's the matter, kiddo?"

She ignored the question. "You were gonna tell me about Bobby Friedman and how you came to be a cop, remember?"

"Okay, wait here."

I retreated into my bedroom and dug deep into my closet to find the galvanized metal box that held the file I was looking for. Slowly thumbing through the file, I hesitated, realizing that this might not be as good an idea as it had seemed earlier. But I was committed. Removing a few old strips of newspaper clippings held together with a single paper clip, I put the rest of the file back in the box. I had only looked at these articles one other time since cutting them out of the papers over forty years ago. The narrow strips of print were like me: yellowed, delicate, fragile, on the verge of turning to dust. I laid them down on the coffee table in front of Sarah. "Read these. It's sort of where the answer to your question begins."

From *Daily News*, December 11, 1966
**Detail of Coney Island Bombing**
Gary Phillips

For the first time since a car exploded on West 19th Street in Coney Island on December 6, the police have released details about the investigation. The two bodies discovered in the wreckage have been positively identified as Martin Lavitz of Mill Basin and Samantha Hope of Gravesend. Both were students at Brooklyn College. The car, a 1965 Chevrolet Impala, was registered to Miss Hope.

Questions have swirled around the case since several unconfirmed reports surfaced that the blast was too power-ful to have been the result of a gas tank mishap. Witnesses to the early morning blast reported hearing an enormous explosion and said they saw a huge fireball rising several hundred feet into the sky.

"I ain't seen nothing like it since Korea," said John Washington, a subway motorman who had stopped at nearby

Nathan's for a hot dog. "Shrapnel was falling every which way. It was just like Pusan all over again."

Police spokesperson Lawrence Light stated, "It was definitely a bomb. We think that they intended to plant the device in or near the draft board offices in the Shore Theater building across from Nathan's Famous. Our bomb squad thinks the explosive device simply detonated prematurely, killing both Lavitz and Hope." The bomb itself was apparently very powerful, but not sophisticated. The police refused to release details on the type of explosives used in its construction.

Sources indicate that both Miss Hope and Mr. Lavitz were known to be affiliated with many campus radical groups and were part of the growing anti-war movement. Ronald Epstein, head of the Students Against Fascism at Brooklyn College, said, "Marty and Samantha are martyrs. They are just the first casualties in a long battle against the military industrial complex's meat grinder war machine. Vietnam is a little war now, but it won't be for long." Others who knew both victims were shocked by the news.

Sarah finished reading the first article and placed it back down on the table. "I guess those were very different times."

"Believe me, kiddo, you've got no idea. Sometimes, when I think back to those days, I can't even imagine I lived through them."

"But what's this got to do with Bobby Friedman and you becoming a cop?"

"Almost everything."

# CHAPTER ONE
# FEBRUARY 1967, BROOKLYN

Bobby was smiling that night I bailed him out of the Brooklyn House of Detention, or as it was more affectionately known in the County of Kings, the Brooklyn Tombs. He was smiling, but things were different. He had changed. I'd known him since I was six years old and he'd always been blessed with a thick layer of woe-proof skin and slippery shoulders off which trouble would run like rainwater. Just recently, though, his skin didn't seem quite so thick nor his shoulders as slippery. Maybe it wasn't Bobby who had changed, but the world had changed around him, and even he'd been powerless to resist its momentum. Listen to me, sounding like I know what I'm talking about. What did I know about the world, anyway? I was just an unambitious schmuck from Coney Island, bumming around Brooklyn College looking for a lifeline. Everything I knew about the world, really *knew* about the world, I had learned on a stickball or basketball court or on the sand beneath the boardwalk.

Bobby Friedman was a happy son of a bitch—quick to smile, slow to anger. The thing about him I could never figure out was how he turned out that way. He certainly didn't get his take-life-as-it-comes attitude from his parents. Hard-boiled, old-school communists, his folks were about as warm and cuddly as a box of steel wool. His mom was a cold fish who'd spent her childhood on a kibbutz in British-occupied Palestine, but she was Blanche Dubois compared to Bobby's dad, a tough monkey who'd fought in the Spanish Civil

War as an eighteen-year-old and had been a union organizer for the last three decades. Bobby used to joke that his mom's favorite lullaby was "The Internationale" and that "Free the Rosenbergs" had been his first full sentence. Needless to say, the guys in the neighborhood didn't hang out much at Chateau Friedman. My pal Eddie Lane used to call their stuffy, oppressive little apartment in Brighton Beach "the gulag." It was kind of hard to cozy up to people who used words like *liberal* and *progressive* as faint damns, and who held nothing but contempt for our parents. As off-putting as their condescension toward our parents' bourgeois aspirations might have been, it was nothing compared to the contempt they had for their own son's cheery and entrepreneurial nature.

Don't misunderstand: Bobby could recite the ABCs of communism, and even believed a lot of what had been drummed into his head since he popped out of the womb. He had joined Students for a Democratic Society before it became fashionable, and was a top-notch recruiter for the cause. He was a charming alchemist, a guy who could organize a protest rally out of thin air. Bobby Friedman was also the poster boy for cognitive dissonance— even if he could tell you what kind of cigars Castro preferred or explain the minutiae of the Kremlin's latest Five-Year Plan, Bobby would always be more Lenny Bruce than Lenin, more Groucho than Karl Marx. And there was something else: Bobby Friedman liked money. He liked it a lot. He liked to spend it. More than that, he liked making it.

He was a hustler. He always had an angle, even when we were kids. For instance, he was great at flipping baseball cards. Instead of hoarding them all, he'd sell the duplicates of the prized cards, like the Mickey Mantle rookie card, to the highest bidder. He understood long- and short-term investment before the rest of us understood that we didn't come from the cabbage patch. Bobby seemed to know where he was going and what the world held in store for him. The future that stretched out before me like a vast desert was, to Bobby, an oasis. He was a man with a plan. I admired that about him.

I guess I shouldn't have been surprised at Bobby's smile that night at the Tombs. I was, though, maybe for the first time since we'd sat next to each other in Mrs. Goldberg's kindergarten class. I was surprised because not only had he chained himself to a police paddy wagon and been dragged along Bedford Avenue for a hundred yards, but because the demonstration was about, among other things, the vicious lies the press and police had spread about Samantha Hope. Bobby'd been dating Samantha Hope for almost a year before the explosion. He had seemed totally smitten by her from the moment they met. I'd been more than a little smitten myself. I suppose all of us guys were. Who wouldn't have been? She was a Brooklyn Jewish boy's wet dream: a golden blonde *shiksa* goddess with crystal blue eyes, creamy skin, chiseled cheekbones, and legs up to here. Forget that she was an older woman—by two years—worldly, at least compared to us, and savvy about all sorts of things, but especially politics, drugs, even sports.

For two months now, our goddess had lain in charred bits and pieces in a lonely grave somewhere in her hometown in Pennsylvania. So yeah, I was surprised Bobby was smiling, and maybe more than a little bit disappointed in him. I didn't say a word. It wasn't my place to judge other people's grief. Besides, Bobby looked in bad shape. Although his face was bruised and scratched up from getting bounced along the pavement at twenty miles per hour, most of the damage was below his neckline. His clothes were filthy; the elbows of his sweatshirt and the knees of his jeans in tatters. The skin beneath his shredded clothes hadn't yet scabbed over, and some of the cuts were still angry, red, and raw.

"You look like shit, man," I said.

He tousled my hair. "Hey, I got dragged behind a police paddy wagon. What's your excuse?" Joking, deflecting, that was quintessential Bobby.

"C'mon, I'll get you home so you can get those cuts washed up and bandaged. Maybe with your fresh battle scars, your mom and dad will finally welcome you into their club."

"Nah. I could shove a Molotov cocktail up McNamara's ass and they would still be ashamed of me. I smell of money, don't ya know? How did the rest of the demonstration go?"

"It didn't," I said. "After the arrests and tear gas, it kinda broke up."

He grabbed my arm and turned me to face him. Finally, that perpetual smile ran away from his face. When it vanished, my disappointment in him went with it. "You know the pigs are full of shit, right? They're lying about Sam and Marty. Samantha believed in fighting for the cause, but she wasn't a bomb thrower. That wasn't her style."

"I know, Bobby. I know. And Marty Lavitz . . . come on! He was about as radical as my Uncle Lenny's Edsel."

"Even if nobody else believes that, it's important that you believe, Moe. Sam wouldn't have done it. You gotta believe me."

"I do, man. You know I do."

Bobby's smile returned and somehow the world felt all right again. When we stepped outside the Tombs, I swear I could feel the heat of the sun on my face, although it was twenty-five degrees and night had fallen over Brooklyn.

# CHAPTER TWO

We didn't have fraternities at Brooklyn College. I suppose the powers that be didn't think we merited them because going to BC was more like a four-year extension of high school than a serious university experience. You took a bus or subway to school in the morning, came home at night to the same apartment you grew up in, slept in the same bed, in the same room, and took the same crap from your parents you had as a kid. But now the crap was worse because not only weren't you a kid, you weren't a man, either. Friends who went away to school in far-flung places like Buffalo and Oneonta might've been expanding their horizons, but not you.

At BC we had these things called house plans, which were a cross between glorified clubhouses and fraternities with training wheels. They were rented apartments in private homes near campus, *sans* fancified Greek letters. Bobby and I belonged to Burgundy House and we did some of the same stuff as frats did—hazing, beer parties, sports teams—only the stakes were smaller, much smaller. No older house brother was going to help land you a position at a white shoe Wall Street firm after you graduated. You'd be lucky if they helped you land a job shining shoes. Mainly, house plans were places where guys could get away from their parents, hang out, get high, listen to music, and ball their girlfriends.

And now that I had bailed Bobby out, balling my girlfriend was exactly what I had in mind when I showed up in front of Burgundy House. This year Burgundy House was a basement apartment in a weird, rundown Victorian on East 26th Street near the corner of Avenue I. I'd been led to believe that Mindy Weinstock and I shared common cause. During a phone conversation I'd had with her not five minutes before I went to fetch Bobby from the Tombs, Mindy had given me every indication that getting laid was of paramount importance to her. Now, as I reached the end of the driveway and turned toward the back entrance of the Victorian, I wasn't so sure.

Mindy was smoking the guts out of a cigarette and coughing up a lung, which, if she normally smoked, might not have shocked me quite so much. As it was, the shock of her smoking was mitigated by the fact that she was holding a half-empty pint bottle of Four Roses in her other hand. Mindy drank, but stuff like Miller High Life or Mateus Rose, not bourbon, for goodness sakes. That was the kind of shit our dads drank.

"Hey, you," I whispered, checking my watch. "I see you started the party without me."

She tilted her head at me like a confused puppy. "Party?" Then she stared at the cigarette in her right hand and the bottle in her left. "This is no party, Moe. Don't you know a wake when you see one?"

Truth be told, I didn't. Maybe half of my friends were Catholic, but I'd never been to a wake and my guess was neither had Mindy.

"What's this about?" I asked.

"Samantha," she said, eyes looking anywhere but at me.

"It's been months, Mindy."

"So what?" she shouted, raising her arms up over her head so that the bourbon spilled onto her coat. A light popped on in the house next door.

I pushed Mindy's arms down. "C'mon, keep quiet. The neighbors are already giving our landlord crap for renting to us. Let's get inside."

I dug my keys out of my pocket with one hand and urged Mindy forward with the other. As confused as I was by Mindy's smoking and drinking, I was now doubly confused, because Mindy never much cared for Samantha Hope. Well, no, that's an understatement. She hated Sam's guts. For one thing, she thought Sam was a poseur who saw politics as fashion: wearing what was in because it was in, and not because she felt strongly about it one way or the other. Mindy was no poseur. She was plugged into every left-leaning political group on the BC campus. She took it seriously. Another thing was that Mindy wasn't stupid. She knew how smitten I'd been by Sam. I had been in Mindy's shoes myself a few times—somebody's Plan B. No one enjoys being someone's fallback position. None of this is to say that Mindy didn't have her charms. She did, in spades, but hers were local charms, dime-a-dozen Brooklyn charms: wavy brown hair, hazel eyes, plush curves.

Given her politics, it was no wonder that Bobby had introduced me to Mindy. They'd known each other since they were little kids, having met at a socialist sleep-away camp upstate. Seems Mindy's folks were old-school lefties just like the Friedmans, though Mindy's parents had in recent years laid down their hammer and sickle for a slice of apple pie. Mindy's dad and I talked about Tom Seaver, not Leon Trotsky. Her mom cooked chicken soup in her kitchen, not revolution. As Bobby's parents were disappointed in him, so too were Mindy's parents with her, but for opposite reasons. Mindy's political indoctrination had stuck, her radicalism untainted by money. I think one of the things her parents liked most about me was that I wasn't political. It was no secret that the only things I believed in fiercely were sports and avoiding the draft. My presence in their daughter's life gave them hope. And in spite of her playing at being my girlfriend, we were mostly about the sex. We were never going to be Romeo and Juliet, and I sometimes couldn't help but feel I was a convenient buffer between Mindy's politics and her folks' concerns.

The basement smelled vaguely of old beer and pot smoke. Only vaguely, because the dank odor of mildew fairly overwhelmed everything else. The décor was strictly Salvation Army chic, and the cheaply paneled walls were covered in posters of the Stones, the Beatles, Dylan, Raquel Welch, and Joe Namath. We had ones of Che and Malcolm X just to keep Bobby happy. Most of the guys in the house were like me: jocks who were into girls and rock and roll, and who couldn't've cared less about Chairman Mao or Ho Chi Minh. We didn't want to be our fathers, but we didn't necessarily want to turn the world on its ear, either.

We weren't inside for more than five seconds before Mindy had the bottle to her lips. Five seconds after that, she was undressing. I don't mean prim and properly either. She was tearing at her clothes as if they were on fire. When she was done removing hers, she started at mine. I grabbed her hands, tried holding her wrists, but she was determined, much more determined to push ahead than I was to stop her.

"What's going on, Min?" I asked as she unbuckled my belt. "What's the matter?"

She said, "Just shut up and fuck me."

I shut up and fucked her and continued doing so for another two hours. I wasn't the most experienced lover in the world, but even I recognized the signs that the sex Mindy and I had that night wasn't about sex at all. It was about hunger and anger and escape. Escape from what, I couldn't say. It was mind blowing because it was both great and terrible, intimate and empty. Every one of her moans, her sighs, her orgasms was like an urgent prayer. But it really got trippy after the fact, when she curled herself up into my arms and cried. And this wasn't gentle sobbing I'm talking about. At first, as the tears rolled onto my chest and down past my ribs onto the mattress of the foldout couch, I held her tight and stroked her hair. Mindy wasn't generally given to tears. I'm not saying she was hard. She just wasn't a crier.

"I know I'm not Don Juan, but I've never driven a girl to tears before."

"You're an idiot, Moe."

"Is this about Samantha again?" I whispered.

"Sort of."

"Huh?"

Then she choked out, "Bobby was my first. Did you know that?"

I felt more than a little pang of jealousy. I'd suspected there was a deeper connection between Bobby and Mindy than hand holding at sleep-away camp, though I never asked. I don't think I really wanted to know. Bobby wasn't the best-looking guy in Brooklyn, but girls loved him. I knew Mindy wasn't a virgin and I never really cared about stuff like that. Besides, my experience as a virgin and being with them wasn't very magical. It was always awkward. The only good thing about those moments was that they didn't last very long. For some reason it really got under my skin about Mindy and Bobby, and it must have showed. Mindy could feel me clench.

As she wiped her tears with the back of her hands, she asked, "What's the matter?"

"Nothing," I lied. "I thought you were upset about Sam. Now all of a sudden you're talking about screwing Bobby. What's this got to do with Bobby?"

"Nothing. Nothing. That was stupid. I shouldn't have said it. Forget it. I think I'm still a little drunk."

She was out of my arms, off the couch, naked and tiptoeing across the cold, gritty linoleum to the bathroom. The light went on and I heard the shower running. I should have warned her to leave the light off. Bobby liked to joke that the place was so filthy, cockroaches would have wanted it fumigated before agreeing to infest.

I must have drifted off to sleep there for a bit because when I opened my eyes, Mindy was pulling her damp hair over the collar of her coat.

"Where you going, babe? I thought we could go get some pizza or something and—"

"Not tonight," she whispered. "I couldn't, not tonight, not with . . ." Then she leaned over and kissed me hard on the mouth, a desperate kind of kiss.

"Is everything okay?" I asked, pulling her down next to me. Her coat still reeked of bourbon. "You're acting kinda freaked out."

Her expression was pained, her lips pressed tightly together. She seemed to want to say something, needed to say something.

"Moe, I need you to do a favor for me."

I wriggled my eyebrows. "Anything, babe. Gimme a second. I think I got another round in me."

She slapped me lightly on the chin. "No, this is serious. I need you to listen to me carefully and do as I ask, but no questions. Say you'll do it for me."

I said, "Sure, whatever you want."

"Promise me you won't question me, and that you'll keep your word."

I sat up, my back against the rear cushions of the couch. "Now you're freaking me out."

"Promise me!"

"Okay, Min, sure. I promise. What is it?"

"Just stay away from Bobby for the next couple of days. Stay away from him, Moe. Far away."

"Are you putting me on? You sound like that stupid robot on *Lost in Space*." I pressed my elbows to my ribs and moved my forearms up and down. "Danger, Moe Prager! Danger! Stay far away from Bobby Friedman. What's with that? It does not compute."

Her face was deadly serious. "I'm not putting you on, lover. Keep away from Bobby."

Before I could say another word, Mindy was out the door. I wasn't exactly dressed to go chasing after her. Even if I had been, she wouldn't have talked to me. I didn't know what was going on, but I knew my girlfriend well enough. It was a struggle for her to say what she had and she wasn't going to say another word. Trouble was, I could be as curious as a litter of Siamese kittens. In the face of curiosity, promises be damned.

# CHAPTER THREE

What had changed? That was the question on my mind when my head hit the pillow on my old familiar bed, and it was still the question when I opened my eyes in the morning. I just couldn't get over how strange Mindy had been the night before. The drinking, the cigarettes, and the angry sex were the least of it. I guess I could make some sense of that. We all do some stupid shit sometimes. But the stuff about her and Bobby . . . it just didn't hang together. Why would she tell me about sleeping with Bobby right after we had screwed ourselves raw? I didn't think she was trying to hurt me. Or maybe she was, I didn't know. And that warning about keeping away from Bobby; what was that about? All I knew was that we had had this really pleasant phone conversation just before I left to bail Bobby out of the Tombs. Then two hours later, Mindy was like a different person. What had happened in those two hours? What had changed?

As I lay there still half asleep, something else, something obvious that hadn't quite registered in my sex-drunk brain the previous evening, occurred to me: Bobby Friedman was in some kind of trouble. What kind of trouble, I couldn't say, but it must've been serious. I couldn't get the pained look on Mindy's face out of my head. It was identical to the look on my mom's face when I was little and she used to warn me about polio. *Never put on another kid's jacket or share food or drinks.* She never used the word polio, but I understood what her warnings meant. She would always try to be really calm when she talked about it. Of course the irony was that the false calmness—that pinched look of hers, her struggling not to use the word polio—was precisely the thing that scared the shit out of me.

"Moe. Get up!" It was my big brother Aaron. "You got class in an hour."

"Eat shit and die."

"Nice thing to say to the man who's gonna make you rich someday."

"Capitalist dog!"

"Woof. Woof."

"You're funny, Aaron. Remind me to laugh."

"I'm serious, Moe. Someday . . ."

"Yeah, my brother the salesman is gonna make me rich, huh? What you gonna do, Willy Loman, rob a bank? Take out a big insurance policy, name me as beneficiary, and jump in front of a train?"

"Listen, little brother, why do you think I'm living at home? You think I wanna still be sleeping in the same room as you, smelling your farts, fighting for who gets to piss first in the morning? I wanna be outta here as much as you, but I'm saving money this way. If you don't get some idea of where you're going, you're gonna be waking up in this room, in the same bed for the rest of your life. The money I'm saving now, we're gonna need someday."

"What's with this *we* bullshit? The only time I'd go into business with you is if I had to choose between that and crucifixion. Even then I'd have to think about it."

"Keep it up, Moe, and you'll end up broke like Dad. I'm not gonna be his age with a wife and a family and begging for crumbs. It's not gonna happen to me, and I won't let it happen to you, shithead. Even Miriam has more of a sense of purpose than you.

How does it feel to have a little sister who's more ambitious than you? Get ready in ten minutes and I'll drop you off at BC on my way into work. There's coffee on the stove."

✦

I cut my poli sci class partially because my professor was as stimulating as chewed gum and old enough to discuss the Civil War from memory. Bobby once asked him if Lincoln had been enjoying the play. The class laughed; the professor didn't. I guess that was the other reason I cut poli sci: it was the one class Bobby and I shared. I had no intention of keeping my promise to Mindy, not if my friend was in trouble. On the other hand, I wasn't going to rush headlong into a situation I knew nothing about. Totally avoiding Bobby was practically an impossibility, anyway. Not only did we have a class together, we were in Burgundy House and, more importantly, he owed me the bail money I'd laid out for him. Five hundred bucks was nearly all the money I had, and I couldn't afford to float that much money for too long.

I decided to go over to Burgundy House and clean up a little. Part of me was embarrassed by the state of the apartment. If the other guys were willing to let their girlfriends navigate a filthy minefield of beer bottles, chip bags, and soda cans just to go to the bathroom, that was their choice. Mindy deserved more than that from me. Of course she would have found my concerns utterly bourgeois. Still, my parents had raised me a certain way and I didn't see anything wrong with respecting some basic social graces. So I pulled up the collar of my ratty pea coat and turned left off the quad and onto Bedford Avenue.

The snow, which had been falling in lazy flurries for most of the morning, was now bombarding the streets of Midwood. I couldn't see twenty feet ahead of me, the wind whipping the snow into little whirling white cyclones. My face was so cold that the flakes felt like pinpricks on my cheeks. I quickened my pace to a steady trot until I got to East 25th. By then, the big gulps of icy air I'd been sucking in were burning my lungs. More than a few times on my way over, I thought about heading down to Ocean Avenue to catch the bus toward home. Would've been the smart thing to do, but even I knew that doing the smart thing wasn't always the right thing, that smart and right were often at odds with each other.

When I came around the corner and saw Bobby's Olds 88 parked across the street, I stopped dead in my tracks. Apparently, I wasn't the only student skipping Myths of Post–Civil War Reconstruction. I'd cut class in part to avoid Bobby Friedman and now here he was; at least his car was. For some odd reason my heart was thumping itself out of my chest and, in spite of the cold, I could feel trickles of sweat rolling down my left side. My half-frozen feet didn't seem to want to budge. I'd known Bobby my whole life, I thought, and what, suddenly I'm afraid to see him? How ridiculous.

I was on the opposite side of the street, no more than thirty or forty feet away, when Bobby came trudging up the driveway toward his car. His long brown hair was blowing every which way. He didn't see me because his face was pointed down against the weather. I slipped and struggled to keep my feet. When I steadied myself and looked up again, Bobby was just passing in front of his car. Something wasn't right. I couldn't say what it was for sure. I just knew it. Maybe it was the rumbling of an engine coming to life beneath the howling wind, or maybe it was the flash of lights I caught out of the corner of my eye. Whatever it was, it sent me running as fast as my legs would carry me. I tossed my books aside as I went.

"Bobby!" I screamed. "Bobby, look out!"

That was exactly the wrong thing to do, because he froze in his tracks. When I was within ten feet of him, I could see the headlights emerging through the swirling sheets of snow. Maybe it was all in my head, but the car seemed to slow down ever so slightly and swerve a hair to my right. They say that in battle the world slows down. Maybe that was it, for in that brief second the world slowed down. No matter. I took one last stride and jumped, arms forward. My palms hit Bobby squarely in the chest and sent him sprawling backwards out of the path of the oncoming car. I wasn't that lucky. The car clipped my right ankle and spun me, slamming my shoulder into the front bumper of Bobby's Olds. I was down, face first in the snow, my right shoulder barking at me. Stunned at my brave stupidity, I lay there for several seconds. Then brakes squealed, tires skidded, and there was a loud crash. The moans of twisting metal cut through the heart of the bellowing storm.

Shaken, I forced myself up onto my hands and knees. Bobby was up too, and pulling me to my feet. We turned, looking down the street, but the snow was falling harder than ever and obscured our view. Without a word, we ran—he ran, I limped—to the corner. There, down Avenue I toward Ocean Avenue, was a silver '67 Coupe de Ville. It had hopped up onto the sidewalk and smashed head-on into a big, old oak tree. The front end of the car was like a steel accordion, and steam gushed out of the radiator. The Caddy's doors were flung wide open. Whoever had been in the car was gone now. They couldn't have gotten very far, but the blinding snow made it impossible for us to tell how far. We carefully crossed to where the Cadillac had come to rest.

"Look at this. There's blood on the steering wheel," I said, rubbing the driver's blood between my fingertips, "and on the seat. A lot of it. The windshield on the passenger's side is all smashed in too." Then, pointing at the spotty red trails in the snow, "People got hurt here and they're bleeding pretty bad too." I dipped my fingers into the snow to wipe the blood away.

"I hope the driver bleeds to death. What a dumb bastard, driving like that in this weather. What was he thinking? The schmuck nearly killed us."

"Yeah, Bobby. It almost looked like he was aiming for you."

"Don't be an idiot, Moe. Why would anyone wanna hurt me?"

I shrugged my shoulders, wincing as I did it. "You tell me."

He ignored that. "You all right?"

"I'll live."

"Come on, let's get outta here before the cops show up asking questions. I've had my fill of the goddamn pigs. Anyway, we need to get some ice on that shoulder of yours."

"Sounds good."

"Moe, one more thing."

"What?"

Smiling that smile of his, he said, "Thanks for saving my life."

He just had to say it, didn't he? I guess he did have to thank me and I guess I would've been pretty pissed off if he hadn't, but it weighed on me. I couldn't recall just where or when I first heard about the old Chinese proverb: *Save a man's life, and his life becomes your responsibility.* Probably on *Captain Kangaroo.* Yeah, thinking back, I'm almost certain it was on *Captain Kangaroo.* I don't suppose it would have mattered one way or the other. In a flash of headlights and metal, Bobby Friedman had gone from being my friend to being my responsibility.

# CHAPTER FOUR

Driving would've been treacherous enough even if Bobby hadn't consumed a six-pack of Schaefer while I iced down my shoulder and we waited for the storm to let up. My ankle was okay, and it didn't swell up much at all. My shoulder was a different story altogether. I didn't need to see the spreading purple bruise to know I'd been pretty badly banged up. It hurt like a bastard, throbbing as steadily as a bass drum.

We had been listening to the Yardbirds, Bobby singing along as he straightened up the place. Who knows, maybe a close brush with death turned him into a neat freak. It certainly hadn't improved his voice. He may have gotten past nearly getting crushed beneath the wheels of a Caddy, but I hadn't. Never mind my aching shoulder; I kept replaying it in my head: the rumble of the engine, the pale headlights emerging from the white veil of snow, the car bearing down on us, the slight swerve. There was something else I couldn't ignore—Mindy's ominous warning.

I brought up her name, but if I thought the mere mention of it was going to get a rise out of Bobby, I was bound for disappointment. He barely reacted, continuing to sing. There was no reason he should have reacted. He and Mindy were old pals—more than that, apparently—but given her warning to stay away from Bobby and his nearly getting turned into roadkill, I figured to see if anything had changed on his side of the equation.

"What's going on with you and Mindy, anyways?" he asked as Jeff Beck took a short solo.

"I don't know. She was kinda weird last night."

He cupped his hand around his ear. "Huh?"

"Turn the goddamned music down, Bobby. You're the one who asked me the question."

He twisted the volume knob on the steel-faced Marantz amplifier, its single dial glowing in the gloomy basement. "Sorry, Moe. What were you saying?"

"I said she was kinda weird last night. Before I went to bail you out—"

"Shit! I owe you five hundred bucks," he said, getting back to sweeping. "I totally forgot. I'll get it to you soon, okay?"

"Fine."

"So what were you saying?"

"I was about to say that before I went to bail your ass out of the Tombs, Mindy and I had this really sweet phone conversation. You know Mindy, she doesn't do sweet and romantic. We were all set for a little action and then to go out to dinner, but when I showed up here, she was crazed."

That seemed to finally get Bobby's attention. His smiling lips went straight as a ruler. He stopped fussing with the broom and went to the fridge. "You want a beer to take the edge off the pain? I want a beer."

"Nah," I said, "Suffering is my duty as a Jew."

He opened his first Schaefer and took a big swallow. "Suffering's nobody's duty, man. Mindy was crazed. How do you mean crazed?"

"I found her outside smoking cigarettes and drinking Four Roses. When we got inside she practically raped me."

"And you're complaining? Half the guys at BC would give their right nut to—"

"No, Bobby. It wasn't like that. Something definitely happened between the time I spoke to her on the phone and when I showed up here. I've seen her in bad moods. I've seen her sad, but I've never seen her like this. She was like a different person."

Bobby got started on his second beer. He seemed unwilling to take a stab at explaining Mindy's behavior, so I pushed a little harder.

"Then, when we were done screwing, she started crying."

"I heard you have that effect on women, Prager." Bobby's smile returned as he finished off his beer. He went for another. "Mindy's a lot of things, but she's not a crier. She must've been putting you on. Or maybe Mindy thinks it's her duty to suffer too. I mean, no offense, but she is dating you."

Bobby was uncanny in his ability to dodge trouble, but I couldn't let him off the hook that easily. Instead of giving him a little push, I gave him a full-on shove, much harder than the one I'd used to save his ass.

"After she stopped crying, she told me about the two of you."

He moved the beer can far enough away from his lips to say, "What about the two of us?"

"Cut it out, Friedman. You know exactly what I'm talking about. That you were her first."

Bobby dropped the charade and went for his fourth beer. "We were kids at camp, man. No big deal. It went the way those things always go. It hurt her and I lasted five seconds."

"No big deal for you, maybe, but it was for her. It always is for girls. You know that. It may be 1967 and the whole world might be going crazy, Bobby, but you know it matters. You have any idea why she would want to tell me that? Why she would tell me about you guys at that moment?"

"Who can understand girls? When you find someone who does, let me know. Besides, she's your girlfriend. Maybe you pissed her off or something."

"Or something," I said. "Do you have any idea what could've happened between the time I talked to her and she showed up here?"

"How the fuck should I know?" he barked back. It was the first time he'd ever yelled at me. Was it the beers? Maybe. He'd had four of them in record time, but I didn't think so. His voice steadied and his smile returned. "As you may recall, dear comrade, I was a guest in the deep cold womb of the fascist state at the time. I have many talents, but knowing what Mindy Weinstock is up to while I'm behind bars isn't one of them."

His words were reasonable, but rang in my ears like a cracked bell. He was pushing back too hard when a simple no would have done the trick. I didn't know much, but I did know when people were full of crap. Bobby was no different than anyone else in that he was sometimes prone to little lies and minor exaggerations, but at the moment the needle on my bullshit-o-meter was off the scale. I left it at that for the time being. He had another beer and chased it down with one more for good luck. A few minutes later we were in Bobby Friedman's rough beast, slouching toward Brighton Beach.

◆

I'd smoked a little grass and hash, dropped acid twice—twice was enough, believe me—and done speed a few times. That was the extent of my drug use. At heart I was a gym rat, and preferred playing ball to getting stoned, but the pain in my shoulder was getting worse. So when Bobby offered me something to help, I didn't hesitate. And almost like magic, I was feeling no pain. Trouble was, I wasn't feeling much of anything else either. Suddenly there was more slush inside my skull than on the ice-slickened Brooklyn streets. The world was an out-of-focus tapestry of red taillights and slow-motion people blurred around the edges, their featureless faces blending one into the next into the next as we rode past. This soft weave of colors and vague figures was set against a slate gray canvas that seemed to darken with each blink of my eyes.

All my senses were dulled but for smell. I was acutely aware of the beer on Bobby's breath, of the sour stink of my own dry mouth, of the chemical pine scent from the green cardboard tree dangling on a string below the rearview mirror. I was conscious of Bobby's mouth moving, of him talking to me, his voice like a muted horn set against the rhythm of the softly slapping wiper blades. It wasn't unpleasant, exactly. I felt as if I was stuck at the edge of sleep, unable but not unwilling to take that last step into the well of dreams.

Time passed in a lazy gallop, and when I looked outside again, I thought I recognized the part of the world we were in. There was thunder overhead, the thunder of subway wheels. I was aware that the car was no longer moving, though the engine kept running and the wipers kept the beat. Now looking right at me, Bobby spoke, the rank smell of beer filling up my head. I could tell there was some urgency to what he was saying, if unable to make sense of the phrases themselves. I was vaguely aware of some words dripping out of my mouth too, words like cold maple syrup. Then Bobby disappeared, and so did I.

# CHAPTER FIVE

Some days it just ain't worth opening your eyes and no matter how fast you shut them again, it's too late. So it was for me . . . way too late. Last night's slush was gone. Now my head was filled with wool, my mouth with cotton. Apparently someone had shoved a harpoon through my right shoulder while I slept. Other than that, I was ready for action. *Put me in, Coach. I'm your boy.* Fuck that! I was nobody's boy. I forced my eyes open again and time-traveled into the present. The air no longer smelled of beer breath or fake pine trees, but of Woolite linens and burnt coffee. The comforting clank and rumble, the *ka-ching, ka-ching* of subway wheels on rails, had replaced the slapping of wiper blades as the backbeat to my life. I was still in my clothes, my Chuck Taylors still on my feet. Not that I remembered how, but I'd managed to get from Bobby's front seat into my bed. And there was something else. Unclenching my left fist, I found five one-hundred-dollar bills folded neatly in my palm—the bail money.

When I sat up, Ahab stuck the harpoon in a little deeper. *The white whale tasks me.* That those were the words that came to mind only proved I was screwed. See, that was the thing about Bobby and my brother: they knew where they were going. I didn't know anything, or how to do anything except quote dead writers and shoot a fifteen-foot fadeaway jumper. Not much of a job market for the former, nor for the latter when the shooter is a six-foot-tall, slow-footed white boy. There were days I wished I woke up with a hunger for adding machines and ledger books. I wanted to know where I was going, or even where I wasn't. I guess that's completely understandable when you're on the verge of choosing a major and minor subject from the mootsville trinity of English, philosophy, and psychology. I hobbled to the bathroom as if on a wooden leg, and thought I was very badly in need of my own white whale. I needed to chase something in my life other than Mindy's ass.

Christ, I looked like shit, but at least no one was home to see but me. When I peeled back my shirt, I got weak at the sight of my shoulder. I was black, blue, yellow, brown, and orange from my right nipple across my chest, around my back, and halfway down my arm. My skin looked like a box of melted crayons. Though puffed and swollen, I could just about raise my arm without losing consciousness. No bones seemed to be broken or sticking out where they didn't belong. I figured I'd live. I swallowed way too many aspirins, finished undressing, showered, and brushed my teeth. It improved my aroma, if not my appearance.

I called Mindy's number and got no answer. That was odd. I knew she was probably at school, but her mom was almost always home. For some reason I couldn't quite explain, I got a sick feeling in my gut. Maybe it was the paranoid afterglow of whatever narcotic Bobby had given me. Yeah, I thought, that was it. Because of my shoulder pain and the drug hangover, getting dressed went about as smoothly as a thumbless man tying his shoes. Still, I managed to do it in less than a week. Of course, the aspirin didn't kick in until I was done. There was the newspaper and a note for me on the kitchen table. I was confident the note was from Aaron, probably lambasting me for coming home drunk, for being a lazy, aimless piece of shit with no ambition and no future. I was getting a little tired of his notes and lectures, so I didn't look at the note until I'd fortified myself with some of my mom's coffee. Fortified being the key word, because if you could survive the over-percolated and burnt black goo that passed for coffee in the Prager household, you could survive almost anything.

I looked at the back page of the paper, the sports section calling to me, but I couldn't stop thinking about Aaron's damned note. I figured I'd read it just to be done with it. The note was from Aaron. That much I'd gotten right. Everything else I'd gotten wrong, as wrong as getting could get. I was out of the apartment almost before I finished reading the note.

✦

What's in a name? Sometimes everything. Kings Highway Hospital was small and privately owned, not one of the bloated gas giants run by the city like Kings County or Bellevue, and it was where Aaron's note said the ambulance had brought Mindy.

Mindy's mom was a heavyset woman who, with a *babushka* around her head and some gold teeth in her mouth, would not have looked out of place in the Ukrainian *shtetl* from which her grandparents or parents had no doubt come. Her large, doe-brown eyes were moist and bloodshot, her voice choked with tears and barely contained panic. She lit up when I came running toward her down the hall. Mindy's father—his burden unlightened by my arrival—was there too: pacing, twitchy, blank-faced. He was a gaunt man, now a scarecrow. Her mother locked me in her embrace, my right shoulder burning in pain. I toughed it out. These people didn't need to hear about my relatively minor woes. Mr. Weinstock gave me a ghost-like pat on the back.

"Beatrice, Beatrice," her husband said, putting his twig arm across her shoulders. "Mindy will be all right. You know how stubborn a girl she is. If anyone will be good, it will be our Mindy."

I wanted to make a joke, to tell them that she had survived my mom's coffee many times, so of course Mindy would be okay. But this was no time for jokes and smiles.

"What's wrong with her?" I asked. Aaron's note had been sketchy on details.

Her mom answered through her tears. "She's . . . she's in . . . a . . . coma."

"A coma! What happened?" I asked.

"They found her on the street last night in the snow, unconscious with a big gash across her forehead," her father said. "The cops think it was a botched mugging."

I didn't understand. "Botched?"

"Yeah, the detective said they found her watch and wallet on her. She must have put up some fight, boy." His sunken chest swelled with pride. He turned to his wife. "She's such a fighter. That's why I know she will be fine."

"Where did they find her?" I asked. "When?"

"In the snow, like I—"

"No, Herbie," Mrs. Weinstock interrupted, impatient. "Moe means where, on what street?"

I nodded. "Right."

"Sorry, Moe. They found her on East 17th and Glenwood Road in front of a house. An old woman looking through her window told the police she saw her struggling with a young, light-skinned colored—black man," he was quick to correct himself. "The old woman said the black man had pink blotches on his hands and face."

"Pink blotches, huh? That should make him easier to find," I said.

"I suppose you're right. Meanwhile, the old woman said that he dropped Mindy to the sidewalk and limped away. Mindy must have given him such a kick or something to make him let go."

There was that sick feeling in my gut again, only this time it was worse, much worse. I was trying to figure out a delicate way to ask the next question, but couldn't find the words. I just asked it raw.

"Were there other injuries?"

Her father shook his head. "You mean . . . was he trying to rape her?"

I didn't, but said yes anyway.

"No, they don't think so," he said, thankful for something. "She was bruised up all over, though, so he must have beat her up pretty bad."

My head was spinning. Suddenly this relationship, which I had been willing to dismiss as mostly about sex, didn't feel that way. I was torn, and torn apart inside. I wanted to fall to pieces and to rip someone to shreds.

"Can I see her?"

"The doctors are in with her now, and they said it will be a while," her mom answered. "Go, do what you have to do. Go to school. We'll call you if she—"

"*When* she wakes up," her dad shouted. "When!"

"Okay, Herbie. Okay, when. Moe, we'll call you when she wakes up or if there's any change."

I hugged them both and drifted back down the hall, down the stairs, and out onto Kings Highway. I just stood there, lost, staring at nothing in particular. Then I heard someone, a woman, say, "Look, Jim, there's Daddy. No, *there*, up on the second floor. See, he's in the window, waving."

I looked up and there in a second floor window was a man, the silhouette of a man, really, in a robe. He was waving down. His wave was weak and unenthusiastic. I turned to look at Jim. He was a boy of six or seven, overdressed against the cold. His face was full of many things: fear, longing, anger, maybe even love. Mostly, he seemed confused.

*Jim*, I thought, *that makes two of us.*

I walked to school from the hospital through the slush and compacted piles of filthy snow. Doesn't take long for hearts and snow to blacken in Brooklyn. Snow in my world only looks white when it's falling, but it's already tainted before touching down. Nothing stays uncorrupted. Nothing. I think I knew that before I could walk. That kid at the hospital, he knew it too. Sometimes I think that was the worst part of having to stay home and go to Brooklyn College. There was no fooling myself that the world could be any different. I thought about the few friends I had who'd been lucky enough to escape to magical places like Ann Arbor or Palo Alto, or even Buffalo. Maybe it's true that you can't run away from your troubles, but fuck me if I didn't want to find out for myself.

The world goes on. That's the first thing I thought when I turned right off Bedford Avenue and stepped onto the quad. Between periods, the quad is a beehive. It looks like chaos from the outside, but not to the bees themselves. Somehow I couldn't reconcile that Mindy had been beaten into a coma and people were laughing, smoking cigarettes. Mindy was in a coma, and people went to their classes. Mindy was in a coma, and people did what they did. The world went on, but how could it? Suddenly, I wanted no part of this place. BC had always been a good place for me to hide. School provided great camouflage for my lack of ambition, but Aaron was right: our kid sister had more of a plan for her life than I did. It was one thing to let myself be carried along with the tide, to be going no place in particular except where the tide took me. This was different. I'd always believed I would bide my time in college, that I would stumble into something or that something would stumble into me. Instead, I'd been steamrolled. I hadn't seen this coming, this thing that happened to Mindy. Now, for the first time in my life, I had a purpose. I needed to find out what had happened to my girlfriend, and I knew where to start looking.

# CHAPTER SIX

I found Lids where I knew I'd find him, selling loose joints and whatever else outside the gates on the other side of campus. Cops walked their beats. Lids walked his. I also knew Lids by his real name, Larry Lester. He was two years younger than me, but had been a year ahead of me at school. He had been Lincoln High School's fair-haired boy, destined for a vastly different trajectory than the arc he was now traveling. Larry was supposed to be at MIT or Princeton or Cornell, doing book-length equations on the relationships between quarks and quasars and how they proved or disproved the existence of God. Larry Lester—Ocean Parkway's answer to Descartes and Einstein—had lasted exactly one and a half terms at MIT before he went flip city. He never got around to smashing atoms. Instead, they smashed him. At least he cracked and wound up in a rubber room before they found him hanging in his closet by his belt. And now here he was, selling joints and getting by in the shadows of Flatbush and Nostrand Avenues.

"Feed your head," was his whispered refrain to familiar passersby.

"Yo, Larry, got a minute?" I said, looping my arm through his. It wasn't a question and he knew it.

"It's Lids. It's Lids out here, man," he repeated, as I swept him along. "I've got a rep to keep."

"Okay, Lids, you look hungry. Eggs? My treat."

"Sure, Moe. Eggs are good."

"Eggs it is."

We turned up Campus Road toward the diner next to the off-campus bookstore. We sat at a tiny table in the corner. The place smelled of fried onions and grilling bacon. That was almost enough to lift me out of the darkness. Almost. Athena, the toothy, horse-faced waitress, took our orders and poured us coffee without looking. She never looked. She never spilled a drop. Athena was half the reason I ate here. I loved to watch her move, how, even built stocky and low to the ground as she was, she flowed like water through the crowd, in and out and around the tightly packed chairs and tables, avoiding book bags and busboys. That day I paid her movements no mind. I could not escape the idea of Mindy in a hospital bed, never waking up.

"What's the buzz?" Larry wanted to know.

"That's what I was hoping you could help me with."

His red, sleepy eyes regarded me with deep suspicion. "You want some of my wares? I didn't think that was your bag, Moe."

I shook my head. "No, no, no. I don't want anything like that."

His eyes turned from suspicion to confusion. "Then I'm even more lost than I was a second ago, and I've been lost since 1965."

"Mindy's in a coma."

"Your old lady?"

"Yeah. She was mugged and beaten. They found her in the snow on Glenwood Road and East 17th."

"Fuck, man. That's heavy, but what do you want from—"

"Two eggs over easy, home fries, bacon, rye toast." Athena slid the plate down in front of Lids. "A toasted corn muffin, butter." She was nearly as suspicious of me as Larry. "You always order eggs," she said in her Greek-inflected English, "scrambled, french fries, whole wheat toast. What's with you today, darling, no appetite?"

"Not much of one, no," I confessed.

She winked at me. "Girl troubles?"

"In a way."

"Don't worry, honey." She tapped her nose with her index finger. "Everything will work out. Athena knows these things."

I hoped so.

Showing me a mouth full of yellow egg yolk and potatoes, Lids asked, "Like I was saying, what do you want from me?" I slid a hundred-dollar bill across the table to him. There was that confusion in his eyes again. "I thought you—"

"It's not for dope. It's for information. I want you to spread it around, and don't tell me you don't know what that means."

The bill stayed on the table, untouched. "What do you need to know?"

"Two nights ago, Mindy was someplace between six and eight o'clock. I need to know where. Also, the cops say the guy who did this to her was a light-skinned black dude, young, with pink blotches on his skin. Anything you—"

"Vitiligo," Larry said.

"What?"

"Those pink blotches, it's vitiligo, a skin pigmentation disease."

"Whatever you say, Larry. But anything you can find out about where she was the other night or the guy that did this to her . . . you know, whatever."

"What you gonna do, Moe?"

"I don't know, but I gotta do something or I'll go fucking crazy. Her parents are wrecks. They're scared. I'm scared. I gotta do something."

Now Lids leaned across the table and whispered, "Listen, Moe, you were always nice to me. In school, you always watched out for guys like me and Spider Thomas. You never asked for anything in return, but I know I owe you. So keep your money." He slid the bill back across the table to me. "If I need to spread bread around, I'll use my own *gelt*. But I probably won't have to. People get stoned and they get stupid. People who want to get stoned can also get pretty desperate. Either way, they'll talk to me."

"I trust you." I took the C-note back. But if I thought Lids was going to leave it at that, I was wrong.

He leaned forward and said, "And whatever you feel you gotta do, don't do it yourself, man. I'm pretty close to people who, you know . . ."

"What kind of people, Larry? Who we talking about, here?"

"I owe you, Moe, but not that much. I know who I know. Leave it at that. You want something done, come to me and it will get done, but you won't know who did it."

"Okay, Larry. I didn't mean to sound ungrateful and I'm sorry for being so nosy. I'm just so mad about what happened to Mindy, I feel like I'm gonna explode." I stood up, threw a five on the table, and patted him on the shoulder.

He grabbed my wrist. "I don't know what I'll hear or if it will help, but whatever I find out . . . you still at the same number?"

"Yeah. If you can't get me there, you can get me at Burgundy House." I wrote that number down for him.

He grabbed my wrist again. "Something's bugging me, Moe." He started doing that twitchy face thing he did when he got overly excited. "Something's bugging me."

"What is?"

"They found Mindy on Glenwood and East 17th, right? That's right near the subway station."

"Glenwood and East 17th, that's what her dad told me, yeah."

"It doesn't make sense. She lives in Canarsie. That's in the opposite direction. What was she doing over there?"

"I don't know. When she comes out of the coma, I'll ask her. It's not important right now."

"If it's not important, then why do you want me to find out where she was the other night?"

"That's different."

He was ticcing like crazy now. "No, it's the same."

"Look, wherever she was when she got mugged, it was the wrong place. Like I said, it's not important."

"But it is important. Where a person is when an event occurs is as important as where particles are when they collide. If they are not in that place, there is no collision. Without that collision, the universe is a different place, subtly different, maybe, but different nonetheless. Don't you understand? It's the key to everything: knowing where things are, or were, or where they will be."

I left him there, mumbling to himself about particles and uncertainty, his tics calmed, his eyes turned inward. I think maybe for the first time, I got a sense of how he'd come undone. I hoped Athena could rescue him from where he had gone to. I couldn't. Even if Athena couldn't do the trick, I had faith Larry would come out of it. He always did, always had. He had to. I needed him.

As bad as I felt for Larry, my internal pressure had eased a bit. If nothing came of our encounter, at least I'd let off some steam. And who knew? Larry was good at finding out all sorts of stuff. People get stoned and they get stupid, that's what he'd said. Yet another reason why I shied away from drugs. I didn't need any help in getting stupid. Just ask my brother Aaron.

# CHAPTER SEVEN

While I was walking back onto campus, Lids's words went round and round in my head. Not the esoteric stuff that had sent him spinning off into his own universe there at the end. No, I was used to that. Even before he went over the edge, even before the drugs, Larry had been out there on an astral plane somewhere. It was the part where he claimed to know people who would do violence on my behalf that surprised me. I guess I shouldn't have been. I mean, Lids was a pusher, and I couldn't help but see him as poor, pathetic Larry. *So he sold a little pot, so what?* But really, I had no idea what he sold, or how much he sold, or to whom. Of course he knew some "people"—everybody in Brooklyn knew someone connected to the mob.

The guy I knew, who Larry and everybody from Coney Island and Brighton Beach knew, was named Tony Pistone. They called him Tony Pizza because he was a fat slob who could demolish two whole pies at a sitting, and because he and his crew hung out at DeFelice's Pizzeria, under the el on Brighton Beach Avenue. Behind his back, though, everyone in the neighborhood called him Tony Pepperoni because he had a red, acne-fucked complexion like a pepperoni pizza. I guess he was okay as far as it went. He was what my dad called a real character. My dad never defined what that meant exactly, but when you looked at Tony you understood. Tony P did magic tricks. You know the kind of thing: pulling quarters out from behind your ear, ripping up five-dollar bills and somehow making them whole again. He was always flirting with the young girls, doing his tricks for them, and joking with us guys when we came into DeFelice's. He'd throw me a dollar sometimes to go get him the racing form or the afternoon paper. The only reason anyone took Tony P seriously was his muscle, a guy they called Jimmy Ding Dong. Jimmy was a stone-cold bastard and we avoided him at all cost. None of us would even look at him if we could help it.

The only business I ever did with Tony P was buying fireworks from him. That didn't make me special. Everybody bought their fireworks from him, even the cops. Of all the kids in the neighborhood, Bobby was closest to Tony Pizza. Two summers ago when I was making quarter tips from the old ladies as a bag boy at the Big Apple supermarket on the corner of Brighton Beach Avenue and Ocean Parkway, Bobby was running errands for Tony. What kind of errands, Bobby wouldn't say. He told me once that he had sworn the Mafia blood oath to Tony never to share. I knew he was full of shit, but some of the other guys believed him. Idiots. Still, Bobby never was very forthcoming about his summer as a mob errand boy. What I did know about that summer was that Bobby earned enough to buy that sweet Olds 88 he drove, and that I earned enough to ride the Cyclone every now and then and to buy a Nathan's hot dog. Like I said, Bobby had a nose for money.

He also had a nose for me, apparently, because when I was just walking past the library and coming down the steps to the snow-covered quadrangle, he grabbed me by the shoulders. I shrank in pain.

"Sorry, I forgot about your shoulder. But Jesus, Moe, I been looking everywhere for you," he said, worry in his voice. And for the second time in the last few days, his smile was nowhere to be seen. "Did you hear about—"

"Mindy? Yeah, I heard. I was at the hospital already."

"Why didn't you call me?"

"I wasn't thinking straight. Aaron left me a note: 'Your girlfriend's in Kings Highway Hospital. It's serious.' I mean, my first thought wasn't that I should call you."

"Sorry, man. What happened to her? I'm not clear on that."

I repeated for him what I had just minutes before repeated for Lids.

"Mugged. Shit." There was a glint in Bobby's eyes—a mixture of puzzlement and mischief. "A light-skinned black guy, you said?"

"Yeah, a young guy, and he had pink blotches on his hands and face. That's what the cops told Mindy's dad. He says the prick beat her up pretty good. She was bruised up all over. Why do you ask?"

He ignored the question. "What was she even doing over there? She lives in the other direction."

Seemed to be a popular question, and I didn't have a better answer for him than I'd had for Lids.

"Don't know, but that's where they found her."

"You doing anything right now?" he asked.

"I was gonna go to class, but I can't think or keep a thought in my head. I don't think I ever cared less about school in my life. I mean, shit, what the hell does any of this crap mean now?"

"Relax, Moe. She'll be okay. She has to be. Since you're not going to class, come with me. I've got to make an airport run."

Airport runs were Bobby's latest and craziest money-making scheme. He would pick you up at your door, drive you to the airport, and carry your bags into the terminal for free. The thing was, if you took him up on the offer, you had to take out flight insurance and name Bobby as the sole beneficiary. If there were two of you, both of you had to take out policies, if there were three . . . I'm not kidding here. Sick as it was, he had about two people a week take him up on the offer. Word of mouth really was the best way to advertise. He'd been doing it for about six months and so far, thank god, he hadn't cashed in.

"Matter of time," he used to say when I'd bust his chops about it. "Matter of time."

"You have a better chance of getting killed in a car crash on the way home from the airport, you sick bastard. What do you do, listen to the radio all day to hear if the plane goes down?"

"Sometimes," he'd answer with a poker face. "You don't understand business very well, do you, Moe? It's a risk vs. reward kinda thing: small risk to me, long odds, big payoff. Besides, you don't need to worry about me, buddy. I got more than this one oar in the water."

He was right. I didn't know much about business, and didn't want to. I don't know whether I was just born this way or if it was that my dad hadn't set a very good example. He wasn't skilled at making money or at business in general. His only talent was for bad investments and failure. As it was, money never much mattered to me. I wasn't stupid. I knew money would be nice to have, but other things just mattered more to me. Love, family, girls, sex, books, sports—they were always more important to me than money. Maybe my outlook would have been different if I'd had any money to begin with. Maybe if I could have experienced what having money was like and then losing it, then I might have invested more of my being into getting more of it or getting it back. I'd tried, I'd really tried to will myself ambitious, to be more like Bobby and Aaron. I'd tried to trick myself into putting money at the top of my pyramid. No luck. And Bobby needn't have bothered to comfort me that he'd be all right even if the airport runs never paid off. Bobby Friedman was golden, bulletproof. Somehow you just knew he would always land on his feet.

As crazy and twisted as his airport runs were, I was glad for the distraction, glad to be invited along, glad to have someone making small talk. For the moment, I conveniently ignored Mindy's dire warning about keeping away from Bobby. My frustration over what had happened to her, my need to do something about it, and my impotence in the face of that need were eating me up. My guts were on fire. We picked up Mrs. Cohen—Stevie Cohen's grandma; he was one of our Burgundy House brothers—at her apartment building on Ralph Avenue, settled her comfortably in the big back seat of Bobby's Olds, and headed off to the Eastern Airlines terminal at Kennedy Airport.

# CHAPTER EIGHT

Nothing had changed, nothing but everything. I just didn't know it yet.

Bobby and I had gone to visit Mindy on the way back from the airport. Only Beatrice Weinstock was there when we arrived. She lit up again at the sight of us. I guess that made me feel a little less useless, but not a whole lot less. She'd sent her husband out to get something for them to eat—"He was making me completely *meshugge* with his pacing." She said the doctors had good news, that her daughter's vital signs had stabilized and that there was brain function. This was all good, according to Bea Weinstock. It was good too, that none of Mindy's other injuries proved to be life threatening. It's funny how when things are really bad, good comes to mean anything less than catastrophic.

Bobby and I took turns comforting Mrs. Weinstock and sitting with Mindy. When I was there with Mindy, I held her hand. I suppose I would have kissed her on the mouth if there wasn't a tube stuck down her throat. I cried some too, for me, I think, as much as for her. You grow up in Brooklyn, you like to think you're tough, that your skin is thick and concrete hard and that you come out of the womb all grown up and prepared for anything life can throw at you. Bullshit! I wasn't any tougher or any more prepared for the darts life throws at you than a Kansas farm boy. The tears? Growing up . . . I think that's why I was crying. I'd had some bad things to deal with before this—my dad losing his business, my *zaydeh* dying, stuff like that—but this thing with Mindy was different. Up to now, my life had been pretty much cake, a nearly twenty-one-year childhood consisting of stickball, the Cyclone, textbooks, stuff served to me on a plate. Real tragedy was always one step removed. With Mindy in a coma, one she might never come out of, I knew the bell had rung. *Ding!* Childhood was officially over.

That was yesterday. When I opened my eyes to the sound of the subway rumbling, I wasn't in a much better frame of mind than when I shut them. At least I opened my eyes. I had a choice about that. I was there, alive, conscious. My first thoughts were of Mindy, of where she was, of wherever one goes in a coma. The motherfucker who did that to her would be wherever he was, doing whatever he was doing. Was he scared? Did he hear footsteps coming up behind him? Did he even give a shit? I brushed my teeth, wondering about where you go in a coma. Was it like a movie? Was it like dropping acid? Was it like a bad trip? Was it Alice through the looking glass? That was the thing, speculating wasn't working for me. Suddenly, taking a philosophical point of view felt like more bullshit, like I was cheating somehow, distancing myself. No, I wasn't going to do that. I wasn't going to protect myself from this. I thought about going to school for about a millisecond, and knew that wasn't going to happen.

The phone rang, and it shook me out of that bad and lonely place. I suppose I should have been grateful. I wasn't. There was a whispering voice on the other end of the line. "This isn't the man, is it? Are you the man?"

"What? Who is this?" I asked, annoyed.

"Are you the man? The pigs?"

"No," I said, like it would matter. *If I was the cops, would I say so?* "Who is this?"

"Never mind who this is."

"Then fuck you. I'm not in the mood for—"

"Lids, man. Lids gave me your number."

"Okay, okay. Sorry." I stopped there and waited for him to say something else, but he needed a prompt. "Lids told you to call me and . . ."

"You got something to write with?"

I grabbed a pencil and the newspaper off the kitchen table. "Yeah, go ahead."

"1055 Coney Island Avenue," he said and stopped.

"What about 1055 Coney Island Avenue?"

"Listen, man, Lids asked me to do him a solid. That's what I'm doing. He said you needed an address. Well, now you got one. He didn't say nothing about giving you more than that. Don't forget to tell him you got a call."

"From who?"

"He'll know."

"You one of Lids's customers?"

"I thought you said you weren't the—"

"I'm not. Forget I asked. Thanks."

A click and dial tone were the last things I heard from him. It took me a second to collect my thoughts. I didn't have a car. I had a license, just no car. With bus and subway stops basically out front of our building, it's not like I needed one. When I went out on dates I borrowed my dad's car, or, in a dire emergency, Aaron's. I hated borrowing Aaron's car. I loved my big brother, but I always felt judged by him. I always felt like he was waiting for me to screw up. I always felt like he was waiting to say, "See, I was right. I knew it." Besides, borrowing his car involved a longer prejourney checklist than a Gemini mission. And the next morning he would debrief me, check the mileage on the odometer, and see if I refilled the tank.

I started dialing Bobby's number, but snapped the phone receiver down before the dial completed its seventh spin. I remembered the timing of Mindy's warning about staying clear of Bobby, and the things that had happened since. I rubbed my still sore shoulder, thinking that someone had already tried to run Bobby down and that Mindy had been savagely beaten. Coincidences? I thought back to the night I'd bailed Bobby out of jail, about how Mindy's whole attitude had changed over the course of two hours. I stared at the address I'd written on the back of the paper and realized that maybe it would be better for both Bobby and me if I left him out of it. If not better, then at least safer.

✦

Other than its name, Coney Island Avenue didn't have much to recommend it. Four potholed lanes that ran in a straight line from the knee bend at Brighton Beach Avenue to the tip of Prospect Park, Coney Island Avenue was a startlingly ugly thoroughfare. It was an endlessly repeating stream of funeral homes, mom and pop groceries, car dealerships, pizzerias, luncheonettes, kosher butcher shops, pork stores, and grubby little storefronts with rental apartments above. Even when the sun shone through a cloudless blue sky, Coney Island Avenue was darker than the neighborhoods through which it ran—louder too. And the soot and stink of diesel fumes from trucks and city buses seemed to stick to the sidewalks and buildings like a layer of rotting skin.

And 1055 Coney Island Avenue wasn't any meaner than the other nasty little storefronts with which it shared common walls. The dusty, sun-faded signage wasn't missing any more letters than the signs on the stores between which it was shouldered. The painted brick façade of the building above the shop at 1055 wasn't in a worse state of disrepair than its neighbors. There was no greater number of chipped bricks, the paint not any uglier or more flaked or pitted. The piles of filthy snow in the gutter out in front of it were no blacker. So in these ways 1055 Coney Island Avenue was unremarkable. I didn't know what Lids had given or promised to the guy who'd called me, but I couldn't help thinking I'd been played for a fool, for a stupid kid desperate for an answer . . . any answer.

The business at 1055 was a fix-it shop. The old vacuum hoses hanging limply behind the smudged glass reminded me of the red-skinned roasted ducks in the windows of Chinatown restaurants. Suddenly, my nose filled with fragrance of garlic and ginger sizzling in hot oil. My mouth watered, but there was no duck, no ginger, no hot oil. There were only broken toasters, round-tubed TV sets, giant radios, and old-fashioned fans in the window, relics. Sun-faded paper price tags were attached to these items with little bits of bakery string. A closer inspection revealed that everything in the window was covered in a fine, downy layer of gray dust.

A cockeyed Open/Closed sign hung in the door above where the store hours had peeled off and never been replaced. The sign said the store was open, but when I pressed my face to the glass, cupping my hands around my eyes, the only sign of movement was the flickering of a fluorescent tube in a fixture above the shop counter. To my surprise, the door gave way when I pushed, and I stepped inside. A rusted bell above the door made a half-hearted attempt to announce my arrival. Instead there was a single shrill and unwelcoming blare. With it, my visions of roasted ducks and the smells of Chinese cuisine vanished. The place was worse inside than out, smelling of machine oil, mildew, and disappointment.

"What?" A man screamed at me from behind the wall in back of the front counter. When I did not answer, he shouted, "What? All right, I'm coming, already. Already, I'm coming." He had a thick

Old World accent like the old folks on the boardwalk in Brighton Beach.

When he stepped out from behind the wall, hardly more than his head reached above the counter. He was short to begin with, and his hunched shoulders and stooped posture weren't helping any. His bald head, paradoxically freckled and pale, had a wreath of unkempt gray hair stretching from temple to temple. He had a furrowed brow and wore heavily rimmed black glasses held together by Band-Aids, with thick lenses on a nose that would have given W. C. Fields a fright. He had that kind of skin with big, ugly pores. He was dressed in pants worn shiny with age that were held up by a length of rope. Over this he had on a T-shirt so frayed and yellowed it might have disintegrated before my eyes.

"What, you picking up or dropping off? Well, you don't got nothing in your hands, sonny boy, so give to me already the receipt."

"I'm not here for that," I said, my voice faltering.

"Then what, you come begging for charity? You come to sell me something? *Gay avek!* Go away. Whatever I had to give, those Nazi bastards already are taking from me."

"I'm not here to ask for money or to sell you anything, mister."

"Then what? I'm a busy man. I have to work hard to be this poor, sonny. So speak up or get out."

"My girlfriend's in a coma in Kings Highway Hospital," I said, panicked. What did I know about questioning someone? I wasn't a cop. I didn't even know how to start. But if I thought telling him about Mindy would at least get me a little sympathy or buy me time, I thought wrong.

He crooked a gnarled finger at me. "At least she's alive. My wife. My kids. All gone. *Pffft!* Smoke out the pipe of the camp. Gone."

"I'm sorry."

"Save your sorrys for when they would matter. On me, they're a waste. Besides, what has this to do with me, your girlfriend?"

"Three nights ago, she was here."

"Here! Who was here?"

"My girlfriend, Mindy Weinstock."

There wasn't even a hint of recognition in his eyes.

"And what time was this when Mindy Weinstock was supposed to be in mine shop?"

"Early evening, between six and eight."

"Sonny, the only things here at those hours are broken toasters and roaches."

Okay, I thought, that was something, a place to start. "How about in the apartments upstairs?"

"How about them?"

"Do you own the building? Do you live upstairs? Do you know any of your neighbors? Stuff like that."

"Look, sonny, it's too bad from your girlfriend in the hospital, but I got no time for this stuff. I've got work. You wanna keep standing there, look for her fingerprints in the dust, be mine guest. But me, I got no time for nonsense." The gnome made to head into the rear of the shop.

"How about a black guy with pink blotches on his face and hands?" I shouted.

That stopped him. He looked up at me. I thought I saw something this time, a glint maybe, behind the thick lenses of his glasses. Or maybe it was wishful thinking on my part.

"You're talkin' crazy now again, a *schwartze* with pink blotches. *Gey avek* before I'm calling the police already." This time the gnome retreated behind the counter wall.

I did not move, not immediately. Although I had no idea of what I might find, I didn't expect to get dismissed out of hand. But even if I had come to the realization that growing up in Brooklyn didn't imbue me with a thicker skin or bless me with magical street smarts, I sensed something wasn't right; not with the old man and not with this musty little place. Okay, sure, camp survivors had it bad. I had seen *The Pawnbroker*. I'd seen the vacant-eyed survivors, their tattooed forearms swinging under the summer sun as they strolled zombie-like along the boardwalk. In their shoes, I might not have been the most pleasant bastard on the planet either. Still, I couldn't shake the feeling that there were things to know here. Screwed onto the countertop was a wooden business card holder that looked like a junior high shop class project. It held a few sun-yellowed cards. I took one because, if for no other reason, I was determined not to walk away empty-handed.

# CHAPTER NINE

I told Aaron I needed his car to see Mindy. It wasn't the first time I'd lied to him. It was unlikely to be the last. What my brother didn't know was that I'd already spent two hours at Mindy's bedside during afternoon visiting hours. Amazing how much time there is in a day when school is no longer a part of it.

I got back to the fix-it shop at around six and parked directly across Coney Island Avenue. It felt much later than six, as if night had already taken hold. That's the thing about winter, isn't it, how it always feels later than it is? Over the last few days I'd come to think that maybe life was like that too.

Now the flickering fluorescent light from inside the darkened shop gave it an eerie feel, like something out of a bad sci fi movie. *Oh, master, look, the creature lives!* I sipped my coffee, ate my bialy with cream cheese, and stared out the car window. At 6:10, the flickering stopped, the shop went completely black. Two minutes later, the hunched old man—Hyman Bergman, according to the business card I'd taken earlier—was on the street, fiddling with the lock. He walked a few paces away, stopped, turned, came back to the door, retried the door handle, and then went on his way. He limped along the street. My eyes followed him until he got into a beat-up '63 Fairlane that was now more rust than steel. He pulled out into traffic and I quickly lost sight of him.

At least I had the good sense to wait a quarter of an hour before making a move. My mom, like old man Bergman, had the habit of checking and rechecking things such as doors and gas jets. I had observed her doing this for nearly twenty-one years and knew that she had a fifteen-minute threshold. If she didn't come back to check something within that amount of time, she wasn't coming back. It was stupid to judge Bergman's *mishegas* by my mother's, but what other measure did I have?

Just as I put my fingers on the driver side door handle, I caught sight of something across Coney Island Avenue. It was a car, a car I recognized—Bobby's car. He parked the Olds 88 between two dirty snow drifts right in front of the fix-it shop. I did not move. I did not breathe. It was as if I hoped my stillness would somehow render me invisible. Not fucking likely, because as Bobby got out of his car he seemed to stare directly across the street at Aaron's Tempest. I could swear he looked right at me, but there was no recognition in his eyes, no change of body language. Maybe it was the darkness, or maybe he didn't make sense of my brother's car being in that setting. Whatever the reason, Bobby acted as if I wasn't there. I let myself exhale, if not relax. I didn't dare risk moving, not yet.

Bobby walked past the fix-it shop's door, heading directly to a white wooden door a few feet to the right of the shop's front window. The white door was the entrance to the apartments above the shop. Bobby reached up with his right arm—to ring the bell, I guess—and waited. About half a minute passed and Bobby rang the bell again. A minute passed. This time, he stepped back on the sidewalk and craned his neck to look up at the apartments. He shook his head, reached into his coat pocket, and pulled out his keys. I recognized his key ring even from across the street. I recognized it because dangling from it was the same stupid rabbit's foot that had been dangling from his key ring since we were twelve years old. It was white and plush back then. Now the fur that remained was dirty gray. He'd won the rabbit's foot in Coney Island for shooting a red star out of a piece of paper with a BB submachine gun.

"Shooting a red star," I'd said. "Don't tell your parents or they'll send you to Siberia."

I remember he'd just kind of laughed, but I think he'd kept the stupid rabbit's foot as a kind of *Fuck you* to his parents.

I was right about the keys, because soon enough, Bobby was stepping through the white door and closing it behind him. I fought my natural curiosity, sat tight, and waited. My patience was rewarded. Less than five minutes after he went in, Bobby came flying through the white door. His head was on a swivel, turning right, then left, then right again. He was breathless, panting, his chest heaving, but it was the panicked look on his face that really got my attention. Sucking in big gulps of frosty air, blowing staccato clouds of steam out of his mouth, he seemed to be trying to calm himself down before taking another step. Then, after he'd seen that no one was walking his way from either direction, Bobby rushed into his Olds and fishtailed away, smoking his rear tires on the slick pavement as he went.

I didn't remember opening the car door or crossing Coney Island Avenue, yet there I was, standing in front of the door Bobby Friedman had just burst through in a panic. And in his panic, Bobby had neglected to shut the door behind him. That wasn't like him. Whatever he'd found upstairs had scared the shit out of him, and he didn't usually scare easy. Under any other set of circumstances, I would have gotten out of there faster than Superman, but these weren't other circumstances. Maybe old man Bergman really didn't know anything, but there had to be a reason Lids's guy had given me this address. There was no chance I was going to walk away from this. No chance. Not now.

The staircase was fairly dark with some very weak light filtering down from the second floor landing. The stairs were crooked and cranky, moaning under my weight. The banister was loose and about as trustworthy as an aluminum siding salesman. The air smelled like my wet gym socks, but there was another raw scent too: the stink of an unflushed toilet. And present between the must and stench was one more pungent odor, one that I didn't quite yet understand. It mixed and mingled with the other smells, but managed to rise above them and crown itself king. It was vaguely familiar. I remembered being at my aunt's house as a kid and finding a broken jar of baby food in a kitchen cabinet. Ground lamb, I think it was. Not only did it reek, but the meat had seemed to be alive. I had noticed the little bits of white squirming about in the sickly gray meat like wiggly grains of rice. Only later did my aunt explain about fly eggs and maggots.

At the second floor landing I was greeted by an unadorned, low wattage bulb and, to my left, a black steel door with two serious-looking padlocks. There was a sign on the door:

**STORAGE**
**KEEP OUT**
**OR ELSE**

God love Brooklyn. Anywhere else, the words "Keep Out" would have been warning enough, but here you had to turn a warning into a threat. Problem with Brooklynites is that we take threats as a challenge. I tried the door. No luck. It didn't budge a millimeter. I had the sense that if a small nuclear bomb hit this building, that door would still be standing. I got down on all fours and sniffed under the door. Nope. Wherever the stink was coming from, it wasn't here. Besides, there was nothing here that would have freaked

Bobby out. I looked up toward the third floor landing. It was totally lightless up there, but sometimes there's just no going back.

These stairs were in even worse shape than the ones leading up to the black door. I think habit was the only thing that stopped them giving way. They bent pretty good as I went. I noticed something else too: the stench was getting more intense as I climbed. The door to the top floor apartment was just cheap bare wood with a lock in the knob like you might find on a closet or bathroom door. It turned in my hand and I pushed it open. When I did, the stink hit me full in the face and it was all I could do not to vomit. Now I understood why Bobby had been breathing so fiercely when I'd seen him out on the street. I put my hand inside the sleeve of my coat and pinched my nose closed. It was incredibly hot inside the apartment, like a sauna at one of those bathhouses my *zaydeh* and all the old European men favored. I touched the cast iron radiator with the tip of my finger. No wonder the apartment felt like a sauna. The radiator was hot enough to cook on. It didn't help that the windows were sealed shut.

I found a wall switch to my left and clicked it on. Two out of three bulbs in the old-fashioned ceiling fixture popped on. The room was barely furnished. There were two blue bean bag chairs, a few plastic chairs, a portable Zenith TV on an upturned milk crate with aluminum foil on the antenna, and not much else. Burgundy House looked like a designer showcase by comparison. I stepped further inside. To my right was a little galley-style kitchen. A few dishes were in the drying rack next to the chipped and rust-stained porcelain sink. In the fridge there were a few six-packs of Piels beer, a paper bag with a few ounces of pot in the vegetable bin, a carton of sour milk, and nothing else. I wished the sour milk was the reason for the awful smell in the place. It was just that: a wish. For when I finally got the courage to go down the short hallway, past the bathroom, and into the bedroom, I saw the real reason lying on the bed.

I was no doctor, and I was no mortician. Still, I knew a dead body when I saw one . . . when I smelled one. Now I understood Bobby's panic. He'd run, and I guess if I hadn't taken a second look at the dead man, I'd have run too. There were some ugly bruises on his face and a big gash across his forehead that was covered in crusted, dried blood. He looked like someone had taken a tire iron to his face. His brown eyes were open, unseeing, and clouded over. I guessed he was about my age and would've stood six-two or -three. He had on a pair of bell-bottom jeans, worn shiny at the knees, and tan work boots. He wore a gray, blood-stained sweatshirt with a horse head logo across the chest, with the words Effingham Mustangs printed below. Yet it wasn't his wardrobe or the color of his eyes or his wounds that kept me there. It was his short-cropped Afro haircut, the light shade of his brown skin, and the once-pink blotches on his face and hands that got my attention. So this poor dead bastard was the son of a bitch who'd put Mindy in a coma. In the movies, they would have had me spit on him or kick him for good measure—*I'll show you to hurt my girlfriend*—but I just didn't see the point. Even though I was close enough to touch him, he was beyond my reach.

I couldn't say if the stench was finally getting to me or what, but I suddenly felt the need to get out of there. I wasn't stupid about it. I didn't want my fingerprints all over the place, so I used my sleeve and wiped down every surface I'd touched: the doors, the light switch, the fridge, the milk carton . . . What was really weird was how the farther away from the body I moved, the more intense my nausea got. I could feel the vomit in my throat, taste it in my mouth. My head was pounding and I was sweating through my clothes. I made it down to the second floor landing before I could no longer hold back. I puked my guts out on the floor, some of it splashing onto the black steel door. OR ELSE indeed.

When I collected what was left of me, I wobbled to the ground floor on very shaky legs. My first lungful of the brutal outside air made me sick again and if I'd had anything left to give, I would have given it up right there on the street. Instead, I dry-retched some and staggered through the sparse traffic until I made it to the safety of Aaron's Tempest. It was strange how much that stupid car seat felt like home. I was in too much shock to drive away, never mind make sense of any of what I'd just been through. My life lessons were now no longer restricted to the stickball court or the sand beneath the boardwalk.

# CHAPTER TEN

I don't know how long it took me to get to Burgundy House. I wasn't sure how I'd gotten there, what streets I'd taken, or if I'd bothered stopping at red lights. The drive over wasn't just a blur; it wasn't even a memory. I was there, then I was here. In that time, however much time it was, I don't believe I'd had one clear thought pass through my brain. It was so bizarre because when I was standing there in front of the body, I'd been pretty calm. Then, in the next second, my calm had begun to unravel. Now, I was a total mess.

In the darkened front seat of the car, I couldn't get warm. I was cold from the marrow out, and the Tempest's heater was as useless to me as corners to a bowling ball. I took my hands off the steering wheel and watched them shake. I was helpless to do anything about it. The harder I tried willing them to stop, the harder they shook. Compared to what was going on inside me, my shaking hands were the least of it. Nevertheless, shock and shaking hands weren't going to stand up in court as reasons for not calling the cops. Sure, the only things I knew about police work I'd learned from *Mannix* and *The Mod Squad*—which I watched because I thought Peggy Lipton was hot—but you didn't have to be J. Edgar Hoover to understand that I was obstructing justice by not telling the cops I'd found a corpse, one that had met a pretty violent end. And that when I'd wiped away my fingerprints, I'd probably wiped away others as well.

To distract myself, I listened to Cousin Brucie on the radio. When I was a little kid, I loved his goofiness. Lately, he drove me nuts. In all fairness, it wasn't only his endless talking over the music that made me crazy. I mean, I liked the Monkees as much as the next guy, but how many times can you stand to listen to "I'm a Believer" in the course of a day before sticking needles in your eyes? I found myself daydreaming about a radio station where DJs talked in human voices, played songs from your favorite albums that weren't hits, and spun long songs that didn't get butchered down to three minutes. Yeah, like that was ever going to happen. I might as well have hoped for wireless telephones or good-tasting American beer. Dream on. After a few minutes, I noticed my hands were no longer shaking and that I could actually put two reasonable thoughts together about something other than AM radio together without freaking out.

That's when it hit me: What the fuck had Bobby been doing at 1055 Coney Island Avenue to begin with, and why did he have keys to the place? I'd been so caught up in what was happening that the illogic of his presence hadn't registered. There was a split second, I think, when I first spotted Bobby's car that I wondered about what he was doing there, but then what followed overwhelmed the question. I guess dead bodies have that effect on me.

Okay, I was pretty confident that Bobby, no matter what he was doing there, hadn't killed the guy. For one thing, Bobby wasn't up there long enough to have struggled with him. Besides, the bedroom window faced Coney Island Avenue, and as I was watching the upstairs windows from across the street, I would have seen a struggle. And though the apartment was pretty much a mess, there were no signs of a struggle: no broken furniture, no cracked plaster, nothing like that. And the body was ripe. My lack of a medical education notwithstanding, even I knew it would take at least a few days for the body to get that way. Still, none of that explained away Bobby's being there and having keys to the place.

Then, a sick, niggling thought wormed its way into my brain: What if Bobby wasn't just going there, but going *back* there? I only had one connection, Lids, and he'd found someone to supply the address to me in less than twenty-four hours. Bobby had a million connections, and he always had money. So it was easy to see that if he wanted an address, Bobby would get it. If he got the address and found the guy who'd attacked Mindy hiding out there . . . Now, you've got to understand this about Bobby: he had the potential for violence. Although he was generally a gentle, happy soul, he wasn't a weak one. He was a tough bastard, thick through his chest and arms. His union-organizer dad wasn't big on hugging his son, but he had taught him all the tricks of the trade. Bobby was a sight to behold when peace demonstrations turned unpeaceful. I'd seen him knock more than one cop and a few construction workers flat on their asses.

So yeah, Bobby had violence in him. It wasn't hard for me to imagine him talking his way into the apartment and then taking a piece of pipe to Mindy's attacker. But why come back? Maybe to see if he had actually killed the guy, or to make sure he hadn't left any evidence behind. Bobby was tough, not stupid. Then there was another possibility, one I really didn't want to think about. What if Bobby was sheltering the man who'd attacked Mindy, and was going there to check on him? The keys—in some ways, it was all about the keys. Maybe Bobby'd taken them from the guy after killing him. If not, that meant Bobby already had keys to the place. And if he did, I was back to square one: What was he doing there, and why did he have keys? Were they Bobby's or the dead man's?

There was only one way to find out.

# CHAPTER ELEVEN

I drove back to the fix-it shop, but made sure to park blocks away and out of sight of anyone who might know me or my brother's car. As I walked, I tried very hard to focus on the cold, on the passing traffic, or just about anything I could other than what I had in mind to do. Did the idea of going back into that apartment and patting down a corpse scare the shit out of me? Yeah, it did, but the thought that Mindy might never wake up scared me more. It scared me more to think that my best friend might've murdered someone. And what scared me most of all was the opposite, that rather than killing the man who had nearly beaten my girlfriend to death, Bobby had a connection to him or had tried to save him.

Again, as I'd done earlier from the safety of Aaron's car, I watched and waited. This time, from the shadows of a doorway directly across the street. A light went on, not from the third floor bedroom where the body was, but from the storage area on the second floor where the sign on the black door had threatened OR ELSE. Frayed and puckered shades covered the windows. They allowed light to leak out their sides, but did not give up anything more than that. I checked the Bulova watch on my wrist that my Aunt Sylvia and Uncle Lenny had given me for my high school graduation. Suddenly, standing out there alone in the biting cold, high school felt like a chapter from someone else's book.

It was a little after eight. Only two hours or so had passed from when I'd first pulled up across the street. Two hours, the same amount of time that had elapsed between my conversation with Mindy and when I found her smoking and drinking outside Burgundy House on the evening this nightmare had begun. I'd been confused by her mood swing that night. What, I'd wondered since, could possibly have happened in two hours to make her change so dramatically? I was no longer as confused. If the events of my evening had taught me anything, it was that a lot more than moods could change in two hours—a lot more.

At 8:16, an old, shit-brown Dugan's Bakery truck, the company logo sloppily painted over, parked in front of the fix-it shop. Two guys about my age, dressed alike in woolen watch caps, army surplus jackets, and gloves, got out of the truck. The back door of the van swung open. When I felt it was safe, I moved four doorways to my right so I could get a better angle on what there was to see. I noticed that the white door to the upstairs apartments had been wedged open and that the two guys, neither of whom were familiar to me, were disappearing up the creaky stairs I'd navigated less than an hour before. For their sakes, I hoped they had nose plugs. The place stank badly enough before I'd deposited the contents of my digestive system on the second floor landing. I couldn't imagine how bad it reeked in there now. I got a little sickly just thinking about it.

When the two of them came down a few minutes later, they were each carrying small, rope-handled, wooden crates that they loaded in the back of the truck. I couldn't make out anything about the crates from where I stood, but they must have been heavy because the truck sat down on its rear tires. Either that or the truck's springs were shot. Frick and Frack made two more round-trips, each time carrying similar crates as on their first foray. On their last trip, Frick had a small duffel bag slung over his right shoulder. Frack was empty-handed. Then when Frick threw the duffel bag onto the floor of the truck box, Frack went nuts.

"What the fuck are you doing, man? You wanna get us killed?"

"Fuck you," said the guy who'd slammed down his duffel. "You're not the boss of me."

Then there was a third voice, a girl's voice, one that cut through the night air like a straight razor. "Shut up! The Committee is the boss of us all, and they won't be happy if these are damaged or if we get caught here. Now let's go. We don't have much time."

When the owner of that third voice stepped out into the ambient street light, my heart caught in my throat. I recognized her. How could I not? I'd sat next to her in Romantic Poetry class three times a week during fall term. Her name was Susan Kasten. She'd said about five words to me during that time, four of which were "shut up" twice. But those were five more than she uttered aloud in the rest of the class. She was a petite, mouse-haired, plain-faced girl who struck me as the kind of person who longs for invisibility. And if it wasn't for her cat-green eyes, she might have been able to disappear into the background. I squeezed my eyelids shut, combing my memory to recall if there was anything about Susan that would connect the girl from class with the one barking orders at Frick and Frack. Nothing came to mind. The sound of the truck door slamming shut broke my trance. I looked up to see the Dugan's truck pulling away, coughing big clouds of exhaust as it went. I was half hoping that Susan had slammed the white door shut behind her so that there'd be no way for me to get back up to the third floor. She hadn't. In fact, she'd left it wide open.

There was a fair amount of traffic in both directions on Coney Island Avenue when I stepped out of the shadows to cross the street. At least a minute passed before I could even make it halfway across. When I got stuck there on the double yellow lines, I looked up at the third floor windows. I got weak in the knees and lightheaded thinking about what I was going up there to do. But when I looked up, I saw orange light dancing in the windows of the bedroom where the body lay. Before I could take another step, flames completely engulfed the room. I was frozen in place. Then I remembered what Sue Kasten had said to her flunkies: "We don't have much time."

As my eyes shifted down one story, there were two loud explosions. The second and third floor windows blew out, showering the street below and the cars below with jagged glass shards, bits of plaster, and wooden shrapnel. The hallway coughed flames out onto the sidewalk. Some of the debris flew over my head. Some of it bit into the blacktop around my feet. More than just fire had caused that blast. Gas, maybe? Molotov cocktails? I couldn't say. The explosion unfroze me and I ran. As I did, I kept thinking that I'd asked Lids to get me an address so I might find some answers. What I got instead were more questions wrapped in other questions. I'd worry about that later. First I had to get back to the car.

◆

*Bang!*

This explosion was of a completely different, more personal nature. I guess I wasn't paying careful enough attention to the world outside my head, because under most circumstances I would've seen it coming. Not only didn't I see it coming, I wasn't even sure what *it* was: a length of pipe, a baseball bat, a two-by-four? That was kind of beside the point as whatever it was knocked the wind so far out of me I felt like I would have go to the Bronx to retrieve it. As if it wasn't bad enough that I had already taken a shot across my midsection and was currently writhing on the sidewalk next to my brother's car, the kick in my ribs was like the cherry on top of the icing on top of my indignity cake. It got even worse still when powerful hands grabbed the shoulders of my coat and flipped me over onto my back. Then those same hands twisted themselves around my collar and yanked me up onto my knees. A big man in a full ski mask stood over me, the knuckles on his fingers pinching off the blood to my brain.

"Listen ta me, ya fuckin' amateur. Stay outta this shit or I'll have ta really hurt ya. Ya understand, asshole? Don't be playin' on the big boys' court no more. Ya understand?"

He could have repeated that question fifty times, but I was in no position to answer. I already couldn't breathe, and he was pressing on my neck so hard I couldn't speak. I suppose he finally figured out my answer when I kind of moved my head in a feeble nod.

"All right, you hippie piece a shit. Remember what I said. Stay outta this."

Hippie! Me? I thought the ski mask was supposed to prevent me from seeing his face, not prevent him from seeing mine. My hair wasn't that long. I was clean-shaven, and there wasn't a peace sign anywhere to be found on my clothes. Anyway, if you came from my family you knew better than to think love was the answer for all the world's ills. I might've even laughed at him if he wasn't busy interfering with the bodily processes required to produce laughter. Then I felt his grip relax. Blood rushed back to my brain, and I could feel my lungs were once again in working order. But when he fully released his grip, I went crashing back down onto the cement. As I lay there like a dishrag on the frozen sidewalk, I realized the bruise on my shoulder would have new friends to keep it company.

# CHAPTER TWELVE

It was early; early enough that I heard the *Daily News* being delivered by our apartment door; early enough so I could swipe the *Post* and the *Times* from in front of my neighbors' doors without fear of getting caught; early enough so that my family was asleep and would remain so for a few more hours.

The stories about the fire in the morning papers failed to mention whether or not human remains were found in the debris at 1055 Coney Island Avenue. In fact, all the articles were stingy on details. No surprise there—according to the papers, the fire department hadn't gotten the blaze under control until around midnight. That was less than seven hours ago. Oh, yeah, that was the other thing: the stories were very vague on whether it was just a fire or an explosion and a fire. The *Post* said one thing, the *Daily News* something else. Even the sacred *New York Times* gave it a few inches, but it didn't exactly usurp the continuing coverage of the fire that had destroyed the Apollo 1 capsule in late January. Nor had it pushed aside coverage of Vietnam. The war was getting out of control, just like Bobby had warned me it would when we were seniors at Lincoln.

"You'll see, Moe. They tell you it's about preserving freedom and about preventing the domino effect in Southeast Asia, but that's a crock of shit, man. It's sleight of hand, like when Tony Pizza does those silly magic tricks. You think it's about this hand when it's really about that one."

"Then what's the war about?"

"What it's always about: money. Even Ike, not exactly anybody's definition of a Commie or a dove, warned us about the military industrial complex. War is a money maker. It's a beast with an insatiable appetite. You just watch what happens. By next year, we'll be so involved in the war we'll never get out. It wouldn't be half as bad if the beast only ate machines, but it doesn't. It eats people and if we don't watch out, it's gonna eat us too."

Until six months ago, I'd thought Bobby was being a little hysterical about the war, spouting his lefty propaganda. Then Michael Ruggio, a guy we knew from the neighborhood, came back home from Nam with no legs, one arm, and brain damage. Seeing Mike like that changed my mind to Bobby's way of thinking. So when I went to register for the draft at the Shore Theatre building on Surf Avenue across from Nathan's, I was scared, really scared. I guess I was still pretty scared, but today it was for different reasons.

I was also in pain. Even before last night, I'd been eating aspirins like Cap'n Crunch. Now, just as the shoulder pain had become tolerable, I had sore ribs, an aching kidney—I'd pissed a little blood when I got up—and swelling above my liver. Whoever the guy in the ski mask was, he understood the mechanics of inflicting pain. At least there weren't any bruises on my neck from his knuckles. Not that I had a clue about any of this, but I was more confused by what had happened to me at the end of the evening than the rest of it. How did that guy know to wait for me by Aaron's car? Who was he? What part of this mess was I supposed to stay out of, exactly, and why? Was I supposed to just sit on the bench? There was already such a jumble of questions in my head, I couldn't deal with any new ones.

One good thing: it was Saturday, and that meant I could swipe my dad's car for the day. And that's exactly what I did. Maybe it was a sign I was getting older that I'd begun noticing the weather. That's an exaggeration, because when you grow up close to the beach, like I did, you know that the weather reports you hear on TV are a waste of time. Near the ocean, the weather is about much more than temperature. It's about a thousand things, large and small— the wind, for instance, or where the sun is in the sky at any time of day. I don't know how or when it happened, but one day I realized I could sense snow. I could read it in the sky's subtle shades of gray, smell it on the breeze. Finally, I understood what my mom meant when she said it was raw outside. And raw was just what it was when I left my building. The wind was up, the air damp. The cold cut right through me as if I was wearing a bathing suit instead of a coat.

It was way too early to visit Mindy, so after buying a cup of coffee and a bialy in Brighton Beach, I turned my dad's Rambler American left onto Coney Island Avenue. Traffic was light at that hour. As I went, I noticed the old Jewish men of Brooklyn going to temple for Saturday services. Like most of my other Jewish friends, I hadn't gone to *shul* on the Sabbath in years. Unlike our fathers, and their fathers, and their fathers' fathers before them, we didn't view our bar mitzvahs as a rite of passage into manhood, but paradoxically as emancipation from the weight of tradition and our legacy of victimization. Still, I sensed I would never truly be free of the tradition and the legacy no matter how far I turned my back on them, no matter how I tried to drown out the cantors' sacred songs with the Rolling Stones.

I could smell the remnants of the fire from a block away: the tang of melted plastic, the soggy charcoal stink of burned-out timbers. I suppose every kind of death has a unique, lingering odor. There was some rubbernecking, so I was already going pretty slowly as I passed what was left of 1055 Coney Island Avenue, which wasn't much. The roof was gone and only the bare bones of the top two floors remained. Hyman Bergman's fix-it shop would need more fixing than it was worth. Its glass door and windows had been smashed in or blown out, and the sooted interior looked like a cancerous lung. I had to laugh at how the ominous storage room door, bowed and twisted, its black paint burned off, still stood, swinging in the wind. Milky gray icicles hung off every available surface. There was char on the buildings to either side of 1055, but they seemed to have survived mostly intact.

There was a black and green patrol car stationed out front, and a rectangle of police sawhorse barricades blocking off the sidewalk. Parked behind the patrol car was a conspicuously unmarked Plymouth Fury. At one side of the barricades, I spotted old man Bergman standing between a tall man dressed in a blue tunic and a white cap—probably a fire inspector—and a squat man in a rumpled trench coat—a detective. Bergman kept gesturing at the upper floors and shrugging his shoulders. He was saying something too. Although I'd only had the displeasure of meeting the gnome once, it was easy for me to fill in his dialogue.

Watching Bergman as I passed, I got an idea for how to move ahead. I hadn't really had one up until then. My original plan, such as it was, was to drive by, see what I could see, maybe go hang at Burgundy House until visiting hours at the hospital. I thought that I'd use the phone at Burgundy House to call Lids and ask him about the guy who'd given me the Coney Island Avenue address in the first place. Maybe I'd ask him to do a little more digging for me to find out about Susan Kasten's scene. Or maybe he could get me some information about the black guy with the vitiligo. As far as I could figure, there were only a few people who knew Pink Blotches was dead: Susan Kasten, Bobby, me, and the man who'd killed him. I hoped Bobby wasn't two out of the four. But as I watched Bergman fading in my side view mirror, I remembered the feeling I got when I was in the shop yesterday, and that glint in his eyes when I mentioned the black guy with vitiligo.

It didn't take me long to find what I was looking for. Even in a borough of bruised and dented used cars, Bergman's rusted wreck of a Ford Fairlane stuck out. It was parked on Coney Island Avenue, about a block past the burnt-out shell of the building. I parked a few cars behind it and waited. I was doing a lot of that lately, waiting. After forty-five minutes and a lot of thumb twiddling, the brilliant idea of following Bergman around seemed a lot less brilliant. When a full hour went by, it didn't seem brilliant at all. I was about to give up on the notion completely when I spotted the old man coming my way. Man, his gait was painful to watch. I imagine it wasn't any less painful for him. Each step looked like it should have been his last. He musta been one tough son of a bitch. He was sure as shit nasty enough. Who knows, maybe that was what had helped him survive the camps. He certainly hadn't charmed his way out.

I followed Bergman back toward my part of Brooklyn, except he went left after crossing the Coney Island Avenue bridge over the Belt Parkway. Five minutes later, he pulled into the driveway of a big—by Brooklyn standards—Tudor house off Oriental Boulevard in Manhattan Beach. Manhattan Beach was the fanciest, wealthiest area in my part of Brooklyn. The working stiffs, blue collar mugs, cops, firemen, fishermen, teachers, clerks, secretaries, and construction workers lived in Brighton Beach, Coney Island, and Sheepshead Bay. The people with money, they lived in the fancy houses in Manhattan Beach. Here, the kids got their own rooms and their own cars, and went on family vacations that ranged a lot farther than hotels in the Catskills. What, I wondered, was Bergman doing here? A guy like him, a guy who used rope to hold up his pants, who drove a car made out of rust, I figured, must do pickups and drop-offs if sufficient money was involved. So I parked and waited for him to leave. The thing was, he never left.

More than a half hour had gone by when I realized I either needed to leave myself or to check out the house. Before getting out of my dad's car, I looked around for something, anything that might prevent Bergman from recognizing me if he spotted me lurking. There it was on the floor of the backseat, my dad's silly pork pie hat. My dad had grown up during a time when most men wore hats, but he hated that Aaron, Miriam, and I teased him about it. He pretended he'd stopped wearing one altogether, though we knew he just stashed it in the car. It was one of those little charades that made a family a family. Secretly, I think the three of us admired him for hanging stubbornly onto his tradition while trying to fool us. It gave us something to admire him for, and there wasn't much else to choose from. Kids, especially sons, need to admire their dads.

I must've looked as ridiculous as I felt with my dad's hat on. I folded the brim down like in *Mad* magazine's Spy vs. Spy bits. Pacing across the street from the Tudor house, I had a good view down the driveway through the winter bare hedges. Besides the rust bucket, a white Renault Dauphine and a blue Chevy Impala were parked there. I also had a fairly unobstructed view of the living room window. When two people appeared in that window a few minutes later, I couldn't quite believe my eyes, because I recognized both their faces. Although I couldn't hear what was going on, it was pretty obvious from their body language, their facial expressions, and their angry gesturing that they were engaged in a nasty fight. I found I wasn't as curious about the subject of the fight as I was about the warring parties. Why, I wondered, was Hyman Bergman shouting at Susan Kasten, and what were both of them doing in the living room of this big house in Manhattan Beach? Just what I needed, more questions.

"Hey, you!" A hand landed hard on my right shoulder at the same time I heard the man's voice.

I was so surprised I nearly pissed myself. Instead, I turned slowly in the direction of the voice. And when I did, I smiled, because this was yet another face I recognized. "Dr. Mishkin," I said. "How are you?" Dr. Raoul Mishkin had a practice in Brighton Beach, and had been our family doctor for as long as I could remember.

"Moses Prager. What are you doing in front of my house?"

"You live here?" I deflected as I about-faced. "Nice house."

"Thank you, but I've known you since you were a little *pisher*. You can't pretend with me, kid. I saw you pacing out here. So come on, out with it, why did you track me down? You got something to talk about with me that maybe you would be embarrassed to discuss in my office. Maybe something you don't want your parents to know about."

Look, if this is what he thought, I wasn't going to try and dissuade him. Making something up was going to be a hell of a lot easier than explaining what I was actually doing there.

"It's my girlfriend," was all I said. He filled in the rest.

Mishkin shrugged his shoulders. "Pregnant, huh?"

"I don't know. Maybe. She's two weeks late."

"Come, let's go inside and talk. My wife will make something for us to eat and we can discuss your options."

Doc took me in, introduced me to his wife, and then we went into his library. Fifteen minutes later, his wife brought us lox and onion omelets with bagels and coffee. We ate pretty much in silence. After some initial small talk, he gave me a lecture about what my girlfriend and I needed to consider. Illegal abortion never came up directly, but he sort of talked around it.

"If you and your girl are thinking about some other path, don't rush to take it. It can be dangerous and you can get in a lot of trouble. Listen, I'm just a doctor, which, to tell you the truth, is like another name for being a fancy mechanic. As just a mechanic, I am not a wise enough man, not a philosopher to know what a life is or when it begins. Death, that I know a lot about, too much, I'm afraid. But once a life is ended, there are no second chances, no turning back, no do-overs. Do you understand what I am saying to you, Moses?"

"I do, Doc. I do."

It was odd how I'd ended up in his library, but somehow I knew I would never forget his talk about a pregnancy that never was.

"Good. You always were a sharp kid."

Then I had an idea, hopefully one that would finally lead to some answers. "So Doc, when I was standing on the street, trying to get up the nerve to knock on your door, I thought I saw someone I know in the house across the way."

"Susan?"

"Yeah, Sue Kasten. We had a class together at BC last term. Does she live across the street?"

"Yes, she lives there now with her grandfather, Hyman. He's a horrible human being. I suppose I should be more forgiving because he lost almost his whole family in the camps, but . . ." Mishkin didn't finish his thought. "Susan moved in two years ago. Her mom and dad live out west somewhere, Oregon or California, I think. They're university professors. Sherry, Susan's mom, is Hyman's daughter. Well, Susan wanted to come east to study and to get to know her family here. Hyman and Sherry hated each other and then she moved out when she turned eighteen, but apparently Susan wouldn't be denied."

"Big house they live in," I said.

"Old Hyman's loaded. Owns real estate all over the place, but he's also a *bisl meshugge*. You understand?"

"I speak some Yiddish, Doc, yeah. The old man's a little crazy. How so?"

"Maybe the camps did it to him. I don't know. He drives a car that's practically falling apart, wears clothes a bum would be embarrassed of, and runs a fix-it shop even though he owns the building it's in and half the rest of the block. The man is wealthy, and doesn't enjoy a penny of his money. He dotes on his granddaughter, though. Bought her that ridiculous French car in their driveway."

I stood to go and shook Doc Mishkin's hand. Thanked him for his advice. Then I remembered the tone in his voice when he'd first approached me outside. It wasn't a very welcoming or friendly tone. I realized that he hadn't recognized that it was me standing in front of his house until I turned to face him.

"Doc, when you came up to me on the street, did you know it was me standing there?"

"Nope. It's that we've had a little crime in the area recently, and I didn't like you loitering out in front."

"Crime?"

"Yes. Earlier this week, Bob Schwartz, a friend of mine from down the block, had his Caddy stolen from right out in front of his house."

"A Caddy. What kind of Caddy?"

"A beauty. A silver '67 Coupe de Ville with a black vinyl roof. They found it smashed up over in Midwood somewhere during the snowstorm. The insurance company took it as a total loss."

I forced myself to answer calmly. "That's a shame. Well, thanks again, Doc. You've given me a lot to think about."

No lie there. He had given me a lot to think about. That, and some answers.

# CHAPTER THIRTEEN

On the way over to visit my real girlfriend—the one in the coma, not the make-believe one whose period was two weeks late—I had a lot to chew on. I believed in coincidence more than the hand of God or fate or karma, but even I had my limits. There were just too many connections here to slough them off as mere coincidence. One thing was for damn sure: Bobby Friedman was, for some reason, the eye at the center of this storm. It seemed to me that all the new violence in my world somehow swirled around my best and oldest friend and I wanted to know why; I needed to know why. If he hadn't shown up at 1055 Coney Island Avenue last night, I might not have seen Bobby as so central to what was happening; but he had shown up and with a set of keys.

No one is immune from willful ignorance. I wasn't. I'd looked the other way and pretended not to see things: friends stealing, friends cheating on tests, friends cheating on their girlfriends. Guys are like that. I can't explain it. Maybe it comes from playing team sports all our lives. It's like we're in some sort of club with a silent understanding that it's always us against them. The "us" was constant. The "them" was situational. I don't really know. What I did know was that this was different. I couldn't ignore the fact that those keys Bobby had weren't just any keys to just any building. There'd been a dead body in that building, the body of the man who'd beaten Mindy into a coma. They were keys to a building that burned to the ground a few hours after his visit. I wasn't willing to ignore the fact that the Cadillac that nearly killed Bobby and me had been stolen off old man Bergman's block. Bergman, the owner of the building that had burned down. It was impossible for me to ignore the fact that Bergman's granddaughter was probably the person who'd torched her grandpa's building, dead body et al. Sitting there in the hospital lobby, waiting the few minutes until visiting hours were to begin, I thought back to the fight I'd seen between grandfather and granddaughter. And as I reflected on what I'd witnessed, it struck me that I wasn't the only man in Brooklyn who thought Susan Kasten, the quiet girl from my Romantic Poetry class, was guilty of arson. Grandpa seemed to think so too.

"Visiting hours have begun. No children under the age of twelve will be permitted on the upper floors. Please do not . . ." came the announcement over the loudspeaker.

I took the stairs to the third floor. I took them slowly as I was still aching pretty bad. Mindy's parents were already in her room when I arrived.

"Moe, it's wonderful. A miracle! Come look," said Beatrice Weinstock, tugging at my arm. "She's opened her eyes."

My heart went from zero to sixty before I could take another breath. I could feel it thumping at the walls of my chest. In that instant, none of the rest of it mattered. None of it. Suddenly, I didn't give a rat's ass if Bobby was at the head of a Soviet spy network, the criminal mastermind behind a plot to rob the Federal Reserve bank, or both. And damn it if it wasn't true: Mindy's eyes were wide open.

"Hi, Min," I whispered in her ear, kissed her cheek. I stroked her hair. "I love you. I love you. I love you. I'm sorry I never told you that before. I'm not sure if I even knew it. I love you."

But she didn't respond in any way. My thumping heart sank into my shoes. It occurred to me that her eyes weren't seeing anything more than Pink Blotches's dead eyes had seen the night before.

When I snuck a peek at Herbie Weinstock, I saw that he had reached a similar conclusion.

"That's wonderful," I shouted to Mrs. Weinstock. "Wonderful. Listen, you guys stay here and enjoy the moment. I'll be back later."

Herbie nodded. I nodded back. There it was again, that guy thing, that silent understanding. It even crossed generations. Beatrice had already returned her focus to her daughter, willing Mindy to do more than open her eyes. I left them that way. Outside the door, I ran into Mindy's doctor, Steven Curtis, a svelte and delicate man with piano fingers and the bedside manner of a wrecking ball. I'd had the displeasure of talking with the good doctor a few times. He wasn't anything like Doc Mishkin. When Doc Mishkin told you the truth, no matter how harsh, you were comforted to know it. The truth from Curtis was a serrated edge. Trailing behind Dr. Curtis were five bright-eyed interns.

I blocked Curtis's way. "Could I talk to you for a second?" I asked, my eyes letting him know there was only going to be one acceptable answer.

"Later, young man. As you no doubt see, I am doing rounds."

"A second," I repeated.

When he saw that I didn't pray at his altar and I wasn't moving an inch, he relented. "Very well."

I stepped away from his pack and he followed.

"Her eyes are open," I said.

"They do that sometimes. It isn't necessarily significant." He said *they* as if he'd been talking about heads of cabbage or fruit flies.

I put my face up close to his. "Well, do me a favor, Doc, don't shit on her mom's joy. She needs to believe Mindy will be okay, and if Min's eyes being open gives her hope, let her have it. If you have to discuss the truth with the interns, ask Mindy's parents to step outside or use terms they don't understand. Okay?"

"Fine. Now, if you'll excuse me . . ."

✦

I found Lids in his bedroom in his parent's apartment in Trump Village. Village, my ass. Trump Village bore about as much resemblance to the traditional sense of a village as an elephant to an oyster. It was a series of huge brick apartment buildings that soared twenty-plus stories over the streets of Brighton Beach and Coney Island. There are pictures in my high school yearbook of the buildings being constructed, their massive girders dwarfing the school. When Trump—none of us called it Trump Village—opened in '64, the influx of the thousands of new families totally changed the nature of the neighborhood. The Lesters, Lids's parents, had moved to here from the Bronx partially in the hope that their son might fit in better in Brooklyn. No such luck. Larry wouldn't've fit in on the Starship *Enterprise*. He wasn't a fitting-in type of guy.

His sad little parents were happy to see my face. For them, I guess I represented a connection to normalcy for their son in kind of the same way I represented a nonradical political connection to Mindy's folks. Funny how I never thought of myself as normal. Does anyone ever consider himself normal? Would anyone want to? My brother Aaron, probably. At my age, I think he'd fancied himself as normal. It's not like I minded Lids's or Mindy's parents seeing me the way they did. I didn't feel any pressure from it. I liked making people feel better. I always had, though I've no clue where that ability came from. My dad maybe. Surely not from my mom. She was so persistently pessimistic that I don't think she would have been shocked if one day the sun didn't come up. She would just say, "I knew it. I knew it."

Larry Lester was sitting in a chair, rocking, staring out the window at the elevated subway ten floors below. He did that. It helped him think and theorize, he used to say. His room hadn't changed in the thirteen years I'd known the guy. I'm serious. It was like he'd died as a kid and his mother, grief-stricken by her son's death, had preserved his room in museum condition. There were posters of Howdy Doody and Davy Crockett on his walls. Even mad genius drug dealers have their quirks. Larry had more than his share.

"Hey, Larry," I said.

It was as if he hadn't heard me. He just kept on rocking and staring. I waited another minute before trying again.

"Yo, Larry. Lids!"

"Moe, did you ever think that time is something that doesn't really exist, that it's something we impose on the universe?" he said, still not turning around, continuing to rock and stare.

"Not really, Larry. I can see myself grow, watch my parents get older, watch things rust away. So how can time not exist?"

"What if things aren't linear in the way you just described them? What if the universe is a solid block of events that occur all at once? Maybe everything that ever happened is happening, and everything that ever will happen has already happened. Maybe it's like a film with all the frames compressed together. We might only experience it one frame at a time, one slice at a time. Maybe time is merely experiential in nature."

"Are you tripping or theorizing now?"

"The latter," he said, finally turning to face me. "How's your old lady?"

"Mindy? She's pretty much the same. She opened her eyes this morning, but apparently Dr. Mengele doesn't think it's significant."

"Too bad."

"Yeah. So I wanted to thank you for getting that guy to call me. What'd it cost you?"

His eyes drifted back to the window. "Forget it. Anything for you, Moe. Did his information help?"

"Yes and no."

That got his full attention. "What does that mean?"

"It means his information left me with a lot more questions than answers. I think I need to have another talk with that guy, face to face."

That set off his nervous ticcing. Larry's head jerked slightly every few seconds and his eyelids fluttered. He touched every fingertip on his left hand to the tip of his left thumb and then reversed the order: index, middle, ring, pinky, pinky, ring, middle, index, index . . .

"Easy, Larry, easy. It's no big thing. I just wanna talk to the guy."

My words had no effect on him. His ticcing just got worse.

"The guy who attacked Mindy is dead!" I shouted at him, hoping his parents wouldn't hear. "The guy with the pink blotches is dead."

His left hand stilled. His eyelids opened wide. "Vitiligo," he said. "I told you, those skin discolorations are vitiligo. He's dead?"

"Yeah."

"How? Did you—"

I cut him off. "Do you have today's paper?"

"On the kitchen table. My dad reads all of them every day."

"Go get 'em."

A minute later, I was showing him the stories about the fire. Like I said, I only had one source for information: Larry. I couldn't afford to lose him, so I made the decision to tell him everything . . . well, almost everything. I sort of neglected to mention Bobby Friedman showing up with a set of keys. And maybe I pretended not to know the identity of the girl who'd dropped by to remove inventory from the second floor store room, the girl who'd torched the place. Other than that, I laid it all out for him.

When I was done, I made my pitch. "So you see why I gotta talk to the guy who got me that address in the first place, right?"

But Larry wasn't there yet. "The body."

"What about it?"

"Were you scared?"

"Really scared, but I held it together for a little while."

"I'm not very brave, Moe. I wish I was, but I'm not. I'm never going to make it in this world. I grew up in this room, and I'm going to die in this room. It's the only place in the world where I feel safe. When I was at MIT, I was scared all the time. It used to take every ounce of strength I had to get out of bed there. I think I knew even before I went there that I wouldn't make it."

"But you deal drugs, Larry. Doesn't that scare you? Aren't you worried about Rikers or the Brooklyn Tombs?"

He answered me with a smile, a smile as sad as a chick shoved out of its nest. "I'll arrange for you to meet him, Moe. I'll call you later." With that, he turned back to the window.

I didn't need to look to see that he was rocking. I could hear the legs of his too-small chair creaking.

# CHAPTER FOURTEEN

Privacy was about all the boardwalk had to offer when the temperatures dipped below freezing and the winds off the Atlantic scoured your exposed skin with grains of sand from the long miles of empty ocean beaches. In spite of the frigid air and biting winds, the throttle on my senses was full out. Tripping was a little bit like this, and that's what people who had never dropped acid didn't get. It doesn't so much fuck with your mind as it removes all your filters. Suddenly, it's like all the instruments in the orchestra are playing all at once, loudly, and as fast as they can. So it was as I walked down from the handball courts toward the midway. The clank and squeals of the elevated subway echoed through the brick canyons, and the sea's low roar was constant and undramatic. It was almost as if the ocean understood drama wasn't worth its while with no one on the beach to be impressed. The salt air carried with it the unpleasant grace notes of the raw sewage from the plant around the bend beyond Sea Gate. The arthritic wood beams and sea-ravaged metal bones of the dormant rides moaned about their sad decay, about having to bear the sneering, taunting wind that whistled through their old bones.

By the time I got to the bench in front of the Parachute Jump, I sympathized with the rides. Even my young bones were stiff with cold. My collection of bruises didn't help. I checked my Bulova and saw that I was a few minutes early. I was always early. In my family, if you were five minutes early, you were ten minutes late. The Pragers were never tastefully late to a party. The phrase had no meaning for us. Don't misunderstand; our promptness wasn't so much out of good manners as gnawing insecurity. Aaron, Miriam, and I were raised with a sense of dread, living in the fear of missing something. What that something was, I couldn't say. I think my parents felt cheated by their lives somehow. That if they had only been more vigilant, had slept with one eye open, had just gotten to where they were going a few seconds earlier, they would have escaped the trap life had set for them.

I turned and looked up at the looming superstructure of the Parachute Jump, Coney Island's central icon and, from now on, its quintessential symbol of impotence. For although it was scheduled to open again in the spring, the rumor was it would be its last season. At least they wouldn't be tearing the damn thing down with the rest of Steeplechase Park. No, this was Brooklyn. We liked our scars. We wore our failures with pride. We lived in a world of what used to be, and what would be no more. Too bad they had bulldozed Ebbets Field. They should have packed it up brick by brick and rebuilt it in Coney Island at the foot of the Jump. Two follies, side by side: a parachute jump with no parachutes, a baseball stadium with no team. Greek tragedy? Nah, a freak show. We always did like our freak shows in Coney Island.

"Hey, you Moe? You Moe?" a raspy whisper cut through the wind.

I tilted my head back to earth and saw him standing there. To call him thin would have been high understatement. He was positively skeletal. If he hadn't been as tall as I was, he might've been able to shop in the boys' department at John's Bargain Store. Maybe it was the lighting, but his skin had a yellow quality to it. When I noticed his beak-like nose running and caught a glimpse of the lit cigarette he held between his fidgety fingers, I decided the sickly shade of his skin wasn't a trick of the light. If it was possible, this guy was even more fidgety than Lids. He moved so much he would have made a hummingbird cross-eyed. But unlike Lids, this guy needed a drink or a joint, not shock therapy. His gesticulations aside, it didn't take a genius to see he was nervous about being here and that he'd rather be somewhere else, anywhere else. Still, Lids had gotten him to show up.

"Yeah," I said, "I'm Moe. And you are . . . ?"

"Sick, man. I'm sick."

I was slow on the uptake. "I'm sorry to hear it, but I was asking for your name."

"You bein' funny, man, or just stupid?"

"Watch your mouth or you'll be getting a lot sicker a lot quicker."

He made a series of rapid snorts that passed for laughter. "That's funny. It rhymes."

"Thanks, Shakespeare, but I'm not trying to be funny."

"Sorry, sorry. It's just that—"

"Yeah, I heard you the first time. You're sick. Now what's your name?"

"Man, forget my name. Just let's get this over with. I need to get well. And I can't get fixed up until I talk to you. So what'd'ya wanna talk about?"

"1055 Coney Island Avenue," I said.

"What about it?"

"Why'd you send me there? What was I supposed to find there?"

"Hey, man, look, I heard you wanted to know where your old lady was on a certain night between certain hours. Well, that's where she was." He wiped his nose on his ratty coat. He'd done that so many times, both sleeves had crusty, damp streaks. "Can I go now, huh? I answered your question."

"Soon, Shakespeare, soon. How do you know that's where Mindy was?"

"Because I know, man."

"Wrong answer." I turned to walk away.

"C'mon, man. Where you goin'?"

"To tell your connection you gave me *gotz* and that you're full of shit."

"C'mon, man, don't do that. Don't be that way." He dropped to his knees. "Don't make me beg you."

"Begging's not the issue. Answers are." The guy was a wreck and I guess I ached for him a little. It would have been hard not to, but aching for him wouldn't get me the information I needed.

He wiped his nose with his sleeve again. "Okay, okay, all right. Answers."

"I'm waiting," I said, acting like a hard guy.

"Mindy, that's your old lady, right?"

"Yeah."

"She's a part of, like, this group."

A little bell went off in my head and I remembered what Susan Kasten had said the night before. "The Committee," I said, "is that the group?"

Shakespeare's bloodshot eyes got wide. He didn't answer, but nodded yes over and over again.

"Is Susan Kasten a member of the Committee?"

"Yeah, man, yeah. Can I go now?"

"You ask me that again and I'm gonna kick your ass. You understand me? And get up off your knees, for chrissakes."

He stood, but immediately doubled over in pain. "Sorry, man. Sorry. It's just that I gotta get well. I gotta."

"Okay. So, Mindy and Susan are part of this Committee. Who else?"

"I can't, man. I can't."

"Just a few more questions and then you can go."

"You'll tell Lids I did the right thing? You'll tell him?"

"I'll tell him."

"You promise, man? You wouldn't fuck with me like that."

"I promise, Shakespeare."

"God bless you." He was back on his knees, grabbing at my hands.

I pushed him away and he toppled over like a rootless tree. "Get up. Get the fuck up, already."

As he struggled to get up, I thought I heard something: the creaking of a boardwalk plank, shuffling feet in the sand. But when I looked around, Coney Island was just as dark and deserted as it had been a few seconds before. Shakespeare got as far as his knees. When I saw that was probably as far as he was going to get, I started up again.

"Black guy with pink blotches all over his face and hands," I said. "Abdul?"

I played along. "Yeah, Abdul. Tell me about him."

"What about him?"

"Anything."

"He calls himself Abdul Salaam. Means soldier of peace." He laughed that snorting, machine gun laugh. "But his real name is Ricky Barnett. He comes from some little town in the Midwest somewheres, Effingberg or Effingham, some shit like that."

"Great. Now that we got his bio out of the way, tell me what he—" I stopped, because whatever it was I'd heard before, I heard again. "Get up, Shakespeare. Get up!" I yanked him to his feet by the shoulders of his coat. He was as light as a bag of leaves. "Get the fuck outta here. Run! Run!"

It was no good and it was too late anyway. Instead of running, Shakespeare just kind of melted. He collapsed into a ball of himself, throwing one arm over his head and the other around his ribs. I spun to look behind me, but before I had fully turned I was tackled from behind. Two sets of strong hands held me down. A gag was shoved in my mouth, and a bag or pillowcase was slipped over my head. Tape was rolled around the bag to hold it closed around my neck, but not so tightly I couldn't breathe. My hands were taped behind my back, my ankles taped together, and I was dragged across the boardwalk—the toes of my Converse sneakers made a dull sound as they caught in the spaces between each plank—down the steps, and onto the sand. I was shoved face first onto the sand and then . . . nothing. I heard the soft shushing of feet walking away from me and then their pounding on the boardwalk stairs. Was I scared? Yeah, I was pretty fucking scared, but for some reason not as much as I should have been. I sensed that whatever this was about, it wasn't about me.

Then I heard Shakespeare doing what he did best: begging. "Please, man, don't hurt me. I'm hurtin' so bad already, man."

There was no response. I winced, expecting Shakespeare to take a beating. I knew this was no mugging. For one thing, the guys who dealt with me had left my watch on my wrist and my wallet in my pocket. For another, muggers in Brooklyn didn't make like the *Mission: Impossible* team just to rob two schmucks on the boardwalk. Besides, one look at the two of us would have told even the most amateur thieves that we weren't worth the effort. No, this wasn't about robbery. As I waited for the beating to begin, I imagined the snap of Shakespeare's bones, his screams. None came. What I heard instead was this:

"Thank you, man. Thank you. God bless you."

A few seconds later I heard something being dragged, *tha-dump, tha-dump, tha-dump*, across the boardwalk. Feet scurried. Then there was just the sound of the subway, the waves, the whining of the wind through the rides to keep me company. When I was sure I was alone, I began moving my wrists in opposite directions. At first the tape gave only a tiny bit, and my arms wearied pretty quickly. Still, in about a half hour I had worked the tape loose enough so that I could free my right hand. I was totally free of everything else in short order. Shakespeare was free, too: free of the cold, free of hurt, free of pain, free of this world. I found him seated on the bench where we'd met, a belt strapped tightly around his left bicep, and a needle sticking out of his left forearm. There were so many needle marks stretching along the underside of his forearm that it looked like a subway map. At rest, without his constant movement, he looked much more in tune with death than life. I suppose that would have been okay with me if dying had been his choice and not someone else's. It might also have helped me a little if I didn't feel like I was as much to blame for his death as the needle sticking out of his arm.

# CHAPTER FIFTEEN

None of it seemed like a dream. People always say this or that felt like a dream, but nothing feels like a dream but a dream or, in this instance, a continuous nightmare. After last night I thought I might never sleep again. I ran all the way from the boardwalk to Lids's building, my legs churning as much out of panic as anything else. First, I ran to get away from Shakespeare's body. Then, as it dawned on me how close I'd just come to my own death, I ran harder. Once I'd been hooded and bound, those guys could have done anything to me and there wasn't a thing I could've done about it. They could have shot me in the back of the head or carried me into the shallows and dropped me in the surf to drown. That really freaked me out, not the drowning so much as the thought of dying cold and alone. I didn't want to die cold and alone. Just thinking about it had me crying as I ran. I'd shed some tears at Mindy's bedside, but before that it had been a long time since I'd cried. I used to pride myself on that. There were no more tears by the time I got to the lobby of Lids's building. He wasn't home.

"Who knows where he is?" his mom said to me when I got to their apartment door. "You know better than me where he goes to, no?"

No, I really didn't. The only places I knew to find him were in his room and just off campus, walking his drug corner. Beyond those two places, his life was a mystery to me. I thanked his mom and asked her to have him call me.

As I walked home, I realized I could have called Lids from any one of ten pay phones I had passed on the way and saved myself the long run to his house, but I hadn't been thinking clearly. It was hard to think clearly when you'd sort of just witnessed a murder. It was one thing to walk in on a body that had been dead for days. It was something else to find the body of someone who'd stood a foot away from you thirty minutes ago. It struck me, too, that a call to Lids wasn't the only call I hadn't made. Two bodies in two nights, and neither time did I call the cops. If I was like Bobby, raised to hate the police, or like Lids, a pusher, not calling the cops would have been consistent with who I was. But that's not who I was. I wasn't raised to hate the cops or to love them. I was raised to avoid them. The preceding two thousand years of Jewish history had taught us to love and respect the law, but to be wary of those who enforced it. I hadn't called the cops because I wanted to protect Bobby and Lids.

So, yeah, I was wound up, my mind so muddled by the time I got home that I was sure there was no way I'd sleep again. Except like with most things I was sure about, I was wrong, dead wrong. Because when the phone rang, waking me from sleep, the sun was in my eyes. I was on top of the covers, still fully dressed, pea coat and all. At first I was startled at the feel of grit on the covers. *Sand? How did sand get in my bed?* Then I remembered how it had gotten there. At least Aaron wasn't home to chide me. He had slept over at his girlfriend's house. Thank heavens for small favors. Then the phone stopped ringing.

"Moses! It's Bobby on the phone," Miriam called to me.

When I got out to the kitchen, Miriam and my folks were seated at the dining room table. I hadn't looked in the mirror, but I didn't have to. Their faces told me everything about my appearance I needed to know. It was also about then I realized I still hadn't taken my coat off. I smiled in spite of myself. Miriam did too. My parents, on the other hand, had that worried look in their eyes. *Is he on drugs? Is he turning into a hippie?* I saw a little something extra in my mom's eyes, the satisfaction of pessimism fulfilled. *See, I knew it. I knew it.*

I tousled my little sister's hair. "Thanks, kiddo," I said, grabbing the phone. "Hey, Bobby. What's up?" I stepped into the kitchen. It didn't afford me much more privacy than if I'd stayed put in the dining room, but with apartment living the illusion of privacy is nearly as important as the real thing. "What's happening?"

"Wanna keep me company? I got another airport run. We can go visit Mindy first. How is she, anyway?"

I filled him in on my brief Saturday visit and how she had opened her eyes.

"That's a good thing, right?" he asked.

"Who the hell knows? Her doctor pretty much dismissed it."

"That guy's an ass. He's got all the charm of Lurch."

"I'm shocked. Your parents used to let you watch *The Addams Family*?"

"Of course. They think it is a perfect representation of bourgeois decadence and how unbridled wealth feeds eccentricity at the expense of the masses."

"I guess they have a point. And what, they think *The Munsters* show how the working class is repressed and scorned by the capitalist lackeys?"

He ignored that. "Moe, you coming with me or not?"

"Sure, but I need to shower and shave." I peeked into the dining room after I said that and saw the palpable relief on my parents' faces. "Give me an hour."

"You got it."

I hung up and walked back into the dining room. I sat down, poured myself some of my mom's death coffee and buttered a seeded roll.

"What did the Knicks do last night?" I asked my dad, as if I wasn't sitting there in my dirty pea coat, sandy Chuck Taylors, and filthy jeans.

Even he had to smile about that. "They won. Beat St. Louis by two. Zelmo Beaty and Lenny Wilkens each scored twenty for the Hawks."

My mom just shook her head. "How did you get all full of sand in the middle of winter?"

"I wore my white trousers rolled and walked along the beach."

"Oy, *gevalt*!" she looked up at the ceiling, arms raised. "I knew I shouldn't have asked."

◆

Bobby picked me up downstairs. I'd agreed to go with him because I thought the time had come to find out from him as much as I could about what was going on. But I didn't get in the car and start with the third degree. Besides, he seemed to be in a melancholy frame of mind. I'm not sure I had ever seen him that way in all the years I'd known him. I mean, he was pretty distraught when that thing with Samantha happened. It nearly wrecked him. That was more than melancholy, though. That was hurt, grief, disbelief. This was different. He just seemed sad.

"I miss her," he said.

I knew who "her" was without asking. "Yeah, Sam was great."

"She was all that, Moe. I don't think I'll ever meet anybody like her again."

"Maybe not, but you'll meet somebody who's great but differently great."

"I like that—differently great." He was smiling now, not his old smile. Like his expression when I got in the car, it was one I'd never seen before. "You should've kept writing poetry. You have a way with words."

Sometimes I forgot about my one literary accomplishment: a poem that had been published in our high school literary magazine. Bobby hadn't forgotten. There wasn't much that escaped him. "Thanks, Bobby, but I just couldn't do it anymore after the fire when Andrea Cotter and the other girls died. Besides, there's about as much money in poetry as there is in blacksmithing."

"Since when did you care about money?"

"I never said I didn't care about it. I just have no idea how to make it or much desire to try."

"Maybe I could help you with that someday," he said, without any guile in his voice.

I took that as my cue to get back to the subject at hand. "I know you don't like talking about it, but do you have any idea of what happened with Sam that night?"

"My girlfriend and poor, stupid Marty Lavitz got blown into little bite-size pieces. That's what happened!" he snapped at me.

"That's not what I mean and you know it."

"I also know you were into her and that you would've done anything to have her."

"Bullshit!" I lied. "I had Mindy. Sam was your girl. I never did anything to—"

"Of course you didn't, Moe. Disloyalty isn't in your genes, but it doesn't mean you didn't want to, and it doesn't mean I'm stupid. I know all the guys were into her. Who wouldn't be? Half the guys in Burgundy House tried to pick her up when I wasn't around. You think I didn't know that?"

I opened my mouth to argue with him, then shut it. He almost had me, almost got me going, but I wasn't stupid either. This was classic Bobby Friedman. When we played stickball and softball, Bobby, a left-handed batter—was there any doubt he'd be a lefty?—always hit to the opposite field. He was a classic opposite-field hitter, and a very good one at that. Deflection was his game, catching people off balance and keeping them that way. Although I'd caught him at it, what did it matter? He wasn't going to answer my questions, at least not yet.

There was something inherently depressing about hospitals that all the yellow and orange paint in the world couldn't change. I wondered what it must've been like before hospitals were available to most people, when you were born, got sick, recovered, and eventually died in your own bed. I wondered how much better off we were as a race for having invented institutions where we could hide away unpleasant aspects of life: hospitals for the sick, sanitariums for the mentally ill, nursing homes for the aged, funeral homes for the dead. And there was something else about hospitals that got to me—their smell. They used pine-scented disinfectant in the same way they used yellow and orange paint—to mask unpleasantness. But like too much sweet perfume on very old women, it only made it worse. You couldn't mask the smell of death and dying with perfume or pine. Death had a particular scent of its own. I knew that now, and I would never forget it.

Luckily, I didn't smell it on Mindy. Her folks had met us out in the hall and though they looked completely spent, they were happy.

"She's coming out of it, Moe," her mom said, hugging me fiercely. "She's moving her lips and blinking her eyes."

"What did her doctor say?" Bobby asked.

"He's not the most optimistic man I've ever met," Herb Weinstock said, "but even he thinks these are signs she's coming out of it. Of course, he followed that up with all sorts of warnings and caveats about the long road ahead and all the things that could still go wrong."

We went and sat with Mindy for about an hour and there were times when it almost felt as if she were conscious of our presence. I know part of that was wishful thinking, but I allowed myself a little hope every now and then. Hope wasn't usually an emotion on the Prager family menu. With my dad's business failures and my mom's dim worldview, it wouldn't be, would it? Still, I'd like to think hope is a very human thing that not even my mom could completely kill in me the way she could cook the flavor out of chicken.

Before leaving the hospital, I stopped at the gift shop to buy a Sunday paper. I hadn't had time to check the papers at home for word of Shakespeare's murder. If there was a mention of it in the paper, I thought I could use it to restart my questioning of Bobby. If not, I'd figure something out. And given that the person we were chauffeuring to the airport lived about fifteen minutes away from the hospital, I had plenty of time to talk to Bobby. And there it was, buried a few inches down among the stories of shootings, rapes, and stabbings. I smiled sadly when I saw that I hadn't gotten Shakespeare's name completely wrong: his first name was William. He had been William O'Day of Gerritsen Beach, Brooklyn. Gerritsen Beach was like the Irish wing of Sheepshead Bay. The cops were treating it like just another OD, though there was some thought it might have been a suicide. His parents claimed that he'd been a good boy, deeply involved in politics at Brooklyn College, but that over the last year Billy'd lost his way. I loved that phrase, "lost his way." It said everything and nothing. Now Billy was just lost.

"You know a guy named Billy O'Day?" I asked calmly as if the question was unrelated to what I was reading in the paper.

"Sure. Everybody knows Billy. His big thing is Irish liberation. He thinks the partition of Ireland was bullshit and that until Northern Ireland breaks away and joins the rest of Ireland that the true republic won't exist. He believes in armed struggle against the British in the North. Why do you ask?"

"He's dead."

But if I thought Bobby would steer off the road or slam on the brakes, I was wrong. What he did say was, "Don't tell me, he ODed, right?"

"How the fuck did you know that? Did you read the papers this morning?"

There was one other way he could have known that I didn't even want to think about.

"I didn't have to read about it. His addiction was the worst-kept secret on campus, Moe. He used to be a big wheel in campus politics, and I don't mean student government."

"I know what you mean. So he was in with Susan Kasten and Abdul Salaam and the other people on the Committee."

That got Bobby's attention, though you would have had to have known Bobby as long and as well I as did to catch the subtle change in his demeanor. Then Bobby made it worse by acting dumb.

"Abdul Salaam. Who's that?"

"He's the guy whose body you found the other night at 1055 Coney Island Avenue a few hours before it blew up. The guy who put my girlfriend in a coma. So you wanna tell me what's going on?"

Bobby resorted to his first line of defense, deflection. "You're following me around now?" he asked, smiling like he was teasing. He wasn't, though. He was annoyed and maybe a little freaked.

"No. I wasn't following you around. I had no idea you were involved in any of this. I was parked across the street from the place in Aaron's Tempest when you showed up. I saw you go up and I saw you come out. I saw that look on your face, Bobby, so don't try and tell me you didn't see the body."

This time he did yank the car over to the side of the road and slam on the brakes.

"Look, Moe, you're the best friend I've ever had or probably ever will have, so I'm gonna say this for your own good. *Stay out of it.* No good can come of you sticking your nose in. Some people don't have a sense of humor. They'll do whatever they need to do to meet their objectives. There's things going on here that . . . well, that just don't concern you."

"You concern me. What happened to Mindy concerns me. What happened to Billy O'Day concerns me."

"What the fuck are you talking about? You didn't even know Billy O'Day. How can that concern you?"

"I was there," I said.

He was confused. "You were where?"

"They found Billy O'Day dead on the boardwalk on a bench in front of the Parachute Jump, a belt tied around his bicep and a needle sticking out of his arm. Here." I shoved the story into Bobby's face. "See?"

He took a second to read the story. "They mention the boardwalk, but it doesn't say anything about a bench or the belt or a needle sti—" He stopped talking when he realized how I knew those details.

"That's right, Bobby. I was there. I didn't actually see it happen because I got hooded and tied up, but I found his body. He didn't OD. He didn't commit suicide. He was murdered."

"Murdered?"

"Yeah, while I was talking to him. So don't tell me to stay out of this or that. This concerns me. It also concerns me that for the first time since we've known each other, you're shutting me out and lying to me."

"Kinda makes my point for me, man," he said. "If Billy was murdered, the people who did it know you know. They were smart enough to hood you so you couldn't identify them. I guess they figured you were an innocent civilian, but if you keep at whatever you think you're doing, that civilian label will disappear and you'll become a target."

"Like you?"

"What's that supposed to mean?" he said.

"That night when I bailed you out of jail and I was with Mindy, she warned me to stay away from you. She wouldn't tell me why, but she made me promise."

He actually smiled that smile of his. "I guess you broke that promise, huh?"

"This isn't funny, Bobby. I think that day in the snowstorm, the Caddy was trying to run you down. That was no accident."

He patted my cheek and laughed. "You worry about me more than my own goddamn parents, you know that? But don't worry about me. I've got it covered."

"What about the other stuff?"

"Leave it alone, Moe. Trust me. Leave it alone. C'mon, we gotta get a move on, or we'll be late."

# CHAPTER SIXTEEN

The airport run that day was pretty much like the last one. We took an elderly couple to Eastern Airlines at JFK. They had come up to New York to visit their kids and grandkids, and were now headed back down to Florida. We parked Bobby's Olds 88 in the same lot and followed the same routine. When we left the terminal to return to the car, Bobby confided in me that if the old folks' plane went down, he stood to make a killing. No pun intended. Then, seeing the horrified look on my face, he put me in a headlock.

"Don't be such a downer, man. I'm only putting you on. If it makes you feel any better, I really hope I never get to collect on any of these policies."

I was not reassured. Bobby didn't do anything out of the kindness of his heart, not for strangers, anyway. Sometimes I even thought the protests he was so good at organizing were mostly self-serving. They made him look good and if we didn't have to go to Nam, neither did he. I don't know. I guess I was feeling less love for Bobby that particular day than I'd ever felt before. Maybe if he'd answered some of my questions or'd given me some sense of what I'd gotten myself into, I might have taken a kinder view of my old friend. And for chrissakes, he was my age. He had to know that giving me that boogie man warning and all that mumbo jumbo about civilians and leaving it alone wasn't going to work. Did anyone my age ever listen to those kinds of warnings? *Stay away from drugs. They're bad for you.*

We didn't talk much as we left the airport and got back on the Belt Parkway west toward home. I wanted to keep at him about the Committee, Susan Kasten, the late Abdul Salaam, and the more recently late Billy O'Day, but knew he wasn't going to give me any more than what he'd already imparted. So I decided to take another tack.

"Before we got sidetracked, you were missing Sam bad. Why so blue about Sam today? It's been months."

"I don't know. You know how you forget things sometimes? I used to really dig waking up next to Sam. She was always so warm and she smelled good in the morning even if we'd spent the whole night balling. Anyways, I must've dreamed about her and I forgot she was dead. When I rolled over in bed this morning, I expected to find her there. But the sheet was cold, and then I had to live it all over again in my head."

"I'm sorry, Bobby."

"That's okay, man. Forget what I said to you before about you and her. It's good to talk about her with you, Moe, because you appreciated her and how special she was."

"You know that night with Mindy, the night I found her drinking and smoking outside Burgundy House . . ."

"The night you bailed me out, yeah. What about it?"

"It was weird, but Mindy said she was acting funny because of Samantha."

"That makes no sense," he said, shaking his head. "It was no secret that Mindy hated Sam's guts. Mindy isn't the jealous type, but when it came to Sam . . ."

"Tell me about it. I had to deal with it."

Bobby smiled. "Yeah, man. One thing about Mindy, she's not good at hiding her feelings."

No matter how mad I was at him or frustrated I was by his deflections, seeing that smile made me smile. It didn't last.

*Bang!* The front end of the car on my side smacked down on the pavement, the rear end fishtailing like crazy. Bobby struggled to keep control of the two-ton monster. Luckily we were in the far right lane when the tire blew, allowing Bobby to slow down and drift onto the shoulder near the Pennsylvania Avenue exit.

I started laughing. "Thank God this happened after we dropped them off. We would've had two heart attack victims on our hands."

"I suppose." But Bobby wasn't laughing. "Stay in the car," he said, pointing his finger at me. "Stay in the fucking car."

Man, the day just kept getting stranger and stranger. I'd witnessed bigger mood swings and shifts in Bobby in less than four hours than maybe in the rest of the time I'd known him. Sure, he was upset about his car, but he wasn't obsessed with it like the Italian guys in the neighborhood who would give up their Sundays to Mass and hand-washing their cars. Mass they did out of obligation. The hours they spent on their cars was devotion. That wasn't Bobby, and I couldn't for the life of me figure out why the hell he was so intent on me not helping him with the flat. Did he remember about my shoulder? Doubtful. And I'd been careful not to mention my encounter with Mr. Ski Mask, so he couldn't know about those injuries.

I turned the rearview mirror—the little pine tree air freshener still dangling beneath it—so that I could use it to see through the back window. All I got for the bother was a great view of the raised trunk lid, but I did hear Bobby rummaging around in the trunk. I didn't get it, because the trunk had been empty after we'd removed the old couple's luggage at the airport. Maybe he was just having trouble getting the spare off the spindle. Yeah, I thought, that must've been it. I'd had to struggle with that occasionally myself. Finally, Bobby slammed the trunk lid shut and, as he rolled the spare past my window, rapped on the window with the tire iron for me to come out.

When I got out of the car, I was hit full in the face by the overwhelming stink of rotting garbage. We had come to a stop directly across the Belt Parkway from the Fountain Avenue dump, one of the largest landfills in the world. When Aaron and I were little, before Miriam was born, we used to call it Stinky Mountain. And man oh man, was that the right name for the place today. The breeze was blowing just wrong off Jamaica Bay, and we were straight downwind. The whirling swarms of opportunist gulls and other hungry birds wheeled across the tops of the garbage heaps like feathered tornadoes, touching down wherever the bulldozer blades churned up likely feasts.

"Here," Bobby said, handing me the tire iron. "Pull off the wheel cover and get started on the lug nuts. I'll get the jack."

Fifteen minutes later, we were done. I carried what was left of the blown tire to the rear of the car and leaned it against the back bumper. He carried the jack and tire iron.

"Go back in the car. There's a ton of those towelettes in the glove compartment. Take a few out for me too."

I didn't think anything of it and did what he asked. It was only when he popped the trunk back open and put the stuff away that it dawned on me that he had closed the trunk in the first place. I never closed the trunk when I changed tires and tried to remember if anyone else did. Aaron didn't. My dad didn't. In the end, I shrugged my shoulders to myself and went back to cleaning my hands. In spite of the faint lemony, chemical tang from the towelettes, I couldn't get the garbage stink out of my nose. It was rumored that among the mounds of garbage in the Fountain

Avenue dump were hundreds of bodies and body parts courtesy of New York's Five Families. That thought sobered me right up as the garbage stink in my nostrils was replaced with the memory of Abdul Salaam's ripe corpse.

I looked up again at the mirror and when I did I saw trouble. Bobby had slammed the trunk lid back down, his head turned to the left, his body gone rigid. In the next second, I understood. A black and green police car, cherry top spinning, was pulling off the Belt and right up behind Bobby's Olds. On good days, Bobby and cops mixed kind of like oil and water. Problem here was that this wasn't a good day, and the guy getting out of the black and green wasn't just a regular cop. No, this cop's hat was squashed down and set at a rakish angle. He had on jodhpurs and knee-high black boots shinier than polished silver. I kept an eye on things in the mirror. Highway Patrol cops were renowned for being psychos and ball busters, and this guy looked the part. He was a big man with broad shoulders and a let's-pull-the-wings-off-the-helpless-fly expression that made me pretty uneasy. I opened the door, figuring it was safer for everyone involved if I went out and made nice. Bobby was out on bail, and I knew that wouldn't stop him from pushing back if the cop gave him a hard time.

I got one leg out the door when the cop screamed, "Get the fuck back in that fucking car until I tell you to get out, asshole. You move and I'll blow your brains out, you draft-dodgin' mothafucka."

I didn't need to be told twice, but it didn't stop me from watching in the mirror. And what I saw was strange and mysterious stuff. The cop gestured at the trunk and, jerking his thumb straight up in the air, motioned for Bobby to open it. Bobby smiled at the cop and began telling him some story. The cop didn't like stories, indicating as much by shoving Bobby against the trunk and snatching the keys from Bobby's hand. He pushed Bobby aside and popped the trunk.

Much as Bobby had fussed with stuff when we first got the flat, the cop was doing so now. Then the trunk lid slammed down again. Then a really curious thing happened. The cop threw Bobby face first onto the trunk, frisked him, then handcuffed him. He grabbed Bobby by the collar, marched him to the black and green and threw him in the back seat.

I opened the door again. This time the cop didn't bark at me. He just turned in my direction, unholstered his .38, and pointed it in my direction.

"You, stay there in that front seat until I tell you to move. Got it?"

"Yes, officer," I said, closing the car door.

I watched the cop get into the front seat, pick up his radio, and call in. It seemed to take a lot of time, but was only about five minutes. Next thing I knew, Bobby was out of the patrol car, the cuffs were off his wrists, and the cop was pulling his unit back onto the Belt.

"What the fuck was that about?" I asked as Bobby got back behind the wheel.

"You know the pigs. They just can't help but hassle us. He got on his radio and made a big show of calling in my name for outstanding warrants and stuff. I think when it came back to him that I was out on bail he thought about really busting my balls. But then another call of an accident on the Belt came in."

"Good thing about that accident, I guess."

"I guess. Let's forget it, okay. You all right?" Bobby asked, readjusting the rearview mirror. "You don't look so good. The stink getting to you?"

"Exactly," I said. "Exactly, the stink. That and having a gun pointed at me."

Bobby pulled back onto the Belt when traffic allowed. We didn't say another word until he dropped me off in front of my building. Even then, the words we did say were meaningless, goodbyes spoken between two friends who were suddenly wary of one another.

# CHAPTER SEVENTEEN

When I got back upstairs, Miriam and my folks were watching *Walt Disney's Wonderful World of Color*. My mom said there was some chicken in the fridge I could heat up if I was hungry. I was pretty hungry, just not *that* hungry. My dad told me to read the messages he'd written down on the pad by the phone in the kitchen. The messages were mostly from Lids.

"Larry called several times."

"Yeah, Dad, I can see that."

"Oy, is that kid Larry a bundle of nerves or what? No wonder he went crackers."

"You shoulda been a shrink, Dad," I said, my voice thick with sarcasm.

"What? Huh? Miriam, lower the TV."

"Never mind. I'm going to use the extension in your bedroom."

"What?"

I sat down on my parents' bed, which always made me feel a little creepy, and dialed Lids's number. His mother picked up.

"Hello, Mrs. Lester. It's Moe, is Larry around?"

"Wait, please wait," she said distractedly, worry in her voice. Then she partially covered the phone with her palm. "It's Moses on the line," were her muted words. She came back on. "Wait, Moses, Larry's father wants to speak with you."

"Moses, I've always thought you were one of my son's good friends and that I could trust you," said Larry's dad in his sad little voice.

"Thanks, Mr. Lester. It's nice to be thought of like that."

"Then can you tell me what's going on with Larry?" The baseline sadness in his voice was compounded with worry.

"I don't know what you mean."

"Since this morning he's . . . Well, you know he's had some problems in the past at MIT and all, but he's been doing much better since he got out of the hospital."

"Yes, sir, he has."

"But not this morning. He was manic, acting all *meshugge* again, spouting gibberish, things his mother and I couldn't make any sense of. We called his psychiatrist, but it's Sunday and he's out of town. Something got him going. Do you know what could have set him off?"

*Maybe the fact that one of his customers got murdered on the boardwalk last night and that he's afraid he'll be next.* "No, Mr. Lester. I'm sorry, I don't," is how I framed the lie. "What makes you think I would know anyway?"

"Well, he ran out of here hours ago and then called with a number to reach him at, but I am only supposed to give the number to you. Even I'm not allowed to call him. You're supposed to call him three times, let the phone ring six times each."

"I'm sorry, Mr. Lester, I wish I could help you. Maybe after I talk to Larry . . ."

"Yes." His voice brightened. "See, you are wise beyond your years, Moses. Yes, call him and see what's the matter." I tore off the top of one of the pages from the paperback on my dad's nightstand. It had a lurid cover of half-naked women holding handguns. I wrote the number down on the scrap. "You'll call after you've spoken with Larry?" It was more a prayer than a question.

"I'll try."

I hung up.

As instructed, I tried the number Lids's dad had given me three times. I knew Lids was still a little crazier than he seemed, even when he wasn't all agitated. Looking back, I realized that Larry having another episode didn't come as a shock to me. How, I wondered, could his parents have been caught so unprepared? I thought about just how blind parents could be to who and what their children really were. Mine were of me, but my parents' blind spots were more mundane. With not a shred of evidence to support their beliefs, they saw me as a younger version of Aaron. But the only things Aaron and I shared were a bedroom, good marks, and a last name. We didn't look alike, didn't act alike, didn't think alike. Hell, Aaron had more in common with Bobby.

Lids picked up on the sixth ring of my third attempt. "Moe?"

Man, sometimes one syllable was all it took to suss a person out. And just the tentative, hushed way he spoke my name told me nearly everything.

"Lids, what the fuck is going on? Your parents are freaked out."

"He's dead. He's dead. He's dead," Lids chanted in a lilt. "He's dead. He's . . ."

"Who, Billy O'Day?"

"O'Day ODed, O'Day ODed, O'Day ODed. O'Day O—"

"Enough, Larry. Enough! I know he's dead. I was there when it happened and just to be accurate, he was murdered."

"You were there. There were you. You were there. There were you. You were—"

"I didn't see it happen, but I was there. What's going on, Larry?"

"Don't know. Don't know. Don't know. All confused. All confused. All confused."

"Tell me where you are and I'll come get you."

There was nothing hushed or tentative in his reply. "No! Have to be alone. Have to figure things out. Have to be alone. Have to figure things out. Have to—"

I understood why his parents were so scared for him. "Let me help you."

"They're coming for me. They're coming for me. They're coming for me."

"Who's coming?"

"They are. *They. They. They.* Aren't you listening?"

"They who? Which they?"

"Don't know. Don't know. Don't know. More than one they. More than one they. More than one they. Have to be alone. Have to figure—"

I cut him off. "Why did you want me to call you?"

"Tony Pepperoni is a fat phony. Tony Pepperoni is a fat fat phony. Tony Pepperoni is a fat fat fat phony. Phony fat fat fat a is Pepperoni Tony. Phony fat fat a is Pepperoni Tony. Phony fat a is Pepperoni Tony."

He was totally lost and now so was I. It seemed the sounds of words, the rhythm of words, how they rhymed, were more important than what they meant. I had no idea if any of this hung together, especially the part about Tony Pepperoni. While I listened, Larry had degenerated into the crazy toothless lady with the wire laundry basket who stood on the boardwalk by the handball courts and cursed at you in a language only she understood. You knew the words were curses because of how she said them.

"Larry, let me come and get you."

"No! No! No!"

I was running out of things to say when it dawned on me there was something worth risking. Given how little progress I'd made with him to that point, I figured I had nothing to lose if it failed.

"Let me come and get you. Let me come and get you. Let me come and get you," I fairly sang.

And for the first time since this mind-bending conversation started, there was a pause on his end. I could hear him take a deep breath. Then he sobbed.

"It is you, Moe. I couldn't be sure. There are enemies everywhere and they can take any shape, speak in any voice."

"It's me, Larry, yeah. How can I help?"

"You can't," he whispered. "You're not invisible."

"Are you safe? At least tell me you're safe."

"As long as I'm invisible I am."

Uh oh, he was losing it again. I went along with him because what else could I do? "Then stay that way."

"I will."

There was a click and dead air. Silence. Invisibility.

Aaron was in our bedroom, doing his weekly paperwork for a job he essentially hated. But that was my big brother for you. It didn't matter that he hated the job. He was learning, getting experience, getting a paycheck. I couldn't see me doing any of that, not for a second. Even when I was little I couldn't understand doing things you hated doing no matter the payoff. That said, Aaron was really smart and a good big brother. He was especially good in bad situations, and a bad situation is what I had on my hands. I was worried about Larry, but I didn't want to tell his parents how worried. He needed help, but to get him that help, his parents would have to bring the cops into it. Once the cops were into it, they might find out about his business and that would just make everything worse for everyone involved. Larry needed a stint in the psych ward at Kings County, not a stretch in Sing Sing.

I opened my mouth to say something to Aaron. Nothing came out. I couldn't figure out a way to tell him what was going on and still protect everyone who needed protecting. Was there ever a way to do that, to protect everyone who needed protecting?

"What?" Aaron barked at me. "You just gonna stand there like a putz staring at me, or you gonna ask me what you came in here to ask me?"

"Can I borrow your car tomorrow?" I asked, because I had to say something, not because I needed or even wanted his car.

He shook his head at me, but reached into his pocket and threw me his keys. "Your lucky day, little brother. We have meetings in the city for the next two days. Taking the subway in and won't be home until Tuesday night. But take good care of it and fill it up. Understand?"

"Thanks, man."

"How's your girlfriend doing?"

"Better, I think," I said. "It's hard to know."

"Okay. Now get outta here and go watch Ed Sullivan while I finish my work."

I closed the door behind me. I had his keys, but no ideas about what I should do to save Larry.

# CHAPTER EIGHTEEN

Koblenz, Pennsylvania, was a tiny town in the Pocono Mountains near the border with New York. It had taken me about five hours to get there. It would've taken an hour or two less had I any knowledge of where the hell I was going. Growing up in Coney Island didn't exactly prepare me for cartography. The only map I knew how to decipher was a subway map. Generally, Brooklynites don't do maps. We give directions in terms of landmarks and number of streets, up and down, left and right. *You go two blocks down, make a left by the Sinclair gas station, go two more blocks up by the new church, and there it is on your right.* Without the sun I wouldn't have known east from west; north from south I learned only because the avenues in Manhattan ran north and south. So now you understand why it took me as long as it did to get to Koblenz. Why I was there in the first place was another matter altogether.

The idea of it came to me in my sleep. Not much else did, certainly not much sleep. How the fuck could I sleep while I was worrying about Lids? Given the state he was in, I had no clue about what he might do to himself or if he really was in danger from the people who'd murdered Billy O'Day. Most people with Larry's financial resources could have found a safe place to hide, at least for a few days. And hell, the guy dealt drugs, so he wasn't stupid about surviving on the street. Then there was the fact that he was a goddamned certifiable genius. Somehow none of that was of much comfort to me. Larry wasn't most people. What did money or smarts or intellect mean when you were as damaged as he was? Pusher or not, he was more fragile than anyone else I knew. My little sister Miriam was made of sterner stuff than him.

I'd called his dad back, neglecting to mention the repetition and rhyming of the words in Larry's answers or his son's extreme agitation or his free-floating paranoia. I just lied some more, telling him that I'd spoken to his son and that Larry was calmer, but needed time alone to sort things out. Who knows how much of it he believed? After I'd finished with Larry's dad, I called the only person I could: Bobby. I told him the bare minimum. I didn't connect Lids to Billy O'Day or Billy O'Day to 1055 Coney Island Avenue. I just said that Lids had cracked again and was out there alone somewhere. It wasn't like Lids and Bobby were best buddies. They knew each other from school, from the neighborhood, and Bobby knew Larry was a dealer. He didn't object. Still, Bobby wasn't enthusiastic about doing me this favor.

"What do you want me to do about it?"

"C'mon, Bobby, you've got a million connections. Please ask around. I'm telling you, Lids is going off the deep end. He could hurt himself, maybe other people too." I gave him the phone number I'd used to get in touch with Larry. "Don't call him yourself. He won't answer. Just see if you can find someone to track him down before it all goes wrong."

"All right . . . for you, Moe. I'll see what I can find out."

Now, driving along the twisting, snowy roads of Koblenz, that conversation felt like it had taken place a lifetime ago and not the night before. Above me, the heartless winter sun hung low in the sky behind a cataract of gray, nearly opaque clouds. It seemed to know I was around, but not where, exactly. That made two of us. Although I'd spent parts of many summers in the Catskills and should have been prepared for a place like Koblenz, I was so out of my element, so utterly out of place in the Poconos. I think I felt a little like Lids must have felt, my grip on things slippery at best. Three hours of fitful sleep and the long hard trip had no doubt messed with my head, but it wasn't lack of sleep or the strangeness of the place that was messing with my head. It was fear, plain and simple. For just like that first time when I walked into the fix-it shop on Coney Island Avenue, I was about to step into a situation I was completely ill-equipped to face. Funny how sometimes the best ideas get worse and worse the closer they come to fruition.

I stopped at a general store to buy some flowers and get directions.

"Flowers?" the woman behind the counter looked at me like I was from Mars. "Notice the weather out there, son? This ain't New York City."

I forgot how obvious a Brooklyn accent was to the rest of the world. "Yeah, sorry. Stupid question."

"I've got some artificial flowers if you'd like, and some nice dried and pressed flowers one of our local church ladies makes." She didn't wait for me to ask to see them and went into the rear of the store. When she returned she was carrying a bunch of godawful pink plastic tulips in one hand, and three small but lovely wreaths of dried and pressed flowers. The flowers were glued to circles of woven twigs.

"Those," I said, pointing at the wreaths. "How much?"

"Ten bucks for the lot of them."

I put a twenty on the counter. "I'll take them and a cup of coffee, milk, no sugar."

She pointed behind me. "Help yourself, son. Coffee's on the house."

When I came back to the counter to collect the flowers and my change, I asked her for directions to the New Lutheran Cemetery.

"Oh," she said, frowning, "now I understand about the flowers. Sorry, that was rude of me before."

"Forget it. And from the cemetery, could you give me directions to 11 Post Road?"

She drew me a map so simple even I could follow it. "Here you go."

"Thanks."

"Samantha was a lovely girl," the woman whispered shyly. "Did you know her up in New York?" I guess she knew Samantha's parents' address. Then it was pretty obvious to her why I had come.

"She was wonderful: beautiful, smart . . . She was my best friend's girlfriend."

"Then why ain't he here?"

"I don't think he's been able to deal with it yet. He really loved her."

"Nice of you, though." I just sort of nodded, but she kept on going. "None of us can figure out how she got involved with all them radicals up there. That wasn't our Samantha."

I asked, "She wasn't like that as a kid?"

She smiled sadly, laughed a little. "Our Samantha? No. Don't get me wrong, son, she cared about people and animals and justice and such, but she wasn't like that at all. Samantha would never have been involved with some bomb plot or nothing like that. She must have gotten tricked into it."

I wasn't there to have an argument, but the Samantha this woman was describing wasn't the one I knew. In spite of Mindy's opinion of Sam as a poseur, Samantha had been really political and understood way more about the radical movements than I ever did.

"I guess," I said. "Sometimes people just lose their way."

"Amen to that, son. Amen to that. When you're at her grave, say hello to her for me. My name is Hattie. Tell her old Hattie misses her."

"I'll do that, Hattie, but I'll leave the old part out." Then I turned back to her as I was leaving. "And just so you know, this accent is from Brooklyn, not New York." I winked and left.

The cemetery was on the same road as the general store, so getting there was easy enough. Even as I turned through the rusting wrought iron gates, the words NEW LUTHERAN in block letters painted in gold above me, I still wasn't quite sure what I was doing there. It was just that in my sleep I'd realized that Mindy *had* told me what was bothering her that night I found her smoking and drinking. I just hadn't wanted to pay attention. Then, when Bobby, so oddly melancholy, brought up Sam's name again, I guess something resonated. After that, it was happenstance. Like I said, I wasn't a big believer in fate or the hand of God, but I couldn't escape the fact that I had asked for Aaron's car as a panicked afterthought. I couldn't ignore that he'd let me borrow it. I mean, the chances of that were like a million to one. Besides, none of us, not even Bobby, had gone to the funeral. Coming to this place just seemed like the right thing to do.

The caretaker pointed the way to Samantha's gravesite. Good thing the snow on the ground wasn't fresh, because if it had been just a little taller, not even the caretaker could have found the grave. Cemeteries, especially in daylight, don't freak me out. I was never big on ghouls, ghosts, and zombies. You're alive, then you're not. The dead were dead. I also wasn't big on talking to the dead. I hated those scenes in movies and on TV where people walk around a grave, yakking at the grass and headstone. But I'd promised Hattie I would say hello for her and I did. Keeping my word means something to me, if not to a lot of other people. Funny, I'd never been in a gentile graveyard before and I found myself wondering if Christians had as many arcane rules as Jews did about who could set foot on a gravesite. Jews, we had rules about everything—some sensible, some not so much. Our rules about cemeteries were like the rules of cricket: the people who play claim to know them, but only pretend to understand them.

There were some obvious differences, of course: crosses instead of stars, no rocks or pebbles on the gravestones, no names like Finkelstein or Cohen. And then there was the fact that this was a country cemetery. It was simpler, no grandiose mausoleums, no granite archways, no marble benches with bad poetry carved into the stone. In fact, most of the headstones were tasteful little hunks of gray granite with beveled faces where the particulars were inscribed. I liked that. It was simple, just a way to acknowledge that the person buried there hadn't always been so. It let a visitor remember the deceased as the visitor wished to. Or, in my case, it let a stranger wandering by imagine the deceased however his mood moved him to.

I got down on my hands and knees by Sam's low headstone and wiped away the snow that had accumulated around it. I laid the dried flower wreaths in an overlapping pattern against the foot of the stone. I didn't pray, didn't talk except to pass along Hattie's message. I just remembered her, remembered the first time we met. I smiled a big smile, recalling that I had been thrilled to know there were women like her out there in the larger world. I stood, wiped off my knees, and almost unconsciously said, "Bye, Sam." I took a few steps toward Aaron's Tempest, then stopped in my tracks. For the second time in less than an hour, I turned back. I stared down at the inscription on the headstone:

## SAMANTHA JANE HOPE
## LOVING DAUGHTER
## 1941–1966

That couldn't be right, I thought. Those dates had to be wrong. Samantha seemed older than us, sure, but she wasn't twenty-five. She couldn't have been twenty-five. I'd find out soon enough.

I had to pass through the actual town of the town of Koblenz on my way to Sam's parents' house. And there, right next to the library and the police station, was Koblenz's town hall. I pulled into a diagonal parking spot in front of the building and went inside. A chubby woman, with a pretty smile and a lazy left eye, pointed me to the public records room.

"You're going to have to help yourself, I'm afraid," she said. "Millie's out with the grippe today."

"That's fine," I assured her, trying to take the Brooklyn edges off my accent. "I appreciate it."

It took me a while to figure out the town's—Millie's, more likely—filing system, but I found it, the record of Samantha's birth on November 5, 1941. There was a doctor's name, but no hospital listed next to her name. I guessed she'd been born at home. I'd never known anyone of my generation born at home. I don't know why knowing that about Sam made me smile, but it did.

As I drove from town hall to the Hope house, I noticed that the sun had vanished completely now and that snow was definitely in the air. I was heartened by the fact that it hadn't started falling yet and that the guy on the radio said I'd have a few more hours until it did. The house at 11 Post Road was a neat, L-shaped ranch with white clapboards, snow-filled window boxes, a white picket fence, and a detached garage at the end of a semicircular driveway. It didn't exactly evoke Norman Rockwell images of God, country, and apple pie, but it sure didn't evoke images of Brooklyn either. It was easy for me to picture Samantha as a little girl playing in the front yard, her blonde hair blowing into her eyes as she ran to greet her dad coming home from work.

I pulled up the driveway, parked by the front door, got out, and knocked. It didn't take long for the door to pull back. There, standing behind the storm door, was a lovely woman who was, at most, in her late forties. It was like looking at Sam's much older sister, but I knew it was her mom. Sam was an only child. She gestured for me to open the storm door and I did.

"You're Samantha's friend from Brooklyn," her mom said. "Old Hattie from the general store called and mentioned you were in town. Please come in."

I wiped my shoes on the welcome mat and stepped inside. "Yeah—I mean, yes, ma'am, I'm Moe, Moe Prager, and I knew your daughter."

"You went to visit with her. Hattie told me about the flowers too."

"I did."

Mrs. Hope asked, "Did you have a nice visit with her?" I must have looked completely confused by the question, so she came to my rescue. "Sorry, Moe, that's between you and Sam."

"No need to apologize, really."

"Moe," she said, "is that short for something?"

"Moses."

"My favorite figure from the Old Testament."

"My brother's name is Aaron, and my little sister is Miriam."

That turned Mrs. Hope's polite smile into a beacon. "Good for your folks. Come in, sit down. You must be hungry. Can I fix you something to eat, get you a drink?"

"Thank you, yes, Mrs. Hope. I'd like that very much."

"That's settled, then. Take your coat off and sit yourself down at the table. We can talk while I get your lunch ready."

I did as she asked. The interior of the house was a mirror of the outside: neat, simple, clean. The furniture was all clean lines and upholstered cushions. The dining room set was colonial. A big copper lamp that had been refitted for electricity hung over the table for light. Then, as I scanned the walls, my heart did that flip-floppy thing. It wasn't the pictures of Sam at different ages that did it to me, but rather all the plaques in the living room that featured the names of various police organizations and images of badges and stars.

"What does Mr. Hope do for a living?" I called into the kitchen, but there was no answer.

"Were you Samantha's boyfriend there in New York?" she asked instead.

"No," I answered, standing up, walking into the living room. "I'm her boyfriend's best friend." Apparently, old Hattie hadn't shared all the information with her friend. "His name is Bobby Friedman and he's still too broken up about what happened to deal with it."

That was the second time I'd said those words or ones just like them in the last few hours, but I hadn't thought about them, really considered them until that moment. Were they true? Yeah, probably, but I couldn't help wondering why Bobby hadn't come here for the funeral after Sam's body was released to her family. We never discussed it. Maybe we should have.

I stood in front of one of the many plaques on the wall and read silently to myself:

*For service above and beyond the call of duty on the date of August 6, 1956, this commendation is awarded to Trooper Samuel Hope.*

All the plaques and awards were much alike except for Samuel Hope's rank; he'd risen to the rank of colonel. I'd often wondered why Samantha didn't talk much about her family or where she was from. I understood now. Tough to think of your dad as the enemy. Samantha didn't resemble her dad at all, but they had had many photos taken together, many of which were on proud display— some on the walls, some on the coffee table, others on the mantel over the fireplace. I went and sat back down in the dining room.

"Was Samantha named for her dad?" I called in to Mrs. Hope.

"Yes. Samuel desperately wanted a son to follow in his footsteps. Strange though, that husband of mine loved his daughter more than he could ever have loved a son, I think. They were close, much closer than Samantha and me. They were inseparable, those two. Here you go," said Mrs. Hope, stepping from the kitchen into the dining room. She carried a floral print metal tray. On it was a glass of milk, a white bread sandwich containing some sort of pink-hued meat—probably ham—potato chips, a pickle spear, and an apple.

Clearly, Mrs. Hope wasn't up on the rules of keeping kosher. Technically, Jews can't eat dairy products and meat together, and they can never eat pork, dairy or no dairy. Me, I would never be mistaken for a Talmudic scholar or an observant Jew, though the concept of milk and meat, ham or otherwise, did make me a little queasy. The queasiness didn't improve when I found that the ham was slathered not with mustard, which I loved, but with mayonnaise. Yet, I didn't want to insult my hostess or lose whatever goodwill I had earned with her.

"Delicious," I said, taking big bites and swallowing with little chewing. I savored the chips and the odd-tasting pickle. Kosher dill pickles weren't sweet, but this pickle spear tasted like it had been cured in sugar syrup. I kind of liked it.

She wouldn't sit. Instead she hovered, fussing over me, brushing crumbs away, getting me another napkin. "I'm so glad you're enjoying it."

"So, Sam's dad is a state trooper. Must've been tough on your husband when . . . I'm sorry."

"No, you're right, Moe. It nearly killed Samuel to think that his girl had gotten all tangled up with radicals and hippie types. We will never understand how that happened. Her whole life, up until the time Samantha left for college, all she ever wanted to be was a trooper like her father. But people change, kids grow up, and you don't know them anymore."

"There are female cops, aren't there?" I said.

She let out a laugh. "Not in this family. My husband wouldn't hear of it. No daughter of Samuel Hope was going to wear a badge and strap on a gun. It was the only thing those two ever fought about. So, Moe, if you don't mind me asking, can you tell me about what Sam was like the last year before . . . you know?"

With that, I regaled Mrs. Hope with tales of her daughter. I explained about how all the guys had secret crushes on her, but not only for her beauty. I told her we thought her daughter was smarter and more worldly than any woman we'd ever met. I explained how, in spite of Bobby's politics, that he was a good and loyal boyfriend who loved her daughter to distraction. I told her how we too were surprised by what had happened, that no one would have expected either Samantha or Marty Lavitz of being involved in any violence.

After I washed up, I told her that snow was in the forecast and that I had to get on the road. She thanked me and gave me a long hug. I hugged her back.

"You take care of yourself, Moses Prager," she said, winking at me. "You come back and visit too. Sam was lucky to have a friend like you."

"Thank you. One thing, Mrs. Hope, if you don't mind?"

"Anything."

"Well, I guess we knew Sam was older than us, but I had no idea she was twenty-five."

"She did always look young for her age and she had that energy, you know?"

I did.

# CHAPTER NINETEEN

I got about an hour outside of town before stopping to fill up. When I pulled out of the station, the flurries began to fall. At first they fell in big, lazy flakes. They would stop for a while and then start up again, but after another half hour, stopping wasn't on the storm's agenda. The snow grew steadier and heavier as the sky darkened. At least I knew how not to get lost on my way home, though the snow and dark made it unlikely that the return trip would take any less time. What I hoped for was that I would eventually get ahead of the weather, because the storm was predicted to stay north and miss New York City altogether.

The roads were getting pretty slick and tricky, the snow accumulating so quickly that I could barely make out the black of the pavement beneath. Look, I'd had my license for less than two years and it wasn't like I was Richard Petty or A. J. Foyt. I was good at city driving, real good. I was never scared of driving into Manhattan, but I knew adults who would break out in hives at the thought of driving over the Brooklyn Bridge and dealing with yellow cabs and crowded streets. This was something else, though. I didn't have much experience with rolling hills and snowy country roads. The pressure of driving in my brother's car wasn't helping any either. I was several miles away from Route 80 when I felt the Tempest's snow tires occasionally losing traction. That always made me nervous, the sense of impending loss of control. Maybe that's why I didn't dig drugs that much.

Each time I felt the tires spin, lose their grip, I slowed down a few miles an hour. Up to that point I'd been lucky in that I seemed to be one of the few idiots out on the road. So when I slowed, I wasn't pissing anyone off. In city driving, that was always part of the equation: Am I pissing off the guy behind me? Is he going to get out of his car at the next red light and beat the shit out of me? Thinking about that made me smile and relax a little bit. Then when I looked in my rearview mirror, I noticed headlights that hadn't been there before. They were back a ways, but the hills made it impossible for me to know how far back. I didn't think anything of it at first. So what if there were two idiots driving around on these roads? But the next time I checked my mirror, I noticed that those headlights had made up a lot of the distance between us. The next time I looked, the headlights were gone. *Well, at least one of us idiots made it home safe.*

Thirty seconds later, I felt my body tense, my hands tightening their grip on the wheel, my eyes wide and alert, my heart pounding. I wasn't consciously aware of the thing that had caused me to react. It was as if my body, independent of my mind, had seen something or heard a sound above the road noise and radio. I clicked the radio off, and just as I did I was blinded by an explosion of light in my rearview mirror. Those headlights hadn't disappeared at all. The driver of the car on my tail had simply shut off his lights in order to sneak up on me without me knowing, and when he was close enough, he hit his lights and brights at once. The shock of it almost sent me off the road. I shielded my eyes with my hand, turning away from the harsh light. I flicked the button on the bottom of the rearview that darkened the light reflected in the mirror. I sped up to try and give myself time to think, but the guy behind me just raced right up to the rear end of the Tempest, blaring his horn, flashing his lights. For about a mile we repeated this pattern, me racing ahead and him charging right up behind me. The last time I thought there was no way he wasn't going to slam into me. I sped up at the last second, and there was no contact.

As I drove, my eyes darted left and right, looking for someplace to turn off or turn around, or for a neon sign from an open store or gas station, but the two-lane road wasn't lit and there was nothing on the roadsides except stone walls, hills, and drop-offs. There wasn't even much of a shoulder to speak of. Basically, I was fucked. So I just floored my brother's Pontiac, wishing it had been a GTO and not just a Tempest. Now I was getting bounced around as I came over the crests of the hills, and getting slammed when the car landed back on the road. Whatever the guy behind me was driving, it was having no trouble keeping pace. Realizing I was never going to outrun him, I lifted my foot completely off the gas pedal. If the pavement had been dry, I might've slammed on the brakes, but in snowy, slick conditions that wasn't an option. Unfortunately, I'd chosen to make the move after coming over the top of a steep hill and the car didn't slow as quickly as I'd hoped.

At the bottom of the hill, the guy behind me let me have the brights again. He blared his horn as the nose of his car came close enough to my rear bumper to give it a kiss. Instead of ramming me, he took the opportunity to pull to my left and try and overtake me. When he did that, I floored the gas and got thrown back in my seat. We climbed the next hill nearly side by side, and that's when I saw a flicker of light ahead of me coming over the crest of the hill in the other direction. I felt the sweat pouring out of me, gluing my shirt to the skin of my back. This was it. I slowed down as we got to the top of the hill to prevent the guy next to me from sliding in behind me. An air horn split open the night as the cab of a semi appeared. Now it was time for someone else to panic. I steered right to give the semi as much room as possible if he swerved to avoid the other car.

The guy menacing me tugged his wheel hard left to avoid the cab of the semi. As I came over the top of the hill, I didn't so much see what happened as hear it. There was a bang as the car smacked into the stone wall that bordered the road, and then there was another sharp bang as the semi clipped the car's rear end. Air brakes chuffed and tires screeched, and a cloud of tire smoke and radiator steam filled up the air behind me.

If I was smart or brave, I'd have gone back to look, to see who it was who'd tried to get me killed, if not kill me himself. But at that moment I wasn't feeling terribly smart or brave. Mostly, I just felt lucky, and kept on going. I don't think I breathed again until hours later when I saw the lights atop the George Washington Bridge come into view.

# CHAPTER TWENTY

As I came off the Gowanus Expressway onto the Belt Parkway, I was less than ten minutes from home. I was unaware I was much closer to eternity. One second I was listening to the radio, driving in the middle lane, doing a rock-steady fifty, and the next second horns blared, tires screeched, and I was bouncing up onto the shoulder of the Belt. When I snapped out of it, the car was a few hundred yards west of the Verazzano Bridge. I was slumped to the side, my head against the window, my hand on the wheel only because that's where it had been when I drifted into sleep. I managed to pull fully onto the shoulder while shaking the sleep out of my head. Pretty ironic, I thought, to have avoided some lunatic trying to run me off the road in the Poconos only to fall asleep at the wheel and almost get killed within pissing distance of my house. The irony didn't keep me awake.

The next thing I was aware of was an insistent rapping of metal against glass. I held my eyes wide open, shook my head, and nearly had a heart attack when I saw a man standing just on the other side of the driver's side door. He was staring in at me, tapping his wedding band against the glass. Then I noticed that he was wearing a squashed-down hat with a badge on its crown above the visor. Great, I thought, just what I needed to complete my night, getting arrested and having Aaron's car impounded. When the cop saw that I was alert, he stopped banging at the window and made a circular motion with his index finger. I got the idea and rolled down the window.

"You drunk, kid? Stoned?" he asked, shining a flashlight past my chin and checking out the interior of the car.

"Just tired," I said. "On my way back from the Poconos."

He was skeptical. "The Poconos, huh? Don't see no skis on your car, buddy."

"Brooklyn Jews don't ski."

He laughed at that. "Funny, kid, but that's not an answer."

"I was visiting the parents of a dead friend, a girl I went to college with."

"How far you live from here?"

"Coney Island."

"Okay. Get outta here and sleep it off in bed, not on the side of the Belt Parkway."

"Thanks, officer."

Two encounters with highway patrol cops in two days on the Belt Parkway. What were the odds of that? Okay, so the first time I wasn't driving and it was ten miles away in the other direction, but still, what were the odds? At least this cop had given me a break, hadn't slammed me against the car, hadn't frisked or cuffed me. Was that because I didn't have long hair like Bobby's, or because this cop had a sense of humor? It was one of those questions that would never get answered, like "Did Oswald act alone?" When I pulled back onto the parkway, something was bugging me, but I was still too cotton-headed to make sense of it.

I looked at the dashboard clock and figured I'd been asleep on the shoulder for about a half hour when the cop rapped on the window. Was I still tired? Sure, but now I was hungry too. I'd probably been hungry the whole time, but I'd been so close to unconsciousness I'd just failed to notice. So instead of heading straight home, I went to

DeFelice's Pizza under the el. The Gelato Grotto in Gravesend was the most celebrated pizzeria in the area. I loved their gelato, but hated their pizza. I'd take slices, regular or Sicilian, from DeFelice's Pizza any day of the week over the Grotto's. DeFelice's regular crust was as thin as a cracker with a perfect char on the bottom, and they used fresh mozzarella, not that gummy crap they used at the Grotto that came in blocks and had the texture of pencil erasers. And DeFelice's sauce was sweet, not bitter like the Grotto's. My mouth was watering even before I got off the Belt at Ocean Parkway.

At that time of night there were spots out front of the pizzeria. I guess if I'd been less hungry or less tired, I would have noticed Tony Pepperoni's '56 Lincoln Mark II stationed out front. He loved that maroon beast almost as much as he loved to eat, which was really saying something. Sometimes he'd pay kids to stand out on the street and guard the car to make sure nobody got too close to his pride and joy. None of us kids ever had the nerve to point out to Tony P that the subway trains passing overhead shot out hot metal sparks and all sorts of shit that rained down on the cars parked below.

"One regular slice, one Sicilian, and a small Coke," I said to Geno at the counter, his face and hands white with flour.

"I got fresh pies comin' out in a few minoots. Go 'ave a seat. I call you when they ready."

I was alone in the tiny dining room, but knew I wouldn't be for long. It wasn't that I was a mind reader or anything. It was that the place was a tiny hole in the wall and the dining room was so cozy that the bathroom was situated just behind a thin wall at the back of the place. When the restaurant wasn't crowded, which was almost never, and no subways were passing overhead—again, almost never—a diner had a pretty good idea of what was going on in the bathroom. So it was that night. The toilet flushed and the sink ran for a few seconds. The gentleman inside whistled "Volare" loudly enough to be heard over the hand dryer. The door creaked open, and into the dining room stepped Tony Pepperoni.

The funny thing is that when he saw me, he looked surprised or maybe confused, like he expected to see anybody else there but me. Maybe it was just that he didn't expect anyone to be there at that time of night. It didn't matter, because whatever I saw in his expression was gone as quickly as it came. Tony may have had a complexion like the lunar surface, but he had a perfect neon smile. He flashed it as he walked up close to me. I thought back to Lids's crazy ramblings about Tony P, and realized it was the first time I'd thought about Lids all day. Tony P didn't give me a chance to worry about Lids or to wonder if Bobby had had success tracking him down.

"Moe Prager, as I fuckin' live and breathe," he said, pinching then patting my cheek. "What a surprise. Hey, what's that behind your ear?" And with lightning speed, he reached behind my left ear and produced a quarter. "Jeez, will ya look at that, a quarter. Do you crap gold bricks?"

He laughed at his joke then proceeded to manipulate the coin, flipping it over and under all of his fingers with great aplomb. He'd been doing this stupid trick, telling that same stupid joke for as long as I could remember. He held the quarter out to me, but I wasn't supposed to take it. The magic part of the show was over. This part was kabuki. There were prescribed roles to play and lines to say.

"You want it, Moe?" he asked.

"Yeah, sure," I answered as expected.

But as I stretched out to snatch it, Tony jiggled his hand and the coin vanished. It was all going according to script until Geno cried out, "You slices, they ready!"

Tony P's face turned even redder than normal, the veins popping out of his neck, his eyes going all crazy. "Shut the fuck up, Geno. Shut your fuckin' mouth!"

"Sorry, Tony, 'scusa me."

"What the fuck did I just say to you? Shut the fuck up!"

This time there was no apology. Tony waited a beat or two, jiggled his hand, and the quarter reappeared.

"You want it, Moe?"

"Yeah, sure," I repeated as I reached for the coin.

Tony jiggled his hand again. The coin disappeared and then Tony got to say the line he'd been building up to, "Maybe next time, kid. Maybe next time."

When Bobby and I were little, there was another line we used to say, but at this stage not even Tony expected us to say, "*Gee, how did you do that? Can you teach me how?*"

Geno brought my slices and Coke over, averting his eyes from Tony P's glare. "On the house," he said.

Tony nodded in approval, then jerked his head at Geno to disappear. Tony sat his three-hundred-plus pounds across from me.

"Been a long time, Moe. How's school?"

I didn't answer right away because not only did I have a mouthful of doughy Sicilian pizza, but because I hadn't given serious thought to school since the day Mindy had been hospitalized. I never imagined a question from a guy like Tony Pepperoni would stump or shake me. The truth is that school felt irrelevant to me. That wasn't what scared me, though. What scared me was the sense that I might never stop feeling that way. For a Jew raised to honor education above all else, you have no idea just how frightening it was to be without that sense of purpose. It was like getting your backbone ripped out and having nothing to put in its place.

I finally said, "Okay, I guess."

"What kinda fuckin' answer is that? Don't be a mook, kid. You're one of the smart kids around here. Don't be pissin' on that."

"I know."

"Bobby was in the other day and told me about your girlfriend. She doin' okay?"

"Better."

"Good, that's a good thing." Tony P looked at his gaudy diamond and gold watch. "You know, Moe, it's pretty late. Where you been that you're comin' in so late?"

"Long story, Tony."

"I got time." Tony P wasn't the type of guy who would take no for an answer.

"I was up visiting in the Poconos."

"That's nice," he said with little enthusiasm. "That's the whole story?"

"On the way home it was snowing like crazy and some asshole tried running me off a road up there."

"No shit? Up there? That don't figure. Why, you cut him off or something? You flip him the bird?"

"Nah. Maybe it was my New York license plate pissing a yahoo off or because I'm young. I don't know. Who knows why people do the things they do?"

Now he was curious. "So what happened?"

"I got lucky. I was coming up to the crest of a hill and a semi was coming up in the other direction just as the guy who was chasing me tried to overtake me. I didn't see what happened, but I heard the crash. It didn't sound as bad as it could have been, I guess. It wasn't head on. There was—"

The phone rang and that got Tony's attention. I took the opportunity to take another bite.

Geno called out, "It's somebody callin' for you, Tony. He says is important."

"Excuse me, kid. I gotta take this. I hope your girl gets better real soon." He took a step away, then turned back. "And hey, Moe, you think maybe you should stick to your schoolwork? It's a lot safer than real life, no?"

Outside, a D train *ka-chunged ka-chunged* along the el tracks, its brakes squealing as it stopped. I gobbled the rest of my pizza, washing it down with the Coke. When I walked to the front of the pizzeria, Tony Pepperoni was gone and Geno looked relieved. I nodded goodnight. As I drove the few blocks back home, I remembered there had been something bothering me about what had happened with the highway patrol cop, but I was even further away from it now than I was before.

# CHAPTER TWENTY-ONE

Ringing telephones seemed to be how I was measuring out my mornings these days now that my class schedule was no longer a consideration. And since the phone that woke me up was still ringing, I could only assume I was alone in the apartment. By the time I got to the kitchen and picked up, all I got for my trouble was a dial tone. I cradled the receiver and went to do my morning business. I didn't get two steps away when the phone started up again.

"Yeah," I growled. "What?"

"Moe, is that you? This is Herb Weinstock, Mindy's dad."

"Oh, I'm really sorry about that, Mr. Weinstock. I'm not feeling so well today."

"Mindy's mom and I figured something must've been up when you didn't come by the hospital yesterday."

Suddenly, there was a king-sized knot in my gut. "Is something wrong? Did something happen? Is Mindy—"

"Calm yourself, Moe. It's all right. It's okay. Mindy woke up a little bit more yesterday and her doctor thinks she should be transferred to a place in Westchester County where they have better facilities to handle her condition and rehabilitation. I'm calling because I didn't want you to get scared if you came here today and found her room empty."

"So you're transferring her today?"

"In an hour. I don't like to do it. She should be by her home, near her friends with her family. That's what her mother and I think, but the doctors say it's best and we have to do what the doctors say. We will call you later with all the particulars and let you know when you can come visit."

"Is Mindy talking yet?"

"Not yet. She seems to recognize us sometimes, Moe. It's wonderful to see a light in her eyes again. Sometimes when she's at her most wakeful, you can swear she moves her lips like she's trying to say words."

"That's great news, Mr. Weinstock. Please kiss her for me and tell her I love her."

"We will do that. Don't you worry. Like I said, we will call."

I hung up the phone and headed for the bathroom. I made it as far as the hallway when the phone started ringing again. Did the world have a conspiracy against my bladder or what?

"Hello," I answered generically, not wanting to offend Mindy's dad if it was him calling back to tell me some forgotten detail.

"Hello? Since when do you answer the damn phone like a receptionist?" It was Bobby. "Where were you like five minutes ago when I called the first time? Then when I called back I got a busy signal."

"That was you? I thought it was Mindy's dad."

"What? What happened? Did something—"

I couldn't take it any longer. "Hang on," I said, letting go of the phone and racing for the bathroom. A minute later and a few pints lighter, I got back on the line. "You still there?"

"What the hell is going on with you?"

I explained the missed phone call, about Mr. Weinstock's call, and about the call of nature.

"That's great news about Mindy."

"It is. So why are you calling this early?"

"I found Lids," he said. "He's safe. I thought you'd wanna know."

"Good, I'll go over and see—"

Bobby interrupted. "You can't see him."

"Is he invisible?"

"I said he's safe, Moe, not home."

I didn't like it. "What's that supposed to mean?"

"What it sounds like it means. He's okay. He's safe. Someone's keeping an eye on him for me."

"You don't even like the guy," I said. "I practically had to beg you to look for him and now what, you're watching over him like a mother hen?"

"Yeah, Moe, something like that."

"Something like that? What the fuck am I supposed to tell his parents? They're gonna want to get the cops involved."

"Make up a story. You're good at that."

"What's going on, Bobby?"

"Look, I don't have time to explain. I've got an airport run this morning and I'm already running behind because I wanted to let you know Lids was okay. I'm taking Ronnie Ackerman's grandma to JFK. You wanna come along? Maybe we can talk about things on the way back."

I said yes before I thought about it.

"Okay," he said. "Fifteen minutes. Be down in front of your building." He was off the line before I had time to change my mind.

I stood there for a moment, the moot phone still in my hand. It wasn't just that I was stunned by Bobby's inexplicable transformation from reluctant searcher to guardian angel. It wasn't about Lids at all, really. What happened is that it finally clicked for me. I understood what it was that had been gnawing at me since the cop woke me up on the side of the Belt Parkway. I thought back to the flat tire, to Bobby fussing with stuff in what should have been an empty trunk. I remembered him making me stay in the car and his keeping the trunk lid shut. I remembered the cop futzing around in the trunk too. I was positive Bobby was going to get arrested. I mean, he was already handcuffed and in the back of the cop car. Then, as if by magic, an accident up ahead forced the cop to kick Bobby loose. See, here's the thing that came to me: *there was no accident anywhere up ahead that day.* After the cop split, we drove from Pennsylvania Avenue past Rockaway Parkway, Flatbush Avenue, Knapp Street, past Coney Island Avenue until we got off at Ocean Parkway. Not only was there no accident on either side of the road; there wasn't even a slowdown. I guess I'd been so freaked out by what had happened between Bobby and the cop that it hadn't fully registered.

Why had it taken two days to dawn on me? I didn't have time to worry about it. Usually, I don't like making excuses, but I had ample cause to be distracted. My girlfriend was comatose. I'd seen two murdered bodies. I'd been tied up, beaten up, nearly run over, and nearly run off the road. A week ago, if you had told me any two of those things would have happened to me over the course of my entire life, I would have called you crazy. So, yeah, I felt comfortable with giving myself a pass. There'd also been a change of plans, only I had no intention of telling Bobby about it.

✦

I was downstairs in ten minutes, not fifteen. After brushing my teeth and throwing on some clothes, I left my building through a rear exit and found Aaron's car where I'd parked it. Heading quickly away from the neighborhood, I kept a close eye out for Bobby's car. For things to work out, I couldn't afford for him to catch me sneaking away. I imagined Bobby's perpetual smile curdling when he saw I wasn't waiting for him in front of my building. His mood wouldn't improve any either when he'd be forced to double-park his car so he could run into my building's lobby to ring my apartment buzzer. He'd be pretty pissed when he finally realized that I wasn't home and that I wasn't coming with him. I didn't like pulling this kind of shit on anyone, least of all Bobby, but I didn't see that I had much of a choice. I had to buy enough time to get over to Ronnie Ackerman's block before Bobby did.

Ronnie was a Burgundy House brother who lived on East 14th Street off Gravesend Neck Road. He lived there with his parents, his sister—pretty sexy in a gloomy, Sylvia Plath kind of way—and his *bubbeh*. I knew all of this because Ronnie'd had all of us over for a barbecue last spring. Good thing too. Otherwise, the mechanics of following Bobby around would have been that much more difficult. As it was, I had no faith I would be any good at playing at *The Man from U.N.C.L.E.* I'd never followed anyone in my life, certainly not in a car, and I understood it wasn't going to be as easy as it looked on TV. I was already behind the eight ball because there was a chance Bobby might recognize Aaron's car in his rearview if I got too close. My one advantage was that I knew where the trip was beginning and where it would end, so I could afford to hang far back. All I had to do was keep Bobby's 88 in sight.

I parked down the other end of East 14th Street, away from Ronnie's house, and waited for Bobby's car to pass. It took quite a while, or maybe it just seemed that way. If I didn't believe that Bobby was lying to me or, at the very least, hiding stuff from me, I probably would've felt guilty about what I was doing. Guilt came as standard equipment in most Jews, and I was no exception. My uncle used to joke that Jews felt so guilty about everything that when the doctors slapped us at birth we felt like we deserved it. In a paper I wrote about Jewish guilt for a psych class, I claimed it was a perverse expression of cultural narcissism. If it turned out that I was misjudging Bobby, I'd eat my heart out with guilt at some later date. Guilt is good that way—it doesn't have a shelf life.

I saw Bobby's 88 coming my way in the side view mirror, and lay down before he passed. Thirty seconds later, I took off behind him. Although following him went pretty smoothly, it wasn't without its problems. Traffic happened to be so sparse that no matter how far I hung back, it was nearly impossible to keep a lot of cars between Bobby and me. Figures I'd pick the lightest traffic day in the history of the free world to start my career as a junior G-Man. It didn't help much that the skies were perfectly clear, and that visibility was basically unlimited. Even so, there was nothing about Bobby's driving that indicated he had any idea I was behind him.

Just as he had done the two times I'd accompanied him, he pulled off onto the Conduit by the Van Wyck Expressway and then onto the road that circled the terminals at JFK. As expected, Bobby drove into the short-term parking closest to the Eastern Airlines terminal. He parked in the same aisle, in the same spot as he had on our two previous trips. I guess I never thought of Bobby as someone who was hung up on consistency. There was very little that was consistent about him other than his friendship. With his happy-go-lucky demeanor, radical dogma, and hustler's heart, he was already a breathing contradiction. It was pretty funny to think of him as the anal retentive revolutionary: *A place for everything and everything in its place.* I pulled into a spot that afforded me a good view of Bobby's car and watched as Bobby ushered Bubbeh Ackerman to the terminal.

A few minutes after they vanished from my view, a white, boxy Dodge van pulled up right behind Bobby's car, obscuring my view. *Shit!* If I wanted to know what was going on, I didn't have much choice but to move myself or my car. I got out of the car, and when I did I felt suddenly very naked. I don't know why exactly. It was silly. There was plenty of activity swirling around me: cars parking, cars pulling in and out of the lot, people heading toward or coming from the terminal. There was no reason that I should be any more or less conspicuous than anyone else. I told myself to just act naturally, and laughed at the inherent contradiction in my own advice. Act naturally; how did that work? I was good at being me, not at acting like being me. At the moment, though, the more pressing issue was finding a way to see what was going on with the white van and Bobby's car.

Too late. By the time I was done being Prufrock, the ship had sailed. The van was pulling away and heading for the exit. If anything had been loaded into Bobby's trunk from the van or from the trunk into the van, I'd missed it. Worse, I had no way of knowing if the van had any actual significance. For all I knew, it had stopped at the rear of Bobby's car because it was having engine trouble. When I got back in the car, I had a tough choice to make and not much time in which to make it. I could wait for Bobby to return and follow him wherever he went, or I could go off after the van. The longer I waited to choose, the less likely the latter option became. I wasn't going to get caught napping a second time. I twisted the ignition key, backed up, and raced for the exit.

I caught up to the white van pretty quickly. It was easier to tail the van at a close distance than it had been to follow Bobby. To the van driver, Aaron's Tempest was just one of a thousand cars just like it on the local roads. My face behind the wheel would be just another humanoid blur, no more significant than the other shadowy faces the van driver passed or would pass during the course of his day. Still, once I fell in behind the van, I didn't tailgate. I tried to keep plenty of cars between the nose of the Tempest and the van's windowless back doors. The van turned off the main terminal road and onto a road that wound its way through unfamiliar ground, areas of the airport I had never seen before. This was the nuts and bolts part of the airfield, where the jets were hangared and their bellies were stuffed with boxes and crates and aluminum containers. The air was alive with the whining of jet engines and the acrid stink of spent kerosene on burning hot metal. I could almost taste the exhaust on my tongue. Crazy as it may sound, the sun that lit the cargo area seemed dimmer somehow, its light more diffuse. Driving through this part of the airport reminded me of the first time I'd walked into the back of a restaurant and seen the ugly bones behind the pretty face shown to the diners.

The van driver didn't seem in any rush, keeping at a steady thirty miles per hour. In fact, he was making it so easy for me to keep pace I worried that I'd been spotted, that he was trying to lure me into a trap. But no, those were my nerves talking. I was just freaked because I knew that once we left the airport I would be on my own. When we had worked our way completely through the cargo area, the van finally turned left out of the airport onto Rockaway Boulevard. We stayed on Rockaway Boulevard past the Belt Parkway and into a neighborhood I was utterly unfamiliar with. I saw some store signs that indicated we were driving through South Ozone Park. I may not have known the neighborhood, but I breathed a little easier when we turned onto Linden Boulevard—an avenue that ran through much of Brooklyn and all of Queens—and I saw the grandstands of Aqueduct Racetrack looming ahead. I was a little too relieved, and got so distracted I wound up directly behind the white van.

He turned right. I kept on straight ahead. I circled back as soon as I could, racing to the corner where he'd turned. No more than thirty seconds had passed, but the Dodge van was nowhere in sight. I drove down the street, hoping to catch a glimpse of a bumper or taillight. Good thing I looked to my left when I did because there it was, the van, parking on a side street. I turned down the side street, keeping my distance. The van door opened, and out stepped a big man dressed in blue coveralls and work boots, a wool cap on his head. He wasn't big as in long, but as in thick. Just the way he walked, circling the van, checking its doors to make sure they were locked, intimidated the hell out of me. There was something else about him too, a vague familiarity. I imagined him with a ski mask over his face and his hands twisted around the collar of my coat. I couldn't be sure, not from as far away as I was, but he certainly reminded me of the guy who'd whacked me across my ribs the night of the fire at 1055 Coney Island Avenue. If I heard him speak, I'd be sure.

When he was done checking that the van was locked, he crossed over to my side of the street, but never got close to me. Instead, he walked into a hole-in-the-wall neighborhood bar. Part of me was very tempted to walk in there after him, but I wasn't in the mood to get my ass kicked. Besides, strangers tend to stick out in neighborhood bars like Hasids at a hoedown. There's no way to just slip in undetected. The minute the door opens in a local joint, everyone in the place turns to see who's coming in. Instead, I took the opportunity to check out the van more closely. I already had its plate number memorized, but I wanted to take a look inside. I pressed my face to the windshield, cupping my hands around my eyes to block out the sun. There wasn't much to see. But for the two front seats, it was as bare as Old Mother Hubbard's cupboard, and not nearly as cozy. Then, when I moved around to the passenger side window to get a different view, I realized it wasn't quite as empty as it seemed. It had one thing in it I was sure Old Mother Hubbard's cupboard had never had: a sawed-off shotgun.

If I had been standing in the street instead of on the sidewalk, the driver's seat would have totally obscured it from my view. The interior door panel had been removed and the window wedged into a permanent shut position. The pump-action shotgun sat in two L-shaped metal brackets welded onto the door's interior. Its stock was gone but for a curved nub, and a few inches had been removed from the end of the barrel. I didn't know much about handguns. I knew even less about rifles and shotguns, but I didn't have to know anything about them to understand that I didn't want to be on the wrong end of a sawed-off.

As I hurried back to the Tempest, I glanced over at the local bar the big man had gone into. It looked like most other neighborhood places. Nothing fancy: a neon Rheingold Beer sign in the window and a porthole window in the front door. The only thing unusual about the joint was its name: Onion Street Pub. Onion Street? I wondered if there was such a street, and where such a street might be. Probably not South Ozone Park. Wherever it was, it sounded like the kind of place my mom would love. Even as a kid I used to think that my mom liked chopping onions, because it gave her license to cry and hide her sorrows behind the onion tears. I wondered if the housewives of Onion Street camouflaged their real tears like my mom camouflaged hers. It's weird what you think about sometimes.

# CHAPTER TWENTY-TWO

The big man stayed in the Onion Street Pub for about a half hour, and when he came out he didn't act any drunker than when he went in. Everything about him—his size, his swagger, the tilt of his head, the way he puffed out his chest—was menacing and seemed to send a warning. *Stay back. Keep away. Just keep the fuck away.* I'd known guys like him in my life. You can't grow up where I grew up and not know guys like him, but the van driver was different. It's hard to explain, but he wore his menace the way a pro athlete wears his grace or a pit viper its tail rattle. I was likely projecting. He probably wasn't half as menacing as his shotgun.

He saved me the trouble of having to turn around, because after starting up the van, he made a U-turn right from his parking spot. I let a few cars pass me before heading out after him. I wasn't sure why I still bothered. The shotgun scared me, but it also intrigued me. What kind of cargo had the van contained that needed a shotgun for protection? What business could Bobby Friedman possibly have with such a man? Besides, I had nowhere else to go. I figured I might as well play out my hand and see what the cards had in store.

Twenty minutes later I was following the van through College Point, another unfamiliar Queens neighborhood. Again, like in South Ozone Park, it became difficult keeping enough cars between Aaron's car and the van. I was forced to hang further back than I wanted to, and twice lost sight of the van for a few seconds. The last time I caught up, I came around a corner and saw that the van was halfway down the block. Its motor still running, it had stopped near a dilapidated wooden garage that looked like a set piece from *The Great Gatsby*. There was even a faded ad for a long-forgotten shirt company painted on the flank of the garage. The name of the shirt company had been lost to history, but the outline of a man's face and some of his slicked-back black hair remained. I think his fingers were buttoning a top button. Oddly, his smile, of all his faded features, had stayed most intact. It was a white, knowing smile. What it knew was another matter altogether. I imagined the doomed Myrtle Wilson living in the tiny apartment above the garage, staring out her filthy window through dingy curtains, longing for escape. There were many such places in New York City, slivers of the past hidden amongst the glories of the space age like Princess phones and color TVs.

The driver got out of the van, undid a heavy padlock on the garage doors, and swung open the old wooden doors. He didn't get back in the van. He disappeared into the garage, and a moment later drove out in a chestnut red '62 Ford Galaxie. He pulled it over to the sidewalk and got out. He loved that car. You could just tell by the way he eased the door shut instead of slamming it. He wiped some dust specks off its fender as he might've wiped a tear from his lover's cheek or tucked a stray hair behind her ear. At that moment, he didn't seem quite so menacing. He got back in the van, turned its flat face out, and backed it into the garage. The driver swung the garage doors closed and locked up, got back in his Galaxie, and was off.

He was like a different person driving the Ford. Whereas he drove the van like the apocryphal little old lady from Pasadena, he drove the Ford with a lead foot. I was pretty proud of myself that I managed to keep up with him, let alone stay undetected. We were almost at the Whitestone Expressway when Aaron's Tempest decided it had had enough cloak and dagger for the day. It coughed a little and decelerated. No matter how hard I pressed my foot on the gas pedal, it wasn't going but for another few feet. Gas pedals, I quickly realized, were kind of moot without gas in the tank to feed the carburetor. I rolled to the side of the street, fished the gas can out of the trunk, and started walking back to the Esso station I'd passed ten blocks back.

✦

First thing I did when I got home was to make a preemptive call to Bobby. He wasn't home. I hated calling his house, because his parents were so damned unfriendly. His mom especially made me feel uncomfortable. She spoke in this condescending monotone that on the one hand sounded like a news reader giving you the crop yields for the state-controlled farms in the central Ukraine and on the other dripped with disdain. Every time I got off the phone with her, I felt like she had spit on me and on everything I believed or ever would believe. I had no faith that she would relay my message to her son, so I tried him at Burgundy House. No one picked up. It was too bad, really. I had my excuse about this morning all worked out. I'd had plenty of time to think it through on my long walk to and from the gas station.

The next call I made was to Lids's house. When his mom answered, I hung up. The palpable desperation in her hello told me all I needed to know. Lids wasn't home yet. She'd answered hoping that it would be her son on the other end of the phone. I didn't need to add to her dread and disappointment with lies she might or might not have believed.

The last call was to our insurance agent, Murray Fleisher. Murray was a nattily dressed charm merchant who was as vain as the day was long. Problem was, Murray had hit the upper limits of middle age, and middle age had hit back with a vengeance. He'd been reduced to wearing a rug, a nice one, but still pretty obviously not something that grew out of his scalp. He was also going a little deaf. I guess all those years with an office on Brighton Beach Avenue under the el had finally gotten to his ears. Unlike with the hair piece, Murray hadn't yet reached a satisfactory compromise with his vanity that would allow him to wear a hearing aid. That worked for me . . . at least, I hoped it would.

"Murray Fleisher here."

"Mr. Fleisher, this is Aaron Prager."

"Who?"

"Aaron Prager," I shouted.

"Oh, Aaron. Sorry, there's so much noise in this office. How's that sexy mother of yours doing?"

I didn't know whether to laugh or gag. Murray's charm was lost on me. "My folks are fine."

"What?"

"My folks are fine."

"Give your mom a kiss for me."

"Whatever you say, Mr. Fleisher," I said, more than a little repulsed by him.

"Huh?"

I yelled, "I'll do that."

"So, what can I do for you, Aaron?"

"I've got a problem," I said loud enough for him to hear.

"Why else would you call old Murray? That's what I do, solve people's problems. Any problem you got, I can fix."

I found myself wishing *I* was deaf. Jesus, this guy was even a bigger schmuck than I remembered him being. "I gave a friend a lift to the airport and when I came out of the terminal, there was a dent in my rear passenger side fender. Two witnesses said they saw it happen and took down license plate numbers. The thing is, Mr. Fleisher, the two license plate numbers don't match."

"I understand."

No he didn't, but that was okay. I kept the volume up so that the Cohens in the next apartment could hear me. "You see, I have no way of knowing if any of this is accurate. Before I put in a claim—"

"I gotcha, kid."

If he had really been speaking to Aaron, my brother would have reached through the phone and strangled Murray for calling him kid. Aaron was born an old man and always hated being referred to as son or kid. And once Aaron hit twenty-one and could vote, forget about it. He was the only person I knew of my generation who liked being called mister.

"You do?"

"Sure. You want me to track down those plates for you, so you can approach the drivers and see if you can reach some sort of 'arrangement.'" Fleisher made the word *arrangement* sound dirty, like it should have been wrapped in brown paper. "While what you're asking me to do is not strictly kosher, it's a clever move, kid. No one needs their premiums to go up for some stupid fender bender, right? Your dad always said you were the shrewd one. How's that lazy brother of yours?"

"Still lazy," I screamed. "So you'll do this for me?"

"Sure, why not? Here's the thing, kid. I want you to think about coming to work for old Murray. I'm telling you, a clever fella like you could make us both rich."

"I'll definitely think about it, Mr. Fleisher."

"What?"

"I'll think about it, Mr. Fleisher."

"Murray, kid. Call me Murray. After all, we're practically partners, right?"

I ignored that. "So, when should I give you a call, Mr.—I mean, Murray?"

I swear I could hear his smile. "Tomorrow afternoon should be good."

"Until then," I said.

# CHAPTER TWENTY-THREE

Besides having to top off Aaron's gas tank and get the car washed and waxed before he got home, I had to buy him a suitable gift as a thank you. Because no matter how full the tank or clean the car, my brother would eventually check the odometer and go apeshit on me. Somehow I doubt that when he tossed me his car keys on Sunday night, he had anticipated I would do a Poconos round-trip and spend the following day driving all over Queens and back. Given that he was going to be pissed at me anyway, I decided to put my few remaining hours with the car to good use.

Samantha Hope's old apartment was in the basement of an attached brick house on Avenue U between West 10th and West 11th Streets in Gravesend. It was only a short walk from her place to the Gelato Grotto. I remember she confided to me that she ate most of her meals there. We laughed when I told her she had my sympathy. I had been to her pad with Bobby many times, and twice for small parties she'd thrown. I'd also been there once on my own. I didn't like thinking about that time. In fact, I'd kind of pushed it so far back in my memory I wasn't sure it had really happened. Even when I was at her graveside and in her childhood home, it hadn't come to mind. It did now.

When she invited me over, I didn't think anything of it. She was my best friend's girlfriend. We were friends. We spent all kinds of time together, and if Mindy could have stomached her, we would have spent nearly all our time together. It was a Wednesday night, and we'd all been hanging out over at the old Burgundy House apartment on Foster Avenue when Bobby stood up and announced he had to split.

"Business," he said, shrugging his shoulders, blowing a kiss at Sam.

I was used to this from Bobby. He always had lots of irons in the fire, but rarely discussed them. I could tell that Sam didn't like Bobby just taking off without an explanation of why he was going or where he was going to. That was the paradoxical thing about Sam: she was so with it and cool, so free-spirited, except when it came to Bobby. She always wanted to keep track of his whereabouts. She even used to bug the rest of us guys about where Bobby was and what he was up to. Sam's jealousy, if that's what it was, seemed strange in a woman as beautiful and worldly as she. I had tried to reassure her every way I knew how that Bobby loved her like he had never loved anyone else. She wouldn't be reassured. I guess there was something about Bobby that made her feel vulnerable.

That night, the night Bobby just got up and split, Sam asked me if I wanted a lift home. I didn't think anything of it. I didn't live more than ten minutes from her apartment and I didn't feel much like schlepping my half-drunk self home on the subway at midnight. But she didn't take me home, not directly. She asked me to come over for a while, that she was feeling sad and needed to talk.

"Sure," I said, "why not?"

It was fine at first. We had a beer, smoked a joint, listened to some Donovan. When Sam excused herself I was still trying to figure out what an elevator in the brain was all about and why, if Donovan was Scottish, he hadn't used the word lift rather than elevator. Grass did that to me. When I was stoned I would latch onto a lyric or something a person said and I would dissect it, parse it, spin it around in my head, play with it. I think it's the only part of getting high I really enjoyed. When Sam came back in the room I was on the floor, back against the couch, head resting on the cushion, eyes closed. Then I felt her straddle me. When I opened my eyes, I was stunned to see she was naked.

She pressed her lips against mine, not softly, and when she pulled her head back, she said, "I've wanted to do that for almost as long as you've wanted me to." Her voice was a breathy whisper.

She kissed me again and I let her. This time I opened my mouth. She opened hers. She grabbed my wrist and put my hand on her breast. When my fingertips brushed against her nipple, she sighed and arched her back. I knew that if I didn't stop then, I wasn't going to stop at all. I took my hand away from her breast, turned my head away, and gently pushed her aside.

I jumped to my feet. With my voice cracking, I asked, "What is this, Sam?"

"Inevitable," she said. "You know we've been headed for this from the day we met." Then she spun around on her knees and rubbed her hand on the crotch of my jeans. She looked up into my eyes, a come-and-get-it smile on her mouth. "Sometimes men should listen to what their bodies are telling them, Moe."

I brushed her hand away. "Stop it, Sam. I'm taken, and Bobby's my best friend."

She put her hands on my belt. "That's like something our parents would say. Besides, Moe, no one's taken . . . not really. And this, the two of us here, now, isn't going to change what Bobby and I have." She skillfully undid my belt, the button of my pants, and slid the zipper down with an aching slowness that made promises I was tempted to let her keep. "You've been curious about what it would be like to be with me, and I've been just as curious about you." Sam placed both thumbs inside the elastic band of my BVDs, and at that same deliberate pace brought my underwear down to my thighs.

She stroked me, first with the back of her hand and then her curled fingers and palm. "Let me, please, Moe. Let me." She didn't wait for an answer, putting me in her mouth.

Her mouth felt like I dreamed it would, better. It was warm, moist, and soft, her tongue eager and deft. I pushed her away, maybe less gently than I should have. "Stop it, Sam. Cut it out," I said, pulling up my underwear and redoing my pants. "Sure, I want you. I have from the minute I met you, but you picked Bobby. Bobby always gets who he wants, and maybe I even resent him enough to let myself do this. So I guess it's a good thing I feel more for him than just resentment. Maybe doing this won't change things for you, but it'll change everything for me."

Sam looked up at me, her vampy smile replaced by something more earnest. "But if we don't do this now, we never will. If we don't scratch this itch, Moe, it will eat away at us." She hugged my thighs. "Please, Moe, let's do this. We'll have this one night together. We'll do anything you've ever wanted to do to me or to any woman, and then we'll let that be enough."

I wasn't the smartest guy in the world, but I knew from what little of her I'd already experienced that if I went ahead with her plan, one night together would never be enough. The kisses, the feel of me in her mouth had already nearly blinded me to my responsibilities to Bobby and Mindy. If I let this go any further, I'd be destroying the things I relied on most in my life: loyalty and friendship. And what had Mindy done to deserve any of this?

"Come on, Moe, let's just do it. We're both high. We're both a little drunk. I'm horny. You're horny. We're here. Let's just do it. It doesn't have to be anything more than that."

"I can't, Sam. I know me. I think I'm a little in love with you and if we do this, I won't be able to turn it off."

"Then if that's what's meant to—"

"I'm leaving."

I ran. I didn't remember grabbing my coat, but I must have because when I was a few blocks away I noticed I was wearing it. I'd never understood what it meant when people said their heads were swimming. I did that night because, man, I was suddenly in the deep end of the pool. As I walked the whole way home, I felt pulled in about a million different directions. I wasn't proud of myself. I didn't feel honorable for turning Sam down. Mostly, I felt naive and stupid. I think I was nearly as angry with myself for not finishing what we started as I was at Samantha for starting it in the first place. I heard my dad's voice in my head, droning on about all the things he should have done and the many opportunities he'd missed.

"I'm telling you, kid," he'd say to me sometimes when we'd go out driving on Sundays, just the two of us. "There have been times in my life when things got served to me on a plate and for some stupid reason or other I didn't help myself. When it's lying on a plate for you, go for it. Take it. Take it! Don't be like me. Don't worry so much about who's looking or what people might think. Take it. Because one day you'll turn around and you'll be old and full of doubts and questions. Sometimes I think that if only I'd taken it just one time, just once . . ." His voice would drift off and the car would go silent.

I never told anybody this, but I think of my dad as the King of Shoulda Done and Mighta Been. As I walked home that night, mostly I beat myself up for being his prince and heir to his throne. That was my greatest fear, I think, that I would be just like him, that the unifying principle of my life would be regret.

Standing in front of Sam's old apartment, I wasn't any more certain of what had happened that night or why it had happened. Thinking back on it, I wasn't sure I believed the reasons Sam had given me for wanting us to be together. She'd kept subtly switching her reasons. First it was that our being together was inevitable. Then it was that we were both curious. Next it was she wanted to please me. Then it was that we were meant to be. Finally it was that we were drunk and horny. I think maybe I believed that last one most of all. Sometimes the lowest common denominator is also the most dependable. It seemed that she would have said or done almost anything to coax me into crossing that line. We'd never talked about it. The next time the three of us were together it was like old times. She knew I wouldn't tell Bobby.

I walked up the brick steps to the brick and concrete porch and rang the bell. A heavyset woman in a house dress answered the door. In her early fifties, she was overly made-up, and her hair was so black it was almost blue. It was a pity because she had a lovely, kind face beneath the too-black dye job and clown mask. I didn't know her name, but I had seen her many of the times I'd been to Sam's place. I thought I saw recognition in her eyes too. Then I saw the sadness.

"You're Samantha's boyfriend, right?"

*No.* "Yeah, right. That's me."

"We never met, but I'm Mrs. Fusco. Call me Gloria. I used to see you and your buddy hangin' around here with her all the time." She held her hand out to me and I gave it a tender shake. "I'm so sorry about what happened . . . you know. I don't believe a word of what they said about Sam. She just wasn't that kinda girl."

"I know, Mrs.—Gloria. I still can't get over it. I think that's why I'm here."

"Come in. Come in . . ."

"Bobby," I said. "Sorry, I forgot my manners."

"That's fine. I understand."

Her house was full of fussy, ornate furniture with bright red and green suede cushions covered in thick, suffocating layers of plastic. Still, the rooms were immaculate and as orderly as a museum. She gestured for me to sit on the couch. In the hot weather, I thought, bare skin would stick to the plastic slipcovers like glue. You'd have to get peeled off to stand up. She offered me coffee to drink and I said that would be fine. I noticed pictures of a boy about my age—her son?—wearing Marine dress blues. Some were of him in green fatigues.

"That's Rocco, my boy," she said proudly when she noticed me studying the photos. Then her voice got brittle. "He's in Vietnam. I hope he's okay and that the damn war gets over soon."

"Me too, Gloria. I mean that."

"He volunteered."

"That was brave of him."

"It was stupid. I already lost his father. I don't know what I'm gonna do if I lose him too."

"I'm sure he'll be fine," I lied.

She handed me my coffee. "Thanks for sayin' that. So what can I do for you?"

I told her the truth. "I'm not sure. We only had a short time together. It's funny, isn't it, how you can be so in love with somebody and not really know them? It was like that with Sam and me. So I guess now that she's gone, I'm trying to find out who she was."

Tears poured out of Gloria Fusco's eyes, ruining her perfect mask. "Bobby, that's so beautiful. What do you want to know?"

First I tossed some easy questions to her about what kind of renter she was. Was she friendly? Did Gloria like her? Stuff like that. Then I got around to asking how it was that Samantha came to rent the apartment from her in the first place.

"She didn't," Gloria said. "Her father rented it for her. Paid a month's deposit and a year's rent in cash."

"Her father? What was he like?"

This was the first question that made Gloria squirm a little. Then when she answered, I got that her discomfort wasn't about the question itself but about what she had to say. "Her dad wasn't a very nice man. When I got to know Samantha, it was hard for me to believe such a hard, crude-talkin' man could have been her dad. If I didn't need the rent money so bad, I wouldn't've rented to him, daughter or no daughter."

"Crude-talking?"

"When he found out I was a widow . . ."

"I understand. What did Sam's dad look like?" I asked, as a throwaway question.

Gloria frowned. "He looked as hard as he was. Short and nasty, with that pasty complexion and the map of Ireland on his face. He had these cold, gray eyes and a crooked mouth. The first thing I thought when I met Sam was that she must look and be like her mom. She sure was nothing like her father."

My head was swimming again. I'd never met Sam's father, but I'd seen more than twenty photographs of him, and the man Gloria Fusco just described wasn't Sam's dad. Sam's dad was tall and kind of regal looking. He was a state trooper, so I was sure he could be belligerent when he had to be, but I couldn't ever see him being described as short and nasty. And then there was the map of Ireland thing. I looked more Irish than Sam's dad, and I didn't look very Irish. What about the fact that Samantha was buried in the New Lutheran Cemetery in Koblenz, Pennsylvania? There were probably more Jews in Ireland than Lutherans. It didn't add up.

"When Sam died," I said, "I didn't really have anything of hers to hold onto. I mean, I have some snapshots and stuff, but no clothes, nothing that smells like her perfume." That got Gloria's waterworks going again. "Do you have any—"

"I'm so sorry, Bobby, but the cops and FBI just came and took everything from her apartment. The furniture and everything."

"That's okay. I under—"

Gloria cut me off. "Oh, my God! Oh, my God. I completely forgot something in all the excitement. Come on with me."

I followed Gloria up the stairs to the second floor and into a small, empty bedroom. She pointed at a short rope hanging down from the ceiling. "Can you grab that, Bobby?"

When I did, I was amazed at the little chute and narrow ladder that swung down. What did I know about attics? I lived in an apartment building my whole life. If we had one of these in our apartment, it would have led into the Spiegelmans's apartment above us. For a heavy woman, Gloria managed to get up into the attic pretty easily.

"Watch your head," she warned as I came up behind her.

You had to love this woman. Even the attic was neat, if a little dusty.

"Now where is it?" she asked herself, as she scanned the nooks and crannies. "There it is. See that suitcase, Bobby?" Gloria said, pointing to a pretty large, old-fashioned, leather-handled case under a stack of cardboard boxes. "That's Sam's. The first week she moved in, she asked me to keep it for her. I totally forgot about it until just now."

I fought the urge to fling the boxes off the suitcase and forced myself to carefully move the boxes above it. The suitcase was pretty beat-up, tattered, and frayed. I moved it aside, and put the boxes back in place. Gloria and I stared at it, both of us a little queasy, I think.

"Take it," she said. "Take it. I don't wanna know what's in it. I don't think I could deal with it. I know it's strange, but with Rocco in so much danger and everything, I don't wanna be reminded of the dead."

"I understand."

When I went to pat Gloria's shoulder, she hugged me with intense conviction. She was really hugging her son, but that was okay with me. We didn't say goodbye. She handed me the case as I made my way down the attic ladder. When I was sure she was down safely, I took the last vestiges of Samantha Hope and let myself out.

I resisted the urge to open up the suitcase only partially due to self-control. The other part was that the suitcase might be locked, and I didn't want to stand out on the street trying to pry it open. I put it in Aaron's trunk and drove home. I got lucky for once and found a parking spot right out front of our building. I put the gift-wrapped bottle of Château Latour on the front seat for Aaron to find in the morning when he got into the car. That was a pretty expensive bottle of red grape juice, but I had kind of abused the privilege with his car. It was still a great shock to me that my brother had become so fascinated by wine. I suppose it appealed to his obsessive side. Although he wasn't adventurous by nature, he did love studying and finding the subtleties in things. He confessed to me once that his dream was to get out of sales and to buy a wine shop. That was cool. The part that wasn't cool was the part where I was supposed to be his partner. Yeah, sure.

I was beat; all the mileage I'd covered over the last two days was catching up to me in a single rush. I felt like once I got upstairs, I would fall into bed and sleep for a week. The thing is, I never made it upstairs. I didn't make it five more feet.

# CHAPTER TWENTY-FOUR

I locked the Tempest's door and took a weary step or two when I saw a car speeding right for me. I squeezed my eyes shut in anticipation of an impact that never happened. Instead, the car swerved past me, skidding, shrieking, screeching to a tire-smoking halt two hundred feet ahead. I was so preoccupied by not being dead that I failed to notice the man coming up behind me. Something hard and round jabbed me in the ribs.

"Don't turn around, you honky mothafucka. Just get in the car."

The car's rear door was flung open and a strong hand hurried me along to it. I wanted to point out that getting pushed was just insult to injury, that I was already sufficiently motivated by the gun in my ribs. Before I got a chance to speak, I was shoved into the back seat of the waiting car, which took off even before the door shut. When I righted myself, I saw that I had plenty of company in the car with me. Besides Strong Hand on my right, there was another man next to me on my left. I assumed he was a man. He was built like one, but I couldn't be sure because he was wearing an LBJ Halloween mask that covered his entire head and neck. The driver had on a Hubert Humphrey mask. Strong Hand was wearing a George Wallace mask—for purposes of irony, I suppose. The person next to Hubert Humphrey in the front passenger seat had on a Robert Kennedy mask. I was pretty sure the front seat passenger was female, her slight build giving her away. All of them were dressed in army surplus jackets and black turtlenecks below their rubber masks.

I should have been afraid, but I just wasn't. In spite of the gun in my side, I couldn't take this bunch seriously. The tough guys I knew meant business. They didn't worry about irony and political statements. Even when I tried to muster up some fear, the best I could manage was bemusement. I felt more confused than anything else and it wasn't profound confusion at that. Mostly, I think my lack of fear had to do with the fact that I recognized the girl in the front seat, her Kennedy mask notwithstanding.

"What does a guy have to do to get a mask around here?" I asked. "I'm feeling left out."

Hubert Humphrey laughed, but George Wallace was not amused. He shoved the barrel into my ribs and said, "Mothafucka, I warned you to shut up."

"What, I'm not a honky mothafucka anymore? And to be accurate, you warned me not to turn around. You didn't warn me to shut up."

Wallace pressed the barrel so hard into my ribs I thought it might go through my coat. "I'm warnin' you now. Shut up."

I turned to him and said, "Listen, man, I don't think sticking the barrel of your gun through my ribs is what Stokely Carmichael meant by Black Power."

Hubert Humphrey laughed again. Wallace was even less amused than before, but he didn't take it out on me.

"Y'all keep on laughin', just keep on laughin' and we'll see how you laughin' with my foot in your damn mouth when I'm kickin' your teeth down your throat."

Robert Kennedy whipped around, angrily shaking her head at Wallace. I guess abducting someone off the street at gunpoint was considered fair play, but insulting your comrade was verboten. I caught a good glimpse of the girl's eyes through her mask before she turned back around. After that, I was sure I knew who she was.

"So, Susan, what did you get on your final paper in Romantic Poetry?" I asked as if we were old friends who just happened into each other on the subway. "It's Susan Kasten, right? I never forget a face."

Nobody was laughing now.

LBJ blurted out, "Holy fucking shit!"

"Shut up!" yelled Hubert Humphrey.

"Man, ain't nobody told you dumb crackers vaudeville is dead?" Kennedy slapped her hand on the dashboard. That got everybody's attention and it shut them all up. I was a little less intimidated by her.

"By the way, Susan, how's Grandpa Hyman doing now that you blew his fix-it shop all to hell?"

With that, she finally spoke, but not to me. "Pull over."

"But the Com—" Humphrey stopped himself mid-word. "But didn't they say to bring him straight to—"

"Now! Pull over right now," she screamed at the driver. When he didn't respond quickly enough to suit her, she yanked the steering wheel hard to the right.

We slammed into the curb, the driver's late braking doing little to slow the car down. When we came to rest, George Wallace said, "I told y'all we shoulda jus' iced this mothafucka and been done with it."

Suddenly, my lack of fear wasn't quite so lacking.

"No!" Kennedy shouted. "We have to know what he knows. We're not the pigs. We're not fascists. We don't just waste people on a whim or because they piss us off."

"I guess Stalin, Mao, and Castro didn't get that memo, huh?"

"Reactionary stooge," scoffed LBJ.

"I was always partial to Curly myself," I joked.

Wallace backhanded me across the side of my head. Some people have no sense of humor. "C'mon. Now let's just ice his white ass."

"We're not cowboys. We must act as we've been instructed."

"By the Committee, you mean?" I said.

Hubert didn't like that. "He knows about the Committee."

Susan was unconvinced. "No, he doesn't. He's fishing, throwing out a word he must've overheard to see our reaction. Well, now he's got his reaction. But that's not important. We have to find out what he *really* knows and how he knows it."

George Wallace didn't give up easily. "I bet he killed Abdul. That's all I need to know."

"I don't even know who you're talking about," I lied. "Do I look like someone who knows people named Abdul?" Then I tried playing one of the few cards I had left to play. "Even if you find out what I know, you'll have no way of knowing who else knows it."

Susan laughed a jagged, joyless little laugh like a shard of glass. "Are you really so stupid, Moe, to suppose we won't do what we have to do to find that out as well?" When I didn't answer right away, she asked, "What, no snappy comeback?" She turned to Humphrey. "Come on, drive. We're late."

It now occurred to me that even if they weren't going to kill me, they were probably willing to get as close as they had to. I was in no mood to find out just how close. As Hubert turned the wheel to pull back into traffic, I planted my elbow smack into George Wallace's nose. It broke with a sickening, dull snap. He dropped the gun to the car floor and kicked it under the front seat as he writhed in pain. Blood gushed through the nostrils of the rubber mask. I hit him with my elbow again, this time in the throat. He slumped against the door, gasping for air. I twisted in my seat, pushed my back up against Wallace for leverage, and kicked LBJ with the flat of my sneaker square on the side of his head. The force of the kick sent his head into the window with a bang. I reached over Wallace, yanked the handle, and tumbled out the door.

I hit the pavement pretty hard and although the car wasn't moving very fast, I rolled into the curb with a lung-emptying thump. I forced myself to get up, to run. My lungs didn't seem to want to work, but self-preservation is a great motivator. I refused to look behind me as I ran. No use wasting time or energy or getting any more frightened than I already was. I recognized where we were, and knew I was not in the best of places if I was looking for someone to help me. Even in broad daylight, the area around Avenue Z and Shell Road was a pretty deserted part of Gravesend. Ahead of me, to my left, under the el and across the old trolley tracks, were the South Highway Little League baseball diamonds, and just beyond their outfield fences, the massive Coney Island rail yards. Further to my left was an area I thought of as Desolation Row: the murky, polluted waters of Coney Island Creek, the litter-strewn underbelly of the Belt Parkway, and the Brooklyn Union Gas Company. I doubted that Susan and her band of unmerry men knew their way around here half as well as I did. There was the additional benefit that most of it was inaccessible to cars.

If I had turned right and made it to Avenue X, I would have been safe. There would be plenty of traffic and people on the street even at that hour of the night. The problem was that there were four blocks separating me from the safety of Avenue X, four blocks where I would be totally out in the open, four blocks that were completely accessible to cars. It would have been easy for them to drive up to me and snatch me again. Somehow I sensed that if they got me a second time, I would have paid a big price for escaping. People with broken noses and bruised egos tend to lose their senses of humor. Still, the choice I made to head for Desolation Row was not without risks of its own. Between the buzzing of cars on the

Belt Parkway and the din of subways passing on the el, it would be nearly impossible to hear someone coming up on me. Once caught, I could scream my head off and not a soul would hear me. And while that area wasn't quite the Fountain Avenue dump, many a body had been left there to rot and gone undetected for weeks. It was too late to change my mind now. I was committed.

I made it across Shell Road and leapt onto the high fence that kept unwanted visitors off the Little League fields. I wasn't a great fence climber, but fear improved my skills. When I came over the top of the fence, I finally looked behind me. It was a good thing I did. LBJ and Hubert Humphrey were close, heading across Shell Road, running not for office but for me. I climbed halfway down the fence, jumping down the rest of the way. I raced across the entire length of the field, from the third base line to the right field corner and hopped the low outfield fence. I got down on all fours. Dark as it was, I wasn't trying to hide. You can't hide behind a cyclone fence. What I was doing was looking for the hole in the fence that separated the ball field from the rail yard. It wasn't a hole so much as a square of fencing that came loose when the Little League officials went to retrieve balls hit into the rail yard. Our parents thought we didn't know about the hole. They thought that if we knew about it, we'd sneak into the rail yard. Of course we knew about it, and of course they were right: we used to sneak into the rail yard all the time. Well, until Pete Malone brought his dog with us once and it got fried like the Rosenbergs on one of the electrified rails. We stopped going after that.

I found the patch. It was held onto the yard fence with six of those little twisty ties your mom uses to close up plastic sandwich bags. I didn't have the time to undo them. Instead I pulled on the patch as hard as I could and it came loose. I wriggled through the hole, replacing the patch as best I could. I hoped that my body had blocked Lyndon and Hubert from seeing exactly where the patch was. Anything that slowed them down, even a little bit, improved my chances. Rows and rows of subway cars lay silent at this end of the yard, but I knew better than to think that it was safe to move about as I pleased. The long lines of subway cars might well have seemed dormant. That didn't mean the rails on which they rested couldn't jump up and bite. Six or seven hundred volts of electricity were running through some of those rails, and guessing which ones were live and which ones weren't would be playing Russian roulette. The rails weren't the only danger, either. Trains were constantly pulling in and out of the yard, and there was the odd chance you might run into a security guard or a yard worker. The rumor was that if you got snagged in the yard, you were going to catch a bad beating.

Carefully navigating my way between trains and across many sets of tracks, I kept in the shadows of the darkened subway cars as much as possible. As I went, I looked for some sort of weapon: a stick, a crowbar, anything I could swing. The best I could do was rocks. I picked a couple of the biggest stones out of the gravel that covered the floor of the yard. My plan, such as it was, was to draw them deep into the yard while I doubled back behind them. Once I got to Coney Island Creek, they'd never find me. I stopped to listen for them, and heard their feet churning up the gravel. It was funny how when there were no passing trains on Shell Road and traffic was light on the Belt, it was quiet enough to hear their clumsy footsteps. I heard something else.

"We have to split up or we'll never find him. You go right. I'll go left."

"I don't like it. What if I find him, what do I do?"

"Hold him and scream for help."

"Me? He's bigger than me and you saw how tough he is. He broke Jimmy's nose and nearly broke your jaw."

"Here, then. You take this. If he runs, shoot him."

"I never fired at a person before. Besides, the Committee didn't authorize—"

"You see anyone from the Committee out here with us?"

"No."

"Then do what I say or I'll shoot *you*. Now take this and get going."

I didn't like the sound of that, but I fought the urge to bolt. I listened to their steps go in opposite directions. Then a subway came rushing over Shell Road and put an end to my hearing anything but its rumblings. Losing track of them forced me to move, but instead of going right or left, straight ahead or back, I went up. I pulled myself onto the rear platform of the subway car closest to me, then climbed onto the roof of the car. I pressed myself flat against the filthy, ice-cold metal, and waited for the subway train on Shell Road to pull out of the station. It seemed to take forever. Eventually, the train's air brakes *psssss*-ed and it slowly moved off toward Coney Island. When it had gone, I lifted my head to see if I could get an idea of where LBJ and Hubert had got to. No luck. Under cover of all that noise, they could have been about anywhere. For all I knew, one of them could be standing just below me.

First I peeked over one side of the car, then the other. No one. I was thankful for that, at least. Quietly as possible, I got onto my knees and scanned the yard. Again, nothing. I reached into my coat pocket, pulled out a stone, and hurled it into the night. I wasn't trying to hit anything in particular. I was just trying to hit something. Mission accomplished. It clanged off metal and the clang echoed through the yard. That set off a chain reaction: the crunch and scrape of running feet on gravel, a short flash of fire, a small explosion, and screams.

"You stupid prick. You shot me! You fuckin' shot me."

"Oh, shit, man. I'm sorry. Where are you?"

"Where did you aim the gun, you moron?"

"Oh, yeah, right. I'm coming. I'm coming."

That was my cue to exit. I jumped down off the top of the subway car and ran for the hole in the fence. I was no longer worried about being stealthy. Five minutes and another climbed fence later, I was heading along the bank of Coney Island Creek. When I made it to Neptune Avenue, I walked back out onto the street and I let myself exhale. I didn't relax, not totally. I wasn't sure I would ever fully relax again, or stop looking over my shoulder.

# CHAPTER TWENTY-FIVE

No ringing telephone this time, just Aaron shaking me awake. Given a choice, I preferred the phone.

"What? What's up?" I said, my head still foggy with sleep.

Aaron dropped me and I collapsed back onto my bed. My big brother didn't let me go back to sleep, though.

"Get up, Moses. Get up right now," he barked at me.

When I didn't respond quickly enough to suit him, he dumped a glass of cold water on my face. The water did a better job of getting my attention than the shoulder shaking.

"What the fuck?" I sat up, wiping the water off my face with my T-shirt.

"Go do your business and I'll meet you in the dining room in five minutes." It wasn't a polite request. It wasn't a request at all.

Normally, I don't respond real well to my brother bossing me around or his attempts at being a third parent, but there was something, maybe the tone of his voice, that compelled me to do as he said. So five minutes later and slightly more awake, I found myself at the table. Aaron had a cup of my mother's reheated death coffee waiting for me. I drank some of it, too much of it, and wondered how much worse could Drano have tasted and how much worse for you could it be.

"Okay, big brother, what's the word?"

"You may be fooling Mommy and Daddy, but not me. What's going on with you? Is it drugs? Are you in some kind of trouble?"

"Nothing's wrong."

"Bullshit."

Of course it was. I didn't believe it myself. How was he supposed to swallow it? He held up a piece of paper and read his car's odometer numbers to me.

"Thanks for the wine. It's a nice gesture, little brother, but I'm not stupid. Where the hell did you go to put on all that mileage?"

"The Sea of Tranquility."

"The moon shot's not scheduled until two years from now. I want the truth."

That's what I gave him, if only a little piece of it. "I went to Koblenz, Pennsylvania."

"Never heard of it. Why would you go there?"

"Because Koblenz, Germany, is too far away and I don't have a passport."

"You're especially not funny in the morning, Moses. What were you doing in Koblenz?"

I gave him another sliver of truth. "I went to visit Samantha Hope's grave."

"Wasn't she the girl who—"

"Yeah. Bobby's girlfriend, the one who got blown up in December in Coney Island."

"Bobby has a car. Why didn't you take his?"

"I didn't go with him. I went alone."

"Why?"

"Because."

"Don't be an ass. You sound like a five-year-old."

"Sounds about right," I said.

"Okay, forget that for now. What's this?" Aaron held up my coat. "And don't say 'it's my coat.' I know it's your coat, but it's filthy and it's torn and there's dried blood all over it. Your sneakers are caked in mud, and the bottoms of your Levis are still damp. Your shirt stinks from sweat."

It was tough to argue with the truth. I had been so full of adrenaline last night, and then so exhausted when I got home, that I hadn't given a second thought to my clothes. Apparently, my brother had done that for me. I had to say something or Aaron would keep pushing. He was like the prosecutors on *Judd, for the Defense*. He was better than them because he didn't lose. He'd missed his calling in life.

"I guess I got into a fight last night."

"You guess?"

"I got into a fight."

"With who?"

"With whom," I corrected. "It's 'with whom did you get into a fight.' It doesn't matter anyway. It's over now. It's done."

"This is Brooklyn, Moe. Fights are never over."

He was right about that too, especially this time. Susan Kasten wasn't done with me, nor did I think Jimmy—George Wallace— was going to forget that I broke his nose and nearly smashed his windpipe. I decided to go on the offensive, or I knew Aaron would wear me down.

"We're not kids anymore, big brother. You can't fight my fights for me. You can't protect me."

"Well, you need protecting because you're acting like an irresponsible idiot. Like I said, you may have Mom and Dad snowed, but I know you haven't been going to school. You can't just not go to school like that."

"How would you know? You haven't taken a fucking risk in your whole life. You've never drawn outside the lines. All you ever do is follow the rules and toe the line."

"I'm not going to apologize for doing the right thing or for having goals and trying to achieve them. What do you have? Do you even know what you want? You're wandering around BC like a moth looking for a flame. Now you're not even doing that. Do you want to be like Dad?"

"I know who I am."

"You don't know anything, least of all who you are."

"You're right," I said, "I don't. The joke is that you don't either. You just think you do. You think you are defined by the rules you follow and the plans you've made. You think being good defines you. It's the other way around. They stop you from defining yourself."

"I hear Psych 1 and Introduction to Philosophy, but I don't hear my brother talking."

"You can hear whatever the hell you want. I wanna go back to sleep."

Aaron shook his head at me in disgust. "Go back to bed. Go do what you want. You'll just do it anyway." He walked away.

"Hey, big brother," I called after him. "You using your car today?"

He stopped and turned. "Why?"

"I need it."

"For what? Wait—" He held up his hands. "I don't wanna know, do I?"

"Probably not."

He tossed me the keys. "If this will help get whatever is going on with you out of your system, fine. Just bring it and you back in one piece. Understand?"

"Loud and clear."

✦

The next time, it *was* a ringing phone that woke me up. I wasn't in a really deep sleep, anyway. I was never very good at going back to sleep after my mind was alert. My mom's coffee hadn't helped. I was tossing and turning over how things had deteriorated since I began digging into what had happened to Mindy. I had found the guy who'd beaten Mindy into a coma. So what? Abdul Salaam was in worse shape than her. There would be no waking from his sleep. I'd practically watched Billy O'Day murdered. Susan Kasten's Committee, whoever the fuck they were, wanted to interrogate and now probably kill me. But everything seemed to come back to Bobby somehow.

Clearly, Bobby was mixed up in smuggling. What sort of smuggling, I couldn't say. At least now I understood the reason for those stupid airport runs. They weren't about hitting old people up for flight insurance policies. They were about giving Bobby cover for what he was really up to, but it was more than that. It had to be. The night 1055 Coney Island Avenue burned down, Bobby had shown up just after me and just before Susan Kasten. He had gone up to the third floor and seen Salaam's body just like I had. Why? What were the odds that Bobby and Susan Kasten didn't know each other? What were the odds they would show up at the same building on the same evening? Had Bobby smuggled in the boxes Susan and her two flunkies removed from 1055 Coney Island Avenue? What was in the boxes?

"Yeah?" I said, picking up the phone.

"Aaron Prager, is that you?" It was Murray Fleisher. "I can't hear so good. Must be a bad connection."

He was right. It was a bad connection between the nerves running from his ear to his brain.

"Yes, Mr.—Murray, it's me, your future partner."

"Wonderful."

"I thought I was supposed to call you this afternoon."

"What? Did I call you too soon?" he shouted at me as if I was the one losing his hearing.

"No, Murray," I upped the volume. "I said I thought I was supposed to call you this afternoon."

"Right, but I figured I would take the chance you'd be home. I got what you asked for . . . mostly."

"Mostly?"

"First, grab a pencil and a piece of paper."

"Got it."

"One of the license plates belongs to a Ford registered to a Wallace Casey of 34 Trinity Street, Oceanside, New York, 11572. You know Oceanside?"

"On Long Island. It's where they got the other Nathan's Famous."

"See," Murray said, "I knew you were the sharp one. That's it. The address is off Long Beach Road and Atlantic . . . around there."

"Thanks, but what about the other plate?"

"What? Now your mother's late? How is she, by the way?"

"No, Murray, sorry for whispering," I shouted. "What about the other plate?"

"The other plate. That's the rub, kid, the other plate. Are you sure you got the numbers right?"

"Positive."

"Then we got a problem," he said.

"How's that?"

"The DMV tells me that plate number is registered to an official city vehicle."

"New York City?"

"Of course. What else?"

"Did DMV tell you what kind of vehicle it is, at least? I think one of the witnesses who saw it clip my car said it was a white Dodge van."

There was silence on the other end of the phone, a long silence.

"Murray, you still there?"

"I don't get it." He sounded almost hurt.

"Get what?"

"It's a white Dodge van, all right, but why would an official city vehicle just pull away like that after denting your car?"

"Then it was the Ford that did it," I said, not wanting Murray to get too curious. I didn't want to have to lie to him anymore than I already had, and I couldn't afford him showing up at our door.

"Sharp kid, very sharp. So, when is Murray gonna see you? We can have a little nosh. Have a drink maybe."

"Soon, Murray. I'll call. Thanks for the help."

"Anytime, partner."

# CHAPTER TWENTY-SIX

What's funny about Brooklyn is that it's not its own place. Brooklyn is actually the westernmost tip of Long Island. Us Brooklynites don't like acknowledging that fact, and it's easy for us to pretend because we've got Queens as a buffer between us and the Nassau County line. Over the county line, Long Island stretches eastward beyond Nassau to the wild netherworld of Suffolk County. Coney Island isn't an island, but a peninsula. Just don't try and sell that notion to a Brooklyn native. If the world's shape doesn't suit us, we'll reshape it as we see fit. Yet in spite of our willful ignorance of geography, there's not another collection of people anywhere on earth who see the world or their place in it with a more honest eye. Good liars have to know the deeper truth of things. If nothing else, Brooklyn teaches you that, how to see those deeper truths.

I hated Long Island, not because Brooklyn was part of it, not for any good reason, really. I always saw it as a kind of suburban East Berlin, a place where parents coerced their kids to go live in the lap of torturous luxury. *You will never again be allowed to wear hand-me-down clothing. You must never play sports on concrete and must suffer with pristine grass fields. You must sleep in your own bedroom. You will never be allowed to share a bathroom again. When you graduate from high school, you will be forced to accept a new automobile. And worst of all, you will be exiled to an actual university.* I suppose if I gave it any serious thought, my hate for the Island had more to do with jealousy than anything else. Don't get me wrong: I love Brooklyn, and I wouldn't trade my childhood for anything. But by the time I hit Brooklyn College, the blinders had come off. Even as a kid I knew my dad was never going to make it big. He wasn't ever going to come home from work one day and say, "C'mon, everyone, we're moving. I just bought a house in Glen Cove." We were doomed to rent, doomed never to have anything to call our own. We were never going to have a little plaque outside our door that read THE PRAGERS. Dad was never going to magically make our lives a little bit easier. No one would.

I took a little ride to Oceanside. It was on the south shore of Long Island, a couple of miles east of JFK airport, across the county line. The town wasn't exactly bustling, but it was loud. Located directly under the glide path for a runway at Kennedy, Oceanside was almost as noisy as Coney Island on a spring Sunday. The difference being that graceful, soaring jets are more majestic than bone-rattling, earthbound subway trains. It wasn't all that fancy a place, either. Many of the houses I saw were smaller than those in Midwood, Mill Basin, Dyker Heights, or Manhattan Beach. For the most part, the homes were modest, well-kept affairs with tidy front lawns and small backyards. Unlike in the city, though, these houses here weren't squeezed in and shoehorned together. People could breathe a little in a place like Oceanside.

Wallace Casey's house was very much in keeping with the other houses I'd seen in Oceanside. His street was a street of such houses. There was nothing showy or chesty about it. Nothing about it cried out for attention. Nothing about it made you want to turn away. I don't know much about architecture, so I can't tell you in what style the house was built. It had red painted clapboards with white trim and black asphalt roofing shingles. The aluminum storm door had some scroll work on it with a fancified letter C in a circle at the center. C for Casey, was my guess. The flashiest things about the place were the white-painted flower boxes that accented the street-facing windows. There was a small gravel driveway and an attached one-car garage. There was no car in the driveway. That didn't mean no one was home. In fact, someone *was* home. As I watched the house, wondering what to do, I saw the shadowy figure of a woman twice pass by the front window.

I didn't have much of a plan. I just sort of hoped Wallace Casey wouldn't be home. After nearly getting run over and run off the road, after getting smacked in the ribs, getting tied up, and nearly getting kidnapped, I wasn't in the mood for a confrontation. Sure, I'd been tough enough to break a guy's nose with a single blow, but that was more a matter of surprise and survival: his surprise, my survival. But those clowns with their stupid masks were strictly amateur hour. If Casey was the menacing bastard I thought he was, I didn't like my chances against him. And even if I was wrong about him and he was a flower child at heart, he was a man who had a fondness for sawed-off shotguns. Either way, I would definitely be the underdog.

When I looked over into the back seat and saw a writing pad from Aaron's company, I got an idea, an idea I hoped wouldn't get me in any more trouble or put me in any more danger than I was already in. I grabbed the pad, found a pencil in the glove box, and hopped out of the car. I crossed to the Casey house side of the street and approached it as if I had just come from their neighbor's house. I rang the doorbell and waited.

"Who is it?" a woman asked, pulling the door back slightly, as far as the door chain would allow. This may have been the suburbs, but many, if not most, of the people who lived here came from the city. Old habits and caution die hard. "Can I help you?"

"Hi, I'm Joseph Jones from the Students for a Fair Draft. We're an organization that—"

She stopped me. "You mean the draft like for Vietnam?"

"Exactly. I'm in your town today to collect signatures for—"

"I don't know," she said. "We're for the war."

It didn't escape my notice that she said *we*, and not *I*. "That's fine. Although I am against the war myself, our organization is neither pro nor con. What we are about is making sure that the draft is fair and that everyone has an equal chance of getting drafted. We don't want the kids of rich and powerful people to be able to dodge the draft while poor kids go off to get killed far away from home." I was encouraged. These were the first sentences she'd let me finish. "I was wondering if I could ask you to sign our petition, which we will present to Congress—"

She stopped me again. "I'm sorry. I don't think my husband would like me doing that. He's a policeman and—"

It was my turn to stop her. "Your husband's a cop?"

"So what if he is?" She got understandably defensive.

"I'm sorry," I said. "Don't get me wrong. It's just that I think a cop, a guy who puts on a uniform and risks his life every day, would really be for our cause."

"Maybe, but I'm sorry. If you want, you can come back in a few minutes and talk to him. He'll be home soon." She closed the door.

I stood there for a few long seconds, stunned, unmoving, completely confused. Then, like a zombie, I crossed the street and got back into the car. If there hadn't been a very real possibility that Casey would be rolling down the block at any second, I might have sat there for hours going over in my head the implications of what his wife had just told me. Instead I twisted the ignition key, put the car in gear, and drove. A few car lengths away from the corner, I caught sight of Wallace Casey's chestnut Ford Galaxie in my rearview mirror. The nagging question repeated itself: What was a cop doing mixed up with the likes of Bobby Friedman? More importantly, why was Bobby Friedman mixed up with a cop? It wasn't so much the questions that bothered me. It was that I couldn't think of many good answers. No, I couldn't think of any.

# CHAPTER TWENTY-SEVEN

I had a sick, uneasy feeling in my gut during the entire ride over from Oceanside. It wasn't that I was scared. I *was* scared. Given my recent history, it made perfect sense to be scared. But it wasn't fear that was making me queasy. My unease was about something more insidious. It was as if I'd been walking around the last week or so with glasses with the wrong prescription and somebody had switched them back when I wasn't looking. Suddenly, all the stuff that had appeared to be so out of focus was now clearer, if not quite crystal clear. I could see a way to connect some of the puzzle pieces that had seemed so utterly random and disconnected: Mindy's warning to stay away from Bobby, the attempt to run Bobby down, Bobby showing up at the apartments above the fix-it shop, the cop on the Belt Parkway letting Bobby go. Even so, many of the events of the last several days still didn't make much sense. There were plenty of puzzle pieces that continued to feel as if they were from a completely different puzzle.

At least I knew the cop was at home. As things were, walking into a neighborhood dive as an outsider was going to be uncomfortable enough. I never would have risked a visit if there was a chance Wallace Casey would be around. And when I stepped into the Onion Street Pub, I realized the only truly unusual thing about the joint was its name. If not for the few horse-racing-related props—an obvious concession to Aqueduct Racetrack's proximity—the place might have been any bar on any street in any neighborhood in any borough in New York City. There were a few framed black-

and-white photos of jockeys on horses in the winner's circle at the nearby track, blankets of flowers tossed over the horses' shoulders. Did the horses ever give a rat's ass about the garlands and the glory? I doubted it. There was a saddle hung on the wall. A whip and riding boots too. There was a dusty, faded display of a jockey's silks, goggles, and helmet, but the place didn't smell like a barn. There was no stink of wet hay or horse shit. There were flies, though. I never understood how in February in New York, every other fly in the city has moved on to that great moldering garbage heap in the sky, yet you walk into any dive bar and *voila*, flies.

Although only two of the three patrons at the bar had lit cigarettes dangling from their slack lips, there was a mighty cloud of smoke hanging in the air like a drawn gauze curtain. Maybe the flies had taken up the habit too. Why not? If the February chill couldn't kill them, smoking wouldn't. The two guys at the bar—one about my dad's age, the other looking old enough to be my grandfather's father—peered up from their copies of the *Daily Racing Form* just long enough to take another drag on their smokes. Their gray stubbled faces, already sour with lifetimes of defeat, barely registered my presence. The woman at the bar, her blonde updo unmoving as she turned her head, gave me a long, hungry look worthy of Cassius. Apparently, I was her type. I think maybe anybody with male plumbing might have been her type. Almost anybody. Not the two losers at the bar, certainly.

The bartender was a different matter altogether. He'd put his eyes on me the second I opened the door and hadn't taken them off me yet. He was an ex-Marine type, the kind with a hard blue stare, gray brush cut, and tattooed biceps. He had some mileage on him, most of it the ugly kind. Too young for WWII and too old for Nam, Korea was probably his war. He looked like he was still fighting it.

I sat down next to Blondie and her updo. She was about thirty going on forty, and had a once-pretty face that had seen way too many last calls for alcohol. Not only did she have trouble pushing away from the bar, she also seemed to have the same issue with the dinner table. She had a good thirty pounds on me. Well, maybe not so good. She smiled at me and I smiled back.

"Buy me a drink?" Blondie asked with a bit of desperation behind the come-on.

I looked at her glass. "Sure. What's that, Scotch?"

"It is, on the rocks."

I got the barman's attention, pointed at Blondie's glass and said, "One more of these and a Rheingold for me." I threw a five-dollar bill on the bar.

The barman looked about as pleased as a fifteen-year-old kid late to his own circumcision. Maybe Blondie was his girl, but I didn't think so. He just didn't like strangers in his place. It upset the balance of the universe, the natural order of things. I decided to prove him right.

"You got a jukebox in this establishment?"

"Yeah, but you won't like it," he said, slamming our drinks on the bar.

"Why's that?"

"No crappy psychedelic hippie shit on it. None of that Motown nigger shit, neither."

I ignored him. Guys like him, they lived to get you going. They were so miserable and rotten inside, they needed to spew their bile on the rest of the world. I wasn't in the mood, not yet, anyway.

Blondie took a swig of her Scotch, looped her arm in mine, and said, "C'mon, lover, I'll show you the way." She took her drink with her. Apparently the trip to the juke was going to be thirsty work.

My tour guide smelled of too much Scotch and too much perfume—the cheap, cloying kind, like motel soap or lavender and lilac-laced potpourri. I wasn't sure which was supposed to overwhelm the other. Didn't matter, really; neither did the trick. The jukebox was at the back of the bar by the bathrooms and next to the cigarette machine. The bartender might've been an asshole, but he was an accurate one. There wasn't a song on the box written by Lennon and McCartney or Jagger and Richards or Smokey Robinson. The Four Seasons was about as radical as the juke got. Mostly there was a lot of Sinatra and Tony Bennett. I was surprised to see some Nat King Cole and Johnny Mathis. I guess only blacks who sang for Motown counted as niggers in the barman's philosophy. When I noticed there wasn't any Neil Diamond or Simon and Garfunkel on the juke, I couldn't help but wonder where Jews fit into his racial cosmology. Well, there were two Sammy Davis Jr. tunes. That was a victory of sorts, but it didn't make me want to raise my fist in defiance and scream, "Power to the people."

I handed Blondie some dimes and told her to play away. She loved it, and knew exactly what tunes she wanted to play and what numbers to press. Sinatra started singing about a summer wind, pretty loudly too.

Blondie spun me around. "C'mon, lover, let's dance."

So we danced, Blondie pressing herself tightly against me. Surprisingly, her touch didn't seem very sexual. It was almost as if she was just happy for the closeness of another human being. That made it more comfortable for me, made it easier for me to return the embrace. Still, her hair kind of got in the way of full enjoyment. When she rested her head on my shoulder, the scratchy, stiff updo brushed against the skin of my cheek. While it didn't draw blood, it came pretty close. Her hair was so saturated with hairspray that I would have been afraid to light a match within five feet of her.

When Sinatra was done, so were we. I bowed to her and she blushed. When we returned to our seats, I decided it was time to see what I could learn from Blondie.

"What's your name?" I asked.

"Angie."

"Pleasure to meet you, Angie. I'm Moe."

"Back at you."

We shook hands.

"So, Angie, I'm curious." When I said that, she sidled up closer to me. "How did this place get a name like Onion Street?"

She laughed and shook her head at the same time. "People are always asking that who drop in here."

"And . . . ?"

She stopped shaking her head, but kept a smile. "The rule is if you don't know, no one who does is supposed to say."

"The rule? I've never liked rules much. You don't look like a woman who's much for the rules yourself."

"My, aren't you a clever one? Nice try, but this is my local and you know how it is."

"I suppose."

I raised my beer to her. We polished off what remained of our drinks. I pointed to the bartender that we needed another round. Angie seemed quite pleased by this. I could tell, because her left hand was now halfway up my right thigh. The barman put the drinks up, and I fed him another five. He didn't like me any more than the last time I ordered a drink. If possible, I think he liked me less. Funny how that worked. I was drinking, but he was the one getting nastier. Angie and I clinked glass to bottle, and sipped. I never figured out where I developed a liking for beer. Aaron says it was at his bar mitzvah when our Uncle Lenny gave me a whole bottle to drink. He told me it was grownup soda. What the hell did

I know? I drank it. I think Aaron is still mad at me because I fell asleep during the reception.

"Okay, Angie, so you won't tell me how this joint got its name. How about who owns it?"

She tilted the top of her piled-up hair at the bartender who was at the opposite end of the bar attending to the older loser. "George owns the place."

"He always so friendly, or am I just catching him on a good day?"

"Clever and funny. I might just have to take you home."

When I didn't jump at that line, she said, "He isn't really so bad. He's an ex-cop. They kicked his ass off the force. He don't like talking about it, so don't go there with him."

"Don't worry about that, Angie. I don't think I wanna go anywhere with George."

"How about with me?" she wanted to know, sucking down her drink for a little shot of courage.

I was hoping it wouldn't come to this, but I guess I knew it would. "Sorry, Angie. I got a serious girlfriend, and she's in the hospital right now."

"Oh, that's terrible."

I wasn't exactly sure what Angie thought was terrible, that I wouldn't sleep with her or that Mindy was in the hospital. She'd been nice so far, so I gave her the benefit of the doubt. "Thank you. She's recovering, but slowly. That's kind of why I'm here."

"How's that?" Even in those two little syllables, there was increased tension. She waved to George for another drink. He poured it for her and looked at me.

"No more for me, thanks." I took out my last five and told him to keep the change. Didn't seem to improve his opinion of me.

When he left, I took out a picture of Bobby Friedman that I'd thought to bring with me. The photo was a year or two old, and I'd had to cut myself out of it. If Angie looked closely enough, she'd see that the disembodied arm slung across Bobby's shoulders was mine. I didn't think she was in the necessary state of sobriety to notice my arm.

I pointed at Bobby's face. "See this guy? The cops think he beat up my girl. Have you ever seen him in here?" So I lied to her, what else could I do? I couldn't tell her who Bobby really was.

"No," she answered too quickly, looking around to see if George was close by. "Listen, Moe, you seem like a nice—"

"They also think this other big guy might have helped," I said before she finished. "I've heard he comes in here." I described Wallace Casey for her.

She took my hand and gave it a squeeze. "Moe, leave it alone. Finish your drink and go, please."

"I thought you said George was okay."

"This is a rough place, kid. You're between the airport and the racetrack. The kinda people who come in here . . . Just take my advice and go."

Kid, huh? She was trying hard to get rid of me. No one likes getting called kid just after they stopped being one. I meant to take her advice, but I had to get something for the fifteen bucks I'd spent in the place.

"Okay, Angie. Just tell me if you've seen the two guys I mentioned in here together. Answer that, and I'll split."

She nodded yes.

"More than once?"

She nodded some again.

To give her cover, I screamed, "Okay, be that way. You don't wanna tell me why this place has such a stupid name, then the hell with ya."

She winked as I stood. I left the bar, but on my way out I noticed a fly was banging against the front window. It kept banging into it as if the window might vanish if the fly hit it hard enough. If fly heaven was a garbage heap, I thought, fly hell must be an endless series of front windows. Good thing for me I knew how to use a front door, although I have to confess that for a good portion of the last week, I'd felt a lot like that fly.

# CHAPTER TWENTY-EIGHT

When I got home, Miriam was the only one there. She told me that Mindy's dad had called, and that there was a long note by the phone. My little sister, she was the best of us. I don't know. Maybe because she was a girl or because she was younger, she seemed untouched by my parents' craziness and failures. She refused to be negative about things, refused to see herself through the prism the rest of the Pragers viewed ourselves through. I just knew she would do good in the world someday.

"Hey, you." I messed her hair. "What's been going on with you lately?"

She hugged me and said, "Nothing." Then she stepped back, twisting up her face. "You stink, Moe. You smell like Aunt Gertie's hall closet. Do you have perfume on or something?"

"Don't be a wise guy or I'll give you such a smack."

She put up her fists like an old-time fighter. "Sure you will. I'll show *you*."

"Oh, yeah?" I put my dukes up too. "Come on, tough girl." I gave her a light slap on the top of her head.

She kicked me in the shin. "There!"

"Ow! That's cheating."

"I have to have some advantage. You're bigger than me."

"I'll give you an advantage right in the jaw, you. Now get outta here and go do your homework, or I'll kick you in the tush."

As Miriam said, the call had been from Mindy's dad. He'd left a phone number with a long distance area code, and detailed directions on how to get from Brooklyn up to the rehab hospital in Westchester County. The note also said Mr. Weinstock needed to speak to me as soon as possible.

"Seventh floor nurses' station, Nurse Havemayer speaking," said the woman at the other end of the line.

"Good afternoon."

"Is it still afternoon?"

"Not for much longer," I said. "It's already getting pretty dark outside."

"Sorry, how may I help you?"

"My name's Moses Prager and my girlfriend's father, Herb Weinstock, left me this number to call."

"You'd be Mindy's boyfriend then."

"Yeah, but—"

"Don't be surprised, Mr. Prager. We spend a lot of time getting to know our patients and their families. Would you like me to get Mr. Weinstock for you?"

"I'd like that very much. Thanks."

"I am going to put you on hold. Don't hang up, okay?"

"Promise."

A minute later, Herb Weinstock got on the phone. "Moe, how've you been?"

"A little worried I haven't heard from you."

"I understand, but we had to get Mindy settled in here and see what was what."

"How's Mindy doing? Is something wrong?"

"She's awake, Moe. She's not talking much yet, but our girl's awake. She knows who we are and she can make herself understood.

She's a little bit confused about things, but the doctors say that's normal with injuries like hers."

"I see you left directions for me. You have any idea of when I'll be allowed to come up?"

"How about now? Her doctor thinks seeing you would be good medicine for her."

"I'm on my way."

✦

Due north of the Bronx, Westchester County was what most Brooklynites referred to as fancy-shmancy. Certainly, my relatives would have called it that. Westchester had lots of big old houses on big old lots, exclusive country clubs, and not many Jews or "coloreds." I had little doubt that most of its churchgoing residents gave thanks every Sunday for those three blessings the Lord had bestowed upon them. I think I half expected the road sign welcoming me to the county to be shaped like a bottle of Scotch and to be painted like plaid golf pants.

For all of Westchester's fancy-shmancy-ness, the first locale a traveler encounters as he or she crosses over the Bronx border is Yonkers, a gritty, working class city, not exactly New York State's garden of Eden. Yonkers functions as a kind of demilitarized zone between the Bronx and the hoity-toity part of Westchester County, a buffer between the ghetto and the eighteenth green. For that reason alone I liked the place. That, and for its harness racing track. I don't think I ever realized just how many horse racing venues there were in and around New York City. There was Aqueduct and Belmont, Yonkers, Roosevelt on Long Island, and Freehold in Jersey. But I guess that's not so many, considering there used to be two racetracks just in my part of Brooklyn. Once upon a time they raced ponies in

Gravesend and Sheepshead Bay. Back then, it seems, racetracks were like high schools: every neighborhood had to have one.

Night was in full bloom by the time I drove through the gates and up the long sloping driveway to the hospital parking lot. In spite of the dark, the grounds were sufficiently lit so that I could get a good idea of the rehab center's bucolic setting. The hospital building itself was a tall, big brick rectangle that looked almost ridiculous perched among the low rolling hills and deep, seemingly endless woods that formed a natural wall around the place. Blankets of white snow still covered the hospital's vast rolling lawns, even though it hadn't snowed for days. *Toto, we're not in Yonkers anymore.*

During the elevator ride up to the seventh floor, it hit me: what if the progress Mindy had made was all the progress she was ever going to make? I was no expert on head injuries, but even I knew life wasn't like on TV or in the movies. You didn't just wake up and have everything go back to normal. At a minimum, you lost some of your memory. At worst . . . I didn't want to think about that. I knew it could get bad. There was this girl from high school, Gloria, who'd been hit by a car on Ocean Parkway. She'd banged her head pretty bad when she landed, and was in a coma for weeks. Most of her other injuries had healed pretty well, but when she came out of the coma she was like a different person. She was angry all the time. She didn't like any of the food or clothes or music she'd liked before the accident. I'd been so obsessed with Mindy's survival that I hadn't ever considered what might lay ahead for her. Suddenly, I wanted to run. Elevator cars, however, kind of limit your options for egress, so when the doors opened on the seventh floor, I went in search of Nurse Havemayer.

You know how sometimes you're sure you'll recognize a person you've never met? Well, I thought it would be that way with Nurse Havemayer. I was wrong. I'd imagined the nurse would be kindly, sweet, and portly. Not all that different from my Angie at the Onion Street Pub, only without the updo and whiskey breath. Instead, another nurse pointed to a lovely, petite woman of some exotic Pacific extraction.

"Nurse Havemayer, I'm Moe Prager."

She saw the question in my eyes. "Havemayer is my husband's name," she said, smiling up at me. "My clan name has too many vowels for most other Americans to pronounce. If I couldn't still hear it in my head, I think I would have trouble with it too. Come, you're here to see Mindy, not make small talk with me." She took me by the arm and walked me down the hall. "Now listen to me, Moe." Her tone was deadly serious.

"Yes."

"Mindy is doing very well, and her doctors believe she should make a nice recovery." Her use of the word *nice* in lieu of *full* did not escape me, but I said nothing. "She can speak a little, but no full sentences yet. You also have to keep in mind that she is still a bit confused. She also gets somewhat frustrated at her inability to express things fully. That's normal. It's even healthy . . . to a point. What we don't want is for her to get agitated. Do you understand?"

"Yep. Don't get her worked up."

"Exactly." She pulled me to a stop and knocked on the door. "Here we are. Her folks are inside. Remember, take it slow."

I stepped into the room, my heart pounding. Mindy's folks gave me a big hug both at once, their heartbreaking smiles dissolving into joyful tears. When they released me, I saw Mindy sitting up in bed, a broad smile on her face. And then, just like in the elevator, it hit me. In the few short days since I'd seen her last, my mind had wallpapered over what she looked like after the beating and replaced it with the image of her face as I had known it before: the hazel brown eyes, the full lips, the slightly crooked nose, the perfect jawline, and the curly brown hair that cascaded over her forehead like a storm. But that wasn't the face I saw smiling at me. Her cheeks were swollen, purple with healing bruises. Her left eye was nearly squeezed shut with swelling. Her nose was no longer just slightly crooked, and a lot of her hair had been cut away. The cuts on her face were scabbed over. As Nurse Havemayer had seen the question in my eyes, Mindy saw the horror. She put her hands to her face and turned away.

As she turned away, I turned to her folks. "Can you give us a few minutes?"

Her mom started to say, "Don't get her—"

"I know," I said. "I won't."

When the door closed behind them, I walked straight over to the bed and gently turned Mindy to face me. I kissed her so desperately that I thought my heart might explode. The rest of the world fell away, and there seemed there was nothing between us. It had never been this way for us, not even when I was deep inside her and our bodies were in harmony. I'd never felt anything like it before and I doubted I ever would again. When I eased back, I saw that we were now both crying.

I said, "I love you."

She blinked her eyes. I knelt by the side of the bed, resting my head on her thigh, her hands on my head. I stayed that way for a few moments until Mindy prodded me to look at her. When I looked up, she brushed my left cheek with the back of her hand. She put her other hand on my heart. No one needed to interpret that for me.

I asked, "Are you okay?"

She nodded yes and smiled. "S-s-oon," she struggled to say.

"I know."

Then the smile ran away from her face. "B-bob—B-bobby?"

My heart sank a little. After everything between us, I thought, it was Bobby whom she really cared about. I was right. For girls, it's always about their firsts. When she saw the dejection on my face, Mindy slowly shook her head no and cupped my face in her hands. It was as if she had read my mind and was saying, "No, that wasn't what I meant." It was amazing what people could communicate to one another with only a very few words and gestures. She took her hands away from my face.

"B-bobby," she repeated, balling her hands into fists and crashing them into each other.

Now I thought I understood. "You were right to warn me. Someone tried to run him over the day this happened to you, but he's fine. You know Bobby, he's always fine. He'll live forever."

She shook her head and the look of consternation on her face was profound. I knew that look. You grow up a Prager, believe me, you know that look.

"Danger!" The word exploded out of her like a cannon shot.

"Look, I'm good. I'm safe," I lied, stroking her face to calm her. "I think I've sort of figured out some of what's going on."

Mindy's eyes widened, but I couldn't tell if it was out of fear or curiosity. I opened my mouth to explain that I had tracked down Abdul Salaam, the man who'd put her in a coma in the first place, and that someone had already seen to it that he paid severely for what he'd done. I said nothing, reminding myself that she might not remember everything that had happened during the time surrounding her attack. I didn't want to confuse her any more than she might already be.

"Relax, Min. It's gonna be okay. I think I know what happened, some of it, anyway. No one's gonna get away with anything."

But instead of relaxing or comforting Mindy, that just seemed to set her off. She shook her head furiously and wagged a finger at me. She struggled to say something, but the words wouldn't come out. Her face bright red with frustration, she pounded her fists into the mattress. When I tried to hug her, she pushed me away. Tears streamed down her cheeks. I reached over and pressed the call button. Mindy was so caught up in her own world that she barely noticed.

If I'd expected to see her parents come rushing in, harsh judgment on their faces, I would have been wrong. Only Nurse Havemayer walked through the door.

"I'm not sure what I did," I said, looking up at her like a panicked little boy. I guess that's just about what I was. "I don't know what to do."

"It will be okay, Moe. Mindy is fine, believe me. Why don't you say so long to her for now. I'm sure she's tired and frustrated at not being able to say what she wants to say to you, in the way she wants to say it."

It was only when Mindy stopped pounding the mattress that I realized Nurse Havemayer wasn't talking to me at all, that she was talking to and for her patient.

I wiped Mindy's tears away with a sweep of my thumbs. I kissed her on the cheek and she let me hold her. "I love you, Min. I'll be back soon."

When I stepped outside the room, Mindy's folks were nowhere to be found. Maybe they'd gone to get a cup of coffee or a lungful of air that didn't smell like a hospital. Wherever they'd gotten to, I was just glad they had gone there. I don't think I could have dealt with their distress or judgment. I was already sick with guilt for upsetting Mindy, and for not loving her fully enough when I had the chance. I may not have slept with Samantha that time at her apartment, but that didn't mean I hadn't wanted to. I think I must have spent half the time I'd been with Mindy, thinking about Sam. There had been so many times I was inside Mindy when the woman inside my head was Samantha, so many times when my mouth was pressed to Mindy that it was Samantha's taste I imagined. The world may judge you only by your deeds, but that's not how we judge ourselves. Even though I don't think we can ever know ourselves, not really, we know things about ourselves the world can never know. We know what's in our hearts. We know our lies and desires. And suddenly I knew something else. I finally knew what I had to do, and I didn't give a shit about the fallout.

# CHAPTER TWENTY-NINE

Knowing what I had to do and doing it wasn't nearly the same thing. I understood that what I was about to get myself into was stupid, and possibly dangerous, and a dozen other things that should have prevented me from even considering it, but there are times when the Brooklyn motto of "Hey, what the fuck!" applies, and you push ahead. The dead winter calm that hung over Manhattan Beach didn't exactly inspire me to action. The only sounds I heard other than the *huuh . . . huuh . . . huuh . . .* of my own nervous breaths were the water gently slapping the wood pilings in the Sheepshead Bay side of the peninsula, and the whispered rush and retreat of the ocean on the other side.

I parked near Doc Mishkin's driveway, staring through the night and the bare hedges at Hyman Bergman's house. With no lights on, the place seemed as black and lifeless as an abandoned coal mine. I think even a single lighted bulb in any window would have given me some hope of success, but there was only darkness. I'm not sure what I had expected. It was, after all, just before midnight and I didn't really see either Bergman or Susan Kasten as night owls. One was more taciturn than the other. I'm not sure I had ever met two less friendly human beings in my life. At least the old man had the Nazis as an excuse.

I got out of the car and made my way across the street. Once there, I hesitated at the edge of the driveway for no good reason, or maybe for the best of reasons: I was scared. Just recently, scared seemed to be my baseline state of being. Forcing myself to move, I slinked quietly down the driveway, which, since I intended to ring the bell or pound on the front door until someone answered, didn't make much sense. So when I got to the door, I went all in and pressed the bell so many times that not even the deaf could miss the sounding of the chimes. It went on that way for more than a minute. My finger was getting tired and I was getting discouraged—discouraged, as in losing whatever little courage I'd mustered up. But I just kept thinking about Mindy, about what her face looked like and how she might never be herself again. Then, just as I was about to stop ringing the bell and start pounding, a light popped on in the front room and the door pulled back.

Susan Kasten stood in the doorway, her usual disdainful glare replaced by a look of utter surprise and grudging respect.

"You wanna talk to me," I said, "then let's talk."

"Come in and close the door behind you."

She stepped back without turning her back to me. It was as if she didn't trust that I wouldn't jump her and kick the shit out of her the second I got the chance. I didn't blame her for not trusting me. Given that she and her band of hapless idiots had tried to abduct me, it would have been very satisfying. But that wasn't why I was here, and so as she moved further into the house, I just followed. I didn't get very far before someone pressed the tip of a gun barrel to the back of my neck. So much for my brilliant plan.

"Look who it is. If it ain't my favorite honky mothafucka. Man, I *am* gonna enjoy taking you apart one piece at a time." I didn't have to turn around to know it was Jimmy.

"How's the nose?" I asked.

Susan Kasten laughed. That was twice in two days, but just like the last time, it was a humorless laugh, the laugh of a mother shark.

"I'll show you how the nose is, mothafucka." And with that, Jimmy whipped the barrel of the gun across the back of my head, sending me to my knees and then to the floor. "That's how it is, funny boy."

I wasn't out of it. I wasn't totally in it, either. The back of my head burned more than ached, and I felt something wet on my fingers when I reached to feel the damage. I was bleeding. I wasn't exactly gushing blood. Still, blood coming out of my head wasn't reason to celebrate. The cobwebs cleared pretty quickly, but I stayed down.

"If you haven't yet deduced it, Moe, Mr. Jimmy doesn't have much of a sense of humor," said Susan, kneeling beside me. "Four hundred years of oppression has blotted out his sense of humor. But please don't misunderstand, he does have a strong sense of purpose."

"Four hundred years, huh? He looks great for his age. What's his secret?"

I heard the revolver's hammer click back and thought my journey was about over.

"Don't be an idiot!" Susan jumped up and stood between Jimmy and me. "We already have enough on our hands. Give me the gun and get back downstairs."

"Don't be orderin' me around, bitch. Jus' 'cause we agreed to be part of this thing don't make you the boss a me. The white oppressor's been orderin' my people around for—"

"Give me the gun and save the speech for after the revolution, Jimmy," Susan cut him off. "And Jimmy, if you call me a bitch again, I will have you crucified."

I didn't see what was happening, but Jimmy stepped past me.

"This ain't over between us," he whispered as he passed, and then a door slammed shut. I heard his boots thudding down a wooden staircase.

"Get up, Moe, and go where I tell you. I think you know me well enough to understand that I'm not like Jimmy. I will just shoot you if you don't answer the questions I ask you or if you make any move I don't like."

Less than a minute later, we were sitting across from each other at a round kitchen table. I didn't know much about guns, but I knew that the table was large enough so that there was no way I could get to her before she would be able to get off a shot. I didn't have a second of doubt that she would shoot me. Whoever had picked her to run things had made the right choice. It wasn't her fault that her soldiers were the student revolutionary equivalents of *F Troop*. Jimmy talked big, but he was just an angry young man. Black or white, it didn't matter; guys my age were angry because they just were. Wind them up, put guns in their hands, and you have an army. Just ask LBJ and McNamara. Susan wasn't like them. She was calculating, committed, and ruthless. She was what Bobby's parents had hoped he would be.

She aimed the gun at me. "You still in the mood to talk?"

"Sure."

"So talk," she said.

"Isn't it weird how Jews always wind up sitting in the kitchen even when one of them is Joe Stalin's love child and she's holding a gun? Where's the sponge cake and coffee?"

Susan smirked. "That's your one smart remark. The next one will earn you a .38 caliber bullet in your kneecap. Once you have killed, what is a bullet in the kneecap? And Moe, be assured, we have killed before."

"Billy O'Day," I said, my voice full of pride. "That was pretty cowardly."

She stared at me coldly. "Do you want a lollipop or a gold star? Remember, no more wisecracks, no more commentary. Now, what do you know and who else knows it? From the beginning."

I didn't hesitate. "The night of the last big campus demonstration, after I bailed Bobby Friedman out of jail, I got together with Mindy Weinstock at Burgundy House. She was in the strangest mood. She was already drunk and smoking a cigarette when I got there. She said some stuff about being really sad about Samantha Hope that didn't make any sense. Mindy always hated Sam, so I couldn't figure it out. What was really strange was that I'd had a great talk with her just before leaving to bail Bobby out. Now, two hours later, my girlfriend was like a different person. And then, before she splits, Mindy says she's got something to tell me only I can't ask her any questions about it. She warns me to stay away from Bobby for a while. Bobby's my best friend and one of Mindy's oldest friends, so you can understand why that confused me and made me curious."

Susan Kasten shook her head. "I knew involving her was a mistake," she said as if to herself. "Go on."

"The next day, the day of the big storm, I cut class and went over to Burgundy House to clean up, but Bobby's car was parked out front. As I was crossing the street, he came down the driveway. All of a sudden, another car comes flying down the block, headed straight for Bobby. I shoved him out of the way. A few seconds later we heard the car crash. When Bobby and I got to the car, the driver and his passenger were gone. So I knew Mindy wasn't just fucking around with me. Somebody *was* trying to kill Bobby, and the car he tried to do it with was a car stolen from your neighbor's house."

She smiled at me, the smile even icier than her usual cold stare. "I would love to sit here and listen to your entire narrative, Moe, but we have other, more pressing matters to deal with tonight. What do you think you know? I don't care about how you came to know it."

"I know that there's this group called the Committee, and that they used to meet in an apartment above your grandfather's shop. I think the Committee is set up like the Mafia's Commission, but that instead of the Five Families, the people who are on the Committee represent all the radical groups on campus: the Panthers, the Weathermen, like that. I think both Mindy and Bobby were connected to the Committee, but I don't know exactly how. Clearly, Bobby did something to piss you guys off, something to do with what happened to Samantha Hope and Marty Lavitz. Mindy heard you meant to execute Bobby and was torn about it. You found out she'd warned me, and you decided you had to get rid of her too. That's why you tried to kill Bobby and sent that Abdul Salaam guy after Mindy to silence her. Then—"

Susan Kasten was laughing again. This time, it almost sounded like human laughter . . . almost.

"Moe, have you ever heard the expression that a little bit of knowledge is a dangerous thing?"

"Sure."

"Well, you have proven it true. I suppose you think yourself very smart for all of your nosing around. You must feel like a real Mike Hammer. Well, Moe, you know nothing. You've gotten to the bottom of nothing. You are just like the rest of the dumb jocks on campus walking around with your heads in the sand. All you care about is not getting drafted. You all think you don't want to be your fathers, that the lives they live aren't worth living. You are a joke, all of you. You can't even see that all you want is to be just like them. At least your fathers had the courage to fight fascism before they were brainwashed into turning on the best ally the working man has ever had."

"The Soviet Union?" I snorted. "Stalin? Yeah, he was great at murdering or imprisoning workers at a faster rate than Hitler. Look,

I think Vietnam is a ridiculous war that's gonna ruin the country. I'm with you there. You want to spew that other propaganda, Susan, feel free. Just don't try and sell Fidel or Chairman Mao to me. You couldn't do that with all the Green Stamps in all the world."

"I was wrong about you, Moe. You are not just another dumb Brooklyn College jock. You're far worse, because you are purposefully blind. I've seen you in class. You have a very good mind. You are more insightful than the other robots, and for that you are a tragic figure. You have no purpose in life, no cause for being. You would have been your father if not for getting involved in this. That will all change tonight." She stood up, her face back to its shark-eyed warmth. "Downstairs. Now!"

She marched me down the same stairs down which Jimmy had gone. As I walked carefully down the narrow, steep steps, I heard that Jimmy wasn't alone there waiting. It was only when I got to the bottom of the steps that I realized my recent fears were justified: I was going to die.

# CHAPTER THIRTY

Bobby Friedman was naked and screaming in agony, his hair wet with sweat and caked with blood. His face was more bloodied and swollen than Mindy's had been that first day I visited her in the hospital. Bobby's eyes were slits and it was hard to tell if he even saw me when I stepped into the basement. If Bobby wasn't exactly handsome before this beating, he was going to be less so now. That was probably a moot issue. I was pretty sure the chances of either one of us getting to see the light of morning were fairly slim—very slim. Bobby's wrists were tied behind him with a rope that was looped over a notched metal beam in the basement's ceiling. A big guy with the body of a linebacker and the face of a choirboy was pulling on the other end of the rope, lifting Bobby off the ground. It was easy to see why Bobby was in such pain. His shoulders were being pulled out of their sockets by his own body weight.

"Enough for now," Susan ordered.

Choirboy let go of the rope, and Bobby crashed to the floor.

"Anything?" asked Susan. "Has he confessed? Do we know if we have been infiltrated by anyone else?"

Jimmy said, "No. And he ain't gonna say nothin' neither. We jus' wastin' time. Let's do what we shoulda done when we snatched the rat. Let's waste him and his little buddy over here. I'll do 'em both." At least Jimmy was consistent. "Besides, ya'll, we don't have much time before—"

"Shut up, you big-mouth moron," a voice came out of the shadows. It was a voice I recognized, Hyman Bergman's voice. Then he followed his voice into the light.

What the hell was the old man doing mixed up in this?

"I don't have to take no shit from some old—"

"You'll shut your mouth and, for once, do as you're told," said Susan, her voice like a scalpel. Then she turned to her grandfather. "It doesn't matter if this one knows too, Papa. No one can stop it."

Papa, huh. Could it be that Susan Kasten had warm blood in her veins after all, and more human emotion than a sharp stick?

The old man shook his head with disdain. "Foolishness, Susan. Bodies are trouble. More bodies, more trouble. Just ask Eichmann."

"It's too late now, Papa," she said with a shrug of her shoulders. She looked at Choirboy and pointed at Bobby. "Ask him again."

With that, Choirboy tugged violently on the rope. Bobby's arms shot up behind him and he was lifted off the floor. He screamed as he struggled in vain to ease his weight off his shoulders.

Susan Kasten walked right up to him. "Why did you sell us out to the pigs?"

"It wasn't me," he said through gritted teeth.

Bobby was stalling because he knew that to admit any relationship with the police was to sign his own bill of execution. There'd be no plea of guilty with an explanation. I had to do something, and fast. If I didn't, I was going to watch my best friend get killed, and odds were good I'd shortly be following him into the great beyond. Problem was, I didn't have a clue about what to do. And then, like that, I knew.

I screamed, "Wait a second, wait a second, for chrissakes! Put him down, put him down. He doesn't know. Put him down."

Jimmy wasn't having it. "Nah, man, this Moe guy here, he don't know shit. He's jus' desperate to save his friend and his own self is all."

"Maybe," Susan said. "Maybe, but he found his way here on his own and though he got some stuff wrong, he actually worked a lot of things out for himself. I want to hear what he has to say." She waved her left index finger at Choirboy for him to release the rope. Bobby went crashing to the floor once again. Susan refocused on me, and she also took dead aim with the gun right at my belly. "Okay, Moe, what is it? And if I think you're just stalling . . ."

"You wanna know who your rat is? That's easy. Whoever ratted out Bobby to you is your Judas. Whoever had the convenient evidence to prove Bobby had sold you out to the cops is who you're looking for. Who was it, Susan? Was it one of those two clowns who chased me into the rail yard? Him?" I nodded at Choirboy. "Jimmy?"

She didn't need to answer. When I saw the look on Jimmy's face, I knew who had fingered Bobby. And all the heads in the room—Susan's, the old man's, the big guy's, mine, even Bobby's—turned to Jimmy.

"Could be possible, what this boy says," offered the old man. "In the camps, the SS would put in the barracks with us spies. They worried we weren't all sheep and trouble for them we could make, so they had people to listen to our plans. To throw away suspicion from themselves, the spies would say *this* one was stealing bread or *that* one was making deals with the guards. But this trick we learned."

"Sure, it's Jimmy," I said.

"Shut your lyin' mouth, mothafucka." He came for me, grabbing at my collar.

It wasn't a big adjustment for Susan to aim the gun away from me and at Jimmy. "Get away from him, Jimmy."

He let go of my collar and stepped back. "Oh, don't go believin' his bullshit."

"It isn't bullshit," I said, "and you all know it. Who's got the biggest mouth here? Who always wants to kill everybody? Jimmy, right? Why? Because if we're dead, we can't prove him wrong."

I didn't know if there was an ounce of truth in what I was saying, but it didn't matter. Jimmy looked so guilty and defeated, he might just as well have betrayed the cause.

Susan had come to a decision. "We'll see about all this later. For now, we'll just wait it out. Moe, sit over there. Jimmy, over there." She looked at Choirboy. "How long now?"

He checked his watch. "Two minutes."

Hyman Bergman seemed suddenly very twitchy. "And you are sure in the building there will be no one?"

She ignored the question. "It will all be over soon and then they won't be able to ignore us."

Now I understood. "Holy shit! The night you torched your grandfather's building . . . those were boxes of explosives you were moving."

Susan was impressed. "Forget what I said about you before, Moe. I misjudged you. You are nothing like those other dumb jocks on campus. Given a little more time, you probably would have been able to stop us."

"Forgive me if I don't say thanks. Obviously, you guys are gonna blow something up."

"Not just something, Moe. The 61st Precinct house on Avenue U. We have been planning this for almost a year. Sorry, Papa, but for the sake of the revolution, I had to lie to you. I knew you wouldn't have built the bomb for us if—"

The old man couldn't believe it. "The clock tower on the campus is not what you are destroying?"

"No, Papa."

"A precinct house! There will be many dead police, no?"

I said, "I think that's the idea, Mr. Bergman."

Choirboy called out, "One minute."

"Stop this, Susan!" Bergman shouted at his granddaughter. "I want no part from this murdering."

"Too late, Papa."

Then it hit me. "You twisted old cocksucker. You built the bomb that killed Sam and Marty!"

"That was not my work," he said. "Susan, you tell him."

But it was too late. I'd gotten to my feet without even realizing it. "You lying piece of shit! I'm gonna—"

Susan swung the gun around to me. "You're not going to do anything, Moe, except shut your fucking mouth. Everyone keep your mouths shut. If it's quiet enough, we should be able to hear the explosion even at this distance. Right, Papa?"

Bergman didn't answer.

Choirboy started the countdown, "Ten seconds to go."

Jimmy moved onto his knees.

*Nine.*

"Don't be an idiot, Jimmy. I see what you're doing." Susan pointed the gun right at him.

*Eight.*

Bobby moaned.

*Seven.*

Susan closed her eyes in rapturous anticipation.

*Six.*

Jimmy knew he was a dead man once the bomb went off. He leapt at Susan.

237

*Five.*

Susan opened her eyes, stepped back, fired.

*Four.*

The gunshot was deafening in that confined space. Jimmy probably didn't much care. He was beyond caring.

*Three.*

The hunched old man backhanded his granddaughter across the side of her head. Stunned, she tumbled over, banging her gun hand against the concrete foundation wall.

*Two.*

Bergman scooped up the gun, turned, shot Choirboy through the heart.

*One.*

Choirboy went down like a huge sack of flour.

*Zero.*

Silence.

The only explosion was the one echoing in our ears. There was nothing from the distance. Susan, her lips dripping blood, scrambled on hands and knees over to Choirboy's body. She grabbed at his wrist, not to check his pulse, but to check his watch.

"Something's wrong, Papa. There was no explosion."

He ignored her, turning to me instead. "Take your friend and get the hell out from here."

I didn't need to be told twice. When I grabbed Bobby's arms he shrieked in pain, but the knot around his wrists was so tight and I had nothing to cut the rope with. Once I got him up, I bent down and folded him over my shoulder. We were about halfway up the stairs when I heard a third gunshot. I didn't go back to look.

# CHAPTER THIRTY-ONE

Coney Island Hospital was a white brick box at the corner of Ocean Parkway and Shore Parkway. It was known in the neighborhood as the butcher shop. It was a city-run hospital and the kind of place where big doses of apathy were handed out like after-dinner mints. Incompetence too. The emergency room was renowned for casts that were put on too tight, and bones that had to be rebroken and reset because . . . well, because they just didn't get it right the first time. I knew guys with broken arms and legs that had driven themselves to other hospitals to avoid the place. But Coney Island Hospital was less than ten minutes away from Hyman Bergman's house, and with Bobby in such bad shape I didn't think I could risk being choosy.

About five minutes after they wheeled Bobby into the emergency room, I was herded into a dark room by two uniformed cops. When I asked what was going on, they told me, "Get the fuck in, sit the fuck down, and shut the fuck up." Charm school graduates, both.

The room was a windowless box with a rolling desk chair that didn't roll, a metal desk, and metal shelves bending under the weight of cardboard boxes dating back to a time before the Dodgers moved away from Brooklyn. I waited in there for a half hour or so, trying to come to grips with what had happened to me over the last few hours. I had just watched two men shot to death in front of me. And I don't mean killed at a distance. One of them, Jimmy, had his brain blown out the back of his head. Neither the Choirboy nor

Jimmy had been more than ten feet from me when they died. I kept waiting to feel something other than numb, but I just didn't. I was cold inside, so cold that I shivered.

There was a knock on the door and it pushed open. In walked a man who didn't exactly bring an end to my shivers. No more than five foot six, he was a nasty-looking little fireplug of a man with a gray and brown brush cut. He wore his face red and angry, and a lit cigarette dangled from his snarly lips. He carried a ridiculous gray fedora in his hand, and he was twenty years too old and thirty pounds too heavy for his John's Bargain Store suit. That, and his black shoes squeaked when he walked. Hanging out of the hanky pocket of his suit jacket was a gold and blue enamel detective shield.

"I'm Nance, Detective Nance," he said, leaning his face right up close to mine. His breath smelled of onions, cigarettes, and whiskey. *Yummy.* He squeezed my cheeks together till they hurt. "We're gonna be pals, you and me."

I said nothing. He didn't like that. Apparently his other pals were more talkative.

He slapped the side of my head and then grabbed my collar. Why did everybody do that to me? My collar had been grabbed more in the last week than in my whole life. "Listen to me, you little shit. You're gonna tell me what happened in that basement tonight and how you came to be there. You don't, I'm gonna slap the cuffs on ya, beat the piss outta ya, and then you're gonna take a ride to the Tombs to spend the night."

I said nothing. What I was in the middle of an hour ago, that was worth being frightened over. This guy bullying me . . . not so much.

He slapped me in the side of the head again, this time a lot harder. "You deaf, asshole?"

"What?"

"Very funny, ya hippie draft-dodgin' piece a crap. Tell me what happened tonight."

This time I had something to say, but I knew he was going to like it even less than my silence. "I'll tell someone, but not you. Get Wallace Casey in here and I'll talk to him, only him."

He was back to tugging at my collar. "You obnoxious little cocksucker. Who the fuck do you think you are, ordering me around like I'm your boy?"

"Wallace Casey," I repeated.

He changed tactics. Instead of tightening his grip on my collar, he pushed me and the chair over backwards. "Start talking."

I obliged him. "*Wallace Casey.*"

Nance kicked me in the ribs. It hadn't escaped my attention that Nance never once asked me who the hell Wallace Casey was. I was pretty sure he knew exactly who Wallace Casey was. I assumed Casey was either standing on the other side of the door or was on his way over. Because there was little doubt that the second an incident involving Bobby Friedman had occurred, Casey would be notified. I knew the truth and the truth was this: the deceased Jimmy might have been a lot of things, a belligerent asshole for sure, but he wasn't the informant. No, Bobby Friedman was. I might have been a little bit in shock, but I wasn't stupid. A lot of things made sense to me now that didn't quite fit before. The only two people who could tell me if I was right or wrong were Bobby and Casey, and Bobby was in no shape to tell me anything.

"All right, ya little kike shit," Nance barked, flicking his lit cigarette into my face. "Stay where ya are and we'll see what we'll see." Then, before leaving, he gave me a goodbye kick for luck.

I really didn't like that man. I hadn't had many direct dealings with the cops in my life, but if Nance was representative of the way most cops acted, it was easy to see why not many people my age gave them much respect. I picked myself up and the chair too, stamped out the cigarette, and waited some more.

This time when there was a knock on the door, it was followed by a question. "Can I come in?"

"Sure."

Wallace Casey stood front and center. He was even more imposing close up than at a distance, but he wore what I guess passed for a smile on his face. He held a hand the size of a baseball mitt out to me. "I'm Detective Wallace Casey. I hear you been asking for me."

I shook his hand. "We've met before," I said. "The night 1055 Coney Island Avenue burned down. You were wearing a ski mask at the time and whacking me across the belly with a baseball bat. You called me something like a long-haired hippie freak."

His smile broadened. "Jeez, you know, for the life of me, I don't remember that," he lied. "Maybe you're confusing me with somebody else. I hear you and my wife are good pals, huh? Students for a Fair Draft, right? You have that petition on you? I'd like to sign it."

"Jeez," I parroted him. "You know, for the life of me, I don't remember that."

"Okay, Prager, now that you got that outta your system, you wanna let me know why you needed to see me so bad?"

"First things first, Detective. I don't suppose this will matter to you or that you'll do anything about it, but that guy, Detective Nance, who was in here before you . . ."

"What about him?"

"Well, in the five minutes we were together, he slapped me, kicked me, pushed me onto my back, choked me, threw a lit cigarette in my face, used a religious slur, and threatened me. Other than that, it was love at first sight. Don't you guys ever stop to wonder why my generation hates you so much?"

"He's an asshole. Aren't any of your friends assholes, Prager?"

"Yeah, sure, but they aren't bullies."

He shook his head. "No, that's right. Your friends just try to blow up entire city blocks and kill as many cops as they can."

"As a general rule, I don't believe in killing people. And just so you know, Susan Kasten and that bunch aren't my friends."

"You sure about that?"

"What's that supposed to mean, Detective?"

"Isn't Bobby Friedman your best friend?"

"Bobby works for you and don't even try to deny it. I saw you pick up or drop off the package in his trunk at the airport the other day. Explosives, right? I followed you and the van to the Onion Street Pub, and then out to that garage in College Point. If I hadn't run out of gas, I probably would have found you out that day."

He applauded. "Keep going."

"Bobby was your way into the group. I don't know how you coerced him to turn on his friends, but you did. You supply the explosives to him. He supplies them to the Committee, and he supplies you with information. I knew that airport run thing he was doing was bullshit. I just couldn't figure out the angle, but I never could keep up with Bobby that way. It was all pretty neat until Jimmy found out about it and ratted Bobby out. So don't talk to me about my friends being involved."

"Some are closer than friends, like Mindy Weinstock, for instance."

"Mindy? Mindy's in the hospital. She just came out of a coma, for chrissakes! I just saw her tonight. She can barely speak. And it was one of Susan Kasten's flunkies, this guy named Abdul Salaam, who put her in the coma in the first place. How can she have anything to do with this?"

"Come on, Moe. I can call you Moe, right?" He didn't wait for an answer. "You're a smart guy, a very smart guy. Look how far you got on your own."

I laughed in spite of myself.

"What's funny, Moe?" he asked. "Most people I know don't think I'm very funny."

"Susan Kasten said almost exactly the same thing about how far I got."

"She was right. Without hardly any resources, you nearly got to the bottom of this thing."

"All I did was stumble around."

"Well, you stumbled around pretty fuckin' good, better than my whole task force and half the federal agencies in this country. Maybe we should try stumbling around a little more often."

"Maybe," I said. "But don't change the subject. Mindy had nothing to do with this."

"She had everything to do with this."

"Bullshit!"

"You think so? I don't. I think your girlfriend's in this up to her eyeballs."

"Prove it."

"I won't have to. You can do it for me."

"What are you talking about?"

He said, "Come with me."

"Where're we going?"

"To open up your eyes that last little bit."

# CHAPTER THIRTY-TWO

Casey refused to tell me where we were going even after we got into his chestnut Galaxie. In a weird way it felt nice to be inside his car instead of following around behind it. As we drove, he asked me to tell him about what had happened at Hyman Bergman's house earlier.

"You know what *quid pro quo* means, Detective?"

"You scratch my ass, I'll scratch yours."

"I've never heard it put that way before, but yeah, like that."

"So who's scratching whose ass first?"

"I'll tell you everything about what happened at Bergman's house and what led up to it, if we can talk about Samantha Hope and Marty Lavitz."

"We'll see," was what he said as he turned left onto Coney Island Avenue from Avenue Z.

"Not good enough."

"For now, it's all that's on the table, Moe. Show me you're as smart as I think you are. Take it."

I took it. I didn't see the point in holding back. Chances were they weren't really going to let Nance beat it out of me, as much as he would have liked to, but I figured the cops had their ways. For all I knew, they would throw my ass in jail and charge me with murder. I could be stubborn, but not to the point of stupidity. I told him everything . . . well, almost everything. I worked backwards from

Bergman's house to the night I bailed Bobby out of the Brooklyn Tombs.

"That was smart thinking, telling them that Jimmy was the rat," he said, turning off Coney Island Avenue onto Avenue I. "It probably saved your lives."

"It was the only thing I could think to do. I knew they were gonna kill Bobby, and they were probably gonna kill me."

"They would've had no choice."

Even after I had a pretty good idea of where we were going, I didn't comprehend why we were going there. We parked outside Burgundy House in the exact same spot Bobby's car had been parked on the day of the big snowstorm. And for reasons I couldn't fathom, I just broke down. I was crying like a little kid, sobbing so fiercely I could swear the car shook. It didn't make any sense. Only a half hour before, I couldn't feel anything about having watched two men shot to death practically within arm's length of me. And now, suddenly, I was overcome at the sight of a darkened driveway at the entrance to a dirty little basement apartment. I might not have understood what was happening to me, but Detective Casey seemed to. He gave me as much time as I needed.

When I settled down, he asked, "Who said that thing about never being able to go home again?"

"Thomas Wolfe, I think. It's the title of a book. *You Can't Go Home Again.*"

"He's right. You can't."

I didn't get it, not then. "So we're in front of Burgundy House, so what?"

"You tell me. What happened here?"

"Like I said, I met Mindy here after I bailed Bobby out of the Brooklyn Tombs."

"And you said she was acting strange, right?"

"Strange isn't the word for it, man. She was drinking bourbon and smoking. There was a sense of desperation about everything she did that night."

"You think you know why?" he asked.

"I do. She must've just come from a meeting of the Committee where she found out that Bobby had betrayed them to you. They no doubt blamed him for what had happened to Samantha and Marty. Look, Detective Casey, didn't I just go over this with you a few minutes ago?"

"I'm just a big dumb cop who doesn't even know who Thomas Wolfe is. Humor me, okay?"

"At the same meeting of the Committee, Mindy also must've found out they meant to kill Bobby for his betrayal. She loves Bobby. They go way back. Bobby introduced her to me. That's why she was so flipped out that night, and why she warned me to stay away from him. She was trying to protect me."

"Okay. What else?"

I shrugged my shoulders. "I don't know. Somehow the Committee found out that Mindy meant to warn Bobby, and they sent this Abdul Salaam guy after her."

"Try again," he said.

"That's the best I got."

"I doubt that, but skip it for now. What happened the next day, the day after Mindy warned you?"

"It was the day of the snowstorm. I cut class and came here to straighten up, but Bobby's car was already here. He was stepping into the street when I saw this car coming at him out of the snow."

"The Caddy stolen from Hyman Bergman's neighbor?"

"Yeah. I ran across the street and shoved Bobby out of the way. The car clipped my foot and spun my shoulder into the bumper of Bobby's 88."

"Then you heard the car crash around the corner, and you and Bobby went to check it out," he said, putting the Ford in gear and slowly driving around the corner. "Show me where you found the car smashed into the tree."

"Here! Right here."

He stopped the car. Even in the dark, we could make out the scar in the bark the Caddy had left in its wake. "Oak tree wins that battle every time. Musta been an ugly scene, huh?"

"Real ugly," I said. "The car was totally fucked up. The windshield was smashed. The driver and his passenger had split, but I knew they were hurt pretty bad. There was blood all over the Caddy's interior and in the snow. I guess we could have tried catching up to them, but my shoulder was killing me and Bobby convinced me to go back to the house and get some ice on it. Besides, the snow was falling like crazy."

Casey put the Ford in gear again. "So the driver and passenger left the scene of the accident? Why do you think they did that?"

"You're joking, right?" I asked. "They didn't want to get caught in a stolen car. Why else would they run?"

"You tell me."

We were moving again, down Avenue I, right onto Ocean Avenue. He drove at a snail's pace. There wasn't much traffic at that time of the morning, so no one protested. As we drove, I got that sick feeling in my gut again. It was a feeling I'd become intimately familiar with in recent days, but I couldn't quite put my finger on why I should have been feeling it at just that moment.

"You don't look so good," Casey said to me as we turned off Ocean Avenue onto Glenwood Road. "What's wrong?"

I didn't answer because a niggling thought forced its way into my consciousness, because I suddenly saw how the dots connected in a way to make me look like a lovestruck idiot. Detective Casey saw the realization in my eyes just as we pulled up to the corners of Glenwood Road and East 17th Street.

I pointed down East 17th. "They found Mindy over there."

"They did."

"Okay, Detective, I get it now. Let's go," I said, never having felt quite so low or so stupid as I did just then. "You made your point."

"I need you to say it, Moe."

"What, that I got it all wrong? That I refused to see the most obvious answer?"

He shook his head. "You know what I need to hear."

"Fuck you!"

"That wasn't it," he said, and we were off again. "Not even close."

Less than two minutes later we were parked in front of the burned-out rubble that had once been Hyman Bergman's fix-it shop.

"The old man's dead. That last shot you heard when you were carrying Bobby out of the basement was Bergman blowing his own head off."

"So where's Susan?" I asked.

"First things first, Moe. You wanna know about Kasten, you wanna talk about Samantha Hope and Martin Lavitz, fine. It's all on the table now, but I need to hear it and *fuck you* better not be the words that come outta your mouth. We understand each other?"

I didn't give him what he wanted. "But why? You already know the truth. What's the value in hearing me say it?"

"We'll discuss that later."

The pigheaded part of me wanted to tell him to shove it up his ass, but I needed him to talk about Sam and Marty. I gave him what he wanted.

"Mindy and Abdul Salaam were the people in the Caddy that tried to kill Bobby, and it was probably Mindy at the wheel. That's why she warned me to stay away from Bobby, and that's why she missed when I shoved Bobby out of the way. Salaam was there as insurance, to make sure she carried out her assignment. It makes a sick kinda sense, really, having Mindy be the one to kill Bobby. It was a way to test her loyalties. After she missed us, when they tried to speed away in the snow, Mindy lost control of the car and smacked into the tree. Mindy wasn't beaten into a coma. Nobody beat anybody. Both Mindy and Salaam were hurt bad in the accident, but they couldn't afford to let us find them. They took off on foot, Salaam probably dragging or carrying Mindy. My guess is that they were coming here," I said, nodding at the rubble.

"Salaam was trying to get them to the upstairs apartment to wait out the storm or to get help from Bergman. But Salaam couldn't make it, not with his injuries and not carrying Mindy. He dropped her on the street to lighten his load. Salaam finally made it here, but the shop was closed because of the weather. He got upstairs, crawled into bed, and probably died of his injuries. That's how I found him. That's how Bobby found him. That's how he was when Susan Kasten lit the place on fire. You happy now, Detective Casey? Pretty ironic how I got involved in all this shit so I could find out who put my girlfriend in a coma. Well, okay, I found out. Joke's on me, I guess. Go ahead, laugh. It's okay. I deserve it."

"I'm not happy and I'm not laughing, Moe. I needed you to say it because, let's face it, if I told you that story, you probably woulda thought I was full a shit. That I was another lying cop trying to set you up."

"You're right. I wouldn't've believed you."

"Now here's the thing," he said. "If I wanted to, I could get your girlfriend sent away for the next hundred years. By the time she got out, she'd be dead or she'd wanna be. You know and I know she was deep in this whole bomb plot thing and I could get her on attempted murder too—"

"But—"

"But I'm not looking to hurt her, and I need a favor from you."

I was more than a little skeptical. "A favor from me?"

"Yeah. Stories are gonna come out in the papers and on the news tomorrow that won't exactly fit the facts of what happened. Your name and Bobby's will be completely kept out of it, but I need you to keep your mouth shut. I need you to promise me that."

"This is the part on TV where you say, *or else*."

"There's no *or else*. This isn't TV and we're not all like that asshole, Nance. I think you're a man of your word, Moe, and I'm asking for your word."

"Where's Susan Kasten?"

"Wish I knew. A year's worth of work setting this up, and now she's gone," he said. "She was the candy inside the piñata, the big prize. We'll never find her now. She'll disappear into the underground and wind up in Cuba or Syria. We figured if we caught her red-handed, looking at life in prison, she'd cut a deal. She'd've given us a way into all the other groups that think bombs are a good way to make a point."

"You mean like LBJ, McNamara, and Westmoreland?"

He wasn't having any. "It's different."

"It's killing."

"People like Susan Kasten kill innocent people."

"You watch the news lately, Detective? You think all the people under those bombs are guilty? A lot of them are guilty of nothing more than being in the wrong place at the wrong time. Besides, Susan Kasten would've chewed her own fucking arm off before making a deal with you. She's a true believer."

"And you're not? A true believer, I mean?"

I laughed. "Me? Are you crazy? I'm not into *isms*. Since my bar mitzvah I don't even do much with Judaism. Sometimes I think that's why Bobby and Mindy like me, because all I believe in is a better world." I turned in my seat to face him. "When I was in that basement, old man Bergman said the bomb that killed Samantha and Marty wasn't his work."

"Don't look at me, Moe."

"Why not?"

"Because that bomb in December nearly blew our operation. It made the Committee suspicious. It's what made Kasten start looking for a rat inside her group. Then there's a very practical reason why it couldn't have been me."

"What's that?"

"Come with me a second."

We got out of the car and walked around to the rear of the Ford. Even though the fire was put out days ago, the air still stank of burned plastic and rubber. Casey keyed open the trunk. And sitting there like a box of groceries was a box identical to the ones I had seen Susan and her two flunkies putting in the back of the old bakery truck. He reached down and pried off the lid with a small crowbar. He picked up a light tan-colored brick wrapped in clear plastic, ripped open the plastic, and handed the brick to me.

"Feels like Silly Putty," I said.

"Essentially, that's what it is. You can mold and shape it any way you want. Stick some blasting caps in it and you're set to go. Of course, there's also supposed to be stuff mixed in there that would blow the both of us into small pieces."

"What do you mean 'supposed to be'?"

"It's inert, Moe. An atomic bomb couldn't set this shit off. We couldn't risk handing over live explosives to these nuts. In the beginning, I gave Bobby a few bricks of the real stuff, so he could prove he could get what the Committee needed. He tested it for them and they bought it hook, line, and sinker. We went through that whole elaborate charade at the airport many times just in case someone from the Committee was watching, but the stuff itself is harmless. You see what I'm saying, right? Whoever it was who blew up Bobby's girl and the Lavitz kid, it wasn't me."

"And I'm just supposed to believe you?"

"That's up to you."

"If it wasn't you and it wasn't them . . ."

"It was somebody else."

"But there isn't any somebody else."

"Let's get back in the car. It's cold, and it stinks out here," he said, slamming the trunk shut. Before we drove away, he held his right hand out to me. "Do I have your word that you won't say anything to the press?"

I shook his hand.

From *Daily News*
**Radical Bomb Plot Blown Up**
Gary Phillips

Late last evening the New York City Police Department prevented a potential disaster. The department's bomb squad defused a large explosive device that was intended to destroy the 61st Precinct house on Avenue U and East 15th Street in Brooklyn. The device, which, according to unconfirmed reports, contained in excess of 40 pounds of plastic explosive, was located in the precinct's basement and was timed to explode at or around midnight. Upon its discovery, the device was quickly rendered inoperable by the bomb squad. The detonation mechanism has been taken to the lab for study. The explosives were removed to an undisclosed site and detonated by the bomb squad.

"The bomb was meant to cause maximum loss of life because it would have detonated during a shift change," explained department spokesman Richard Pioreck. "And not only would the precinct house have been destroyed, with that excessive quantity of explosives, the buildings surrounding the precinct house would have sustained serious damage as well. It may well have taken out the entire block."

Although police won't confirm it, sources have linked the group responsible for the planning and carrying out of this attack with this past December's explosion of a smaller device in the Coney Island section of the borough. Two Brooklyn College students, Samantha Hope and Martin Lavitz, lost their lives in that explosion. Hope and Lavitz are alleged to have been members of a heretofore unknown radical group. It is thought that the explosive device they were transporting detonated prematurely, resulting in their deaths.

Asked how the investigation was progressing, Pioreck said that the department had not made any arrests directly related to either the December explosion or the plot to bomb the 61st Precinct house. "We have some strong leads, but no suspects at this time. We will continue to investigate both incidents. In any case, we believe our efforts have dealt a serious blow to the group or groups who believe such dangerous activities are the way to pursue a political agenda."

From *Daily News*

**Murders in Manhattan Beach**

Scott Montgomery

Responding to reports of shots fired, the police discovered the bodies of three men in the basement of a private house in the Manhattan Beach section of Brooklyn. The owner of the residence, Hyman Bergman, was among the deceased. The other men have not yet been identified. Neighbors feared that Bergman's granddaughter, Susan Kasten, also known to reside at the home, might have been harmed as well. However, she does not seem to have been at home at the time of the incident.

"All three of the deceased appear to have died as a result of gunshot wounds," said a police spokesman. "We're working on the theory that it was a botched robbery."

Neighbors said that Bergman, a concentration camp survivor, kept to himself. "He was a troubled man," said neighbor Dr. Raoul Mishkin. Bergman is known to have large real estate holdings, and was recently the victim of arson. Last week, one of Bergman's properties was intentionally burned to the ground. Police refused to speculate whether the two incidents might be connected.

# CHAPTER THIRTY-THREE

Bobby's parents visited only once during his stay in Coney Island Hospital, and then it was only to fill out the requisite paperwork. There was no tearful hand-holding or get-better-soon bouquets, nothing that even remotely resembled what had transpired between Mindy and her parents. There was only the superior disdain that Bobby's parents exuded. I had known these people nearly all my life without really knowing them at all. They were disappointed in Bobby. Believe me, they did nothing to camouflage it. But I had created a fantasy that beneath their icy, Warsaw Pact exteriors, they loved their son beyond description. That they secretly held dear all those bourgeois rituals and milestones—Bobby's first day of school, losing his first tooth, his high school graduation—that other parents so proudly celebrated. Now I came to see that my stubborn belief was naive and self-serving. The equation was simple: If Bobby's parents really loved him, mine loved me. It's not that my folks were stoic and unexpressive. They told me they loved me. It was just that they were such damaged goods, always so hungry for love and approval themselves, that I never trusted theirs for me. I couldn't speak for Aaron and Miriam.

For the first few days, the hospital was crawling with cops and it was impossible for me to get anywhere near Bobby. I stopped trying. I wasn't even sure why I wanted to see him other than to tell him to go fuck himself. Below the surface, I think I felt almost as betrayed by him as Susan Kasten had. It was one thing for Detective Casey to have done what he did. It was his job. He believed he was doing right.

It was different with Bobby. I still couldn't get a handle on the angle he'd been playing. Look, I knew Bobby believed the war was wrong and that America was a profoundly inequitable place. On some level he might even have truly believed in revolution, but he wasn't a bomb thrower. Nor was he Dudley Do-Right. At first I just assumed Casey had coerced Bobby into it, that he had something to hold over Bobby's head to get him to act as an informant. I don't know. Maybe he'd caught Bobby moving some real explosives, or transporting a fugitive. Something like that. Something where Bobby had no choice but to cooperate, or go away to prison for twenty years.

"He volunteered," Casey'd told me the night it all came down.

"Get the fuck outta here!"

I could only imagine my ancestors spinning in their graves at the disrespect I was showing to a cop. Such a display flew in the face of the Diaspora's mantra: *Keep your head down and keep your mouth shut.*

Casey laughed at me. "It's true, Moe, whether you believe it or not. He came to me."

"How did he find you?"

"I can't tell you that."

I wanted to believe the detective was lying to me, but in my gut I knew he wasn't. That really sent me spinning off my axis. It might have been the Age of Aquarius, but not in my dark corner of the universe. Not only did I feel used and betrayed by Bobby, there was Mindy too. Forget that she was willing to kill Bobby, that she had tried. I could almost understand the rationale behind that. For a few days I pretended that what I couldn't get over was her willingness to kill innocent people, whether they wore uniforms or not. But that was only part of it. It was more that I felt so completely stupid. It was one thing to be Polonius, to be unaware that you're the fool. It's another thing to be the fool and know it. Here were my best friend and a woman I thought I loved, and I didn't know either of them, not really, not deeply. It made me start to question everything I thought I knew.

I was no longer even feigning interest in school. Oddly, my parents didn't pester me about it. My parents were uneducated people, not dumb people. And when my dad read those articles in the papers about the failed bomb plot and the murders in Manhattan Beach, he seemed to sense that the missing thread in the fabric of those stories had a connection to his youngest son. Only Aaron bothered asking me about it at all, and when I refused to say anything, he let it go. Aaron never let anything go. Not anything. Not ever. On Saturday morning, when an unexpected visitor showed up at our apartment door, no one needed to guess or speculate in silence any longer.

When my mom came into the room I was still in bed. I was half-watching a rerun of *Sky King*. People said my mom kind of looked like a cross between the young Joan Crawford and the aging Shelley Winters. Her weight was definitely more on the Shelley Winters side of that equation. But the expression on her face was purely and distinctly her own. It was an odd mix of panic and smug satisfaction, like the look on Chicken Little's face when the sky actually fell. *See, I told ya.* It was as if the worst coming to pass was worth it because it confirmed her darkest fears.

"Someone's at the door for you."

"Yeah, I heard the bell."

"He's a detective."

That got my attention more than Sky King's plane *Songbird*, or his niece Penny. I sat up. "What's he look like?"

"He's a big—"

I didn't hear what she said after that because I was already out of the bedroom.

Casey stood just inside the door. He curled his lips into a small smile and then quickly undid it.

"Throw on some clothes," he said. It wasn't a request.

I opened up my mouth to ask the first of ten questions that came to mind. When I did, he shook his head at me not to bother. I about-faced and headed into the bedroom to change. My mom was still there as if hiding out.

"Ma, get outta here. I gotta get dressed."

"Why is that cop here? What did you do? Is it Mindy? Was it you who—*Oy gevalt!* It was you who did this to her. Was she cheating on you? I never liked her, you know. I knew she was no good."

"Sorry to disappoint you, Ma."

"What's that supposed to mean?"

"That the sky's not falling. C'mon. I gotta get dressed. I have to go."

✦

I never experienced the same kind of buzz or rush my friends claimed to feel the few times I smoked pot, but, man, I felt it there in the front seat of Detective Casey's chestnut Galaxie. Somehow I was a part of something in a way I'd never been before, something bigger than me. It was good to crawl out of the little hole of self-pity and bewilderment I'd dug for myself. It was good to feel important. Maybe this was what Aaron and Bobby felt like. Maybe this was what it was like to have purpose. Fifteen minutes into the trip, Casey still hadn't explained to me where we were headed or why we were going there. Didn't matter. He needed me.

We pulled off the Belt Parkway at Pennsylvania Avenue. In D.C., the White House is on Pennsylvania Avenue. In Brooklyn, Pennsylvania Avenue leads to the Fountain Avenue dump. These days, there were plenty of people who had more respect for the latter than the former. I remembered back to the day Bobby and I stopped on the opposite shoulder to fix his flat tire, the day Bobby was almost arrested and then let free. At least now I understood why the cop let him go. Bobby must have given the cop a code word or a number to call that gave him a free pass. I asked Casey about it.

"If Bobby got snagged by a cop when he was carrying the dummy explosives, did he call you?"

"He had a number to use, yeah. It couldn't be me directly because if I was out in the field I might be outta reach, but there was always someone there to clear his way if he got jammed up. Why you wanna know?"

I ignored the question. "Why didn't he use it the day he got arrested at the demonstration? I had to go bail his ass out that day."

"Because getting Bobby arrested was the whole point," Casey said, turning the car toward the dump instead of away from it. Although all the windows in the Ford were rolled up tight, the stench of rotting garbage seemed to seep through the glass and metal as if through tissue paper. "As the plot to bomb the Six-One was getting closer, I needed a way to reassure Susan Kasten and her crowd that Bobby hadn't betrayed them, that he wasn't the mole. I figured if Bobby got arrested and they saw that he didn't have a magic get-outta-jail card, it would erase any doubts they mighta had about him."

"Didn't work."

Casey shrugged his shoulders. "Guess not. He'd already been ratted out."

We pulled up to a little shack. A guy with bad knees in a green sanitation uniform limped out of the shack and motioned for Casey to roll down his window. When he did, it was all I could do not to puke my guts up onto the floor of the front seat. The detective turned a few shades of green himself as he waved his shield at the gate man. The guy waved us through and Casey set a world's record getting his window rolled back up. We both took big gulps of air to no good end.

"Listen, Moe," he said as we snaked our way along the rough dirt road deeper into the huge mounds of garbage. "This isn't gonna be pretty."

"Is it Susan Kasten?"

"Nah. I wish."

And suddenly, even before he said another word, I knew why he'd brought me here. It was Lids. Had to be. It was the only thing that made sense. In all the commotion of the last few days, I'd almost forgotten about Lids. His parents had called a few times, but I'd been so freaked out by things that I never got back to them. Trust me, nearly getting killed screws with your head and tends to rearrange your priorities. The other night, when I'd recounted how I'd stumbled onto the bomb plot for Detective Casey, I'd fudged Lids's part in helping me. I'd strategically neglected to mention Lids's connection to the late Billy O'Day. I'd emphasized Lids's nervous breakdown and his paranoia, and left out the part about him being a pusher. The way I'd told it, Lids was pure as a spring lamb, sort of an innocent bystander who got caught up in stuff he had no part in.

"If I hadn't asked Bobby to find Lids for me and to keep an eye on him, I wouldn't even be mentioning him to you," was what I said to Casey the night we'd met at Coney Island Hospital. "Bobby told me Lids was safe, but that was all he told me. He didn't tell me who he was with, or where he was. Do you know where he is?"

Casey had sworn he didn't have a clue. That was days ago. Now I was pretty sure he had a good idea of exactly where Lids was.

"It's Lids's body, isn't it? You found him." That strange smile of Casey's cracked across his lips, so I asked, "Why are you smiling?"

"I know he was your friend and all, but you've got a good head for this work. You're sharp."

I didn't say anything to that. As we came over the crest of a last fetid hill, he eased off the gas. About a hundred yards ahead of us was a huddle of official-looking vehicles: two black and green patrol cars, a ridiculously conspicuous unmarked police car, a city ambulance, a bulldozer, and a few Department of Sanitation vehicles. There was another car parked there too, one that was foreign to me: a black or dark brown station wagon with blackened back windows.

"What's that car there?" I asked.

"The meat wagon," he answered as if those two words explained it all. I suppose they did. The Galaxie came to a stop. "Listen, Moe. The first time is a little rough. It's rougher when it's someone you know. You sure you wanna do this?"

Of course, this wasn't my first time. There was Billy O'Day and Abdul Salaam. "No, but I'm gonna do it anyway," is what I said. "You didn't drive me all the way here to have me sit in the car."

"This kid, Lids. He's not my case, you understand?"

"Yeah."

"This isn't my crime scene either. After we spoke the other night, I put the word out on your friend and I got a call this morning. These guys called me as a courtesy. The detectives will want you to take a look before they contact his parents."

"Okay."

"You listen to what the detectives tell you. Your friend, he's in pretty rough shape. That's what they told me over the phone. You understand what that means?"

"I can imagine."

"No, you can't."

When I opened the door, I got smacked full in the face with that rotting garbage smell. The odor was acrid and sour and sickly sweet all at once. It was burnt rubber and curdled milk and rotted vegetables and decayed flesh blended together. And it was worse than just a smell. It hung heavy in the air like a film, tainting my exposed skin, my clothes, my lungs. I could taste it too. It was meat spoiling on my tongue, maggots and beetles sliding down my throat as I swallowed. I didn't make it five feet before I bent over at the waist and heaved up my breakfast. Man, was I happy I'd only had toast. Looking up, I noticed a group of older men—some in uniforms, some not—having a good laugh at my expense.

"Don't sweat it, kid," one of them said. "Welcome to the club."

Then, having had their laughs, the old men turned back around to whatever was the focus of their attention. It wasn't hard to guess what that was. Detective Casey stood me upright, urging me forward. Above our heads, set against a steel gray sky, swirling gyres of feathered scavengers chirped and cawed and wailed, raining stained white streaks of feces down on the piles of garbage below. What from a distance looked so poetic, so much like an aerial ballet, was raw and feral, a thing much more menacing and desperate from where I now stood. *Nature red in tooth and claw.* I think I finally understood what that meant.

I walked up just behind the line of uniforms. Casey stopped me, asking me one more time if I was ready for this. I wanted to ask him if anybody was really ready for this. Was he? How could anyone be ready for this? Some people were. Some people had to be.

"Malone," Casey called out.

"That you, Casey?" a voice asked from beyond the line of uniforms.

"Yeah."

"Hold your water, I'm comin'."

A few seconds later the line of uniforms parted, and through them stepped a rotund, bald man in a cheap, ill-fitting overcoat. He couldn't have closed the buttons on that thing for all the money in the world. He was smoking the shit out of a cigar that wiggled like a hula dancer when he moved his lips. Never in my life had I so welcomed the smell of cigar smoke.

"You Casey?" Malone asked, holding his hand out to the man who brought me. He jerked his head at me and spoke as if I wasn't there. "This the friend?"

Casey nodded yes, shaking Malone's hand.

"Over here, kid," Malone said, tugging me by the arm. We climbed up a low mound of churned up garbage. "He don't look so good, your friend."

"I know, Detective Casey warned me."

"Look out, Phil," Malone barked at his partner standing over the body. "The vic's friend is here."

Malone walked me over to where the other detective had been standing. The body was nude and the colored parts of his eyes had gone kind of milky white. His skin was a waxy gray-white in most places, but it was battered and bruised in others. There was a really nasty ring of bruises around his neck. Jagged spikes of broken bones jutted out through the skin of his left thigh and right arm.

Malone seemed to anticipate my question. "The bones stickin' out like that probably happened after he was dead. They found him when the bulldozer was pilin' up the garbage. We think it was the bulldozer that done the damage to him like that."

"But not the bruises?"

"No, kid. The murderer done that."

I was okay until a bug crawled out of one of the body's nostrils into the other. After that things got hazy there for a second and my knees got rubbery. I felt arms holding me up.

"Easy, kid, easy."

"It's not him," I said. "He's the right height and age and everything. His hair's the right color, but it's not him."

"It's not who?" the other detective, Phil, shouted at Malone.

I shouted back. "It's not Lids. It's not my friend."

"You sure about that, kid?" Malone asked. "Fifteen seconds ago you was so lightheaded I thought you was gonna take a dive. Take another look to be sure."

Even though I knew it wasn't Lids, I looked again. "Sorry, Detective Malone. It's not him."

Phil wasn't happy. "Ah, shit! Just what we needed, another John fucking Doe."

"Okay, kid," Malone said. "Thanks. You done yourself proud. You can get outta here now."

The line of uniforms stared at me in anticipation as I walked back toward them. I just shook my head. While they didn't seem disappointed, they didn't seem pleased either.

"It's not him, Detective," I said to Casey.

Casey didn't ask me if I was sure. "Let's split. I swear if I have to breathe this stuff in another minute, I'm gonna throw up everything I ate since I was ten years old."

I was all for leaving. I was relieved to be getting away from the stench and away from the birds. I was relieved that the body wasn't Lids. I was relieved, sure, but I wasn't exactly happy, either. Whoever John Doe was, he had a family too. Somewhere they were worrying themselves sick, and someday only grief would end their worry. And then I had a sadder thought: What if his family didn't care? What if there was no one to worry about him? I think I learned more about life in those few minutes in the Fountain Avenue dump than I had during the rest of my time on earth.

# CHAPTER THIRTY-FOUR

I knew I had to get in to see Bobby, but the first thing I did was go home and take a hot, soapy shower. And even though I got the film and smell off me, I couldn't get it out of me. I brushed my teeth so long I was in danger of wearing away the enamel. I dipped a Q-tip in a Dixie cup of Aqua Velva and stuck it up my nostrils. It stung like hell and it proved to be a waste of time. The sting lasted longer than the relief and when the alcohol evaporated the stink of the dump filled up my head once again. I would've burned my clothes in the building's incinerator if I could have afforded to. Instead I gave my mom my clothes to wash.

"I just washed these," she yelled, shaking them at me. "They're fine." I thought she was going to puke when she put them to her nose to prove me wrong. She didn't yell at me after that.

When it came to my Converse All-Stars and my pea coat, I didn't have many options. Hell, they smelled even worse than the rest of my clothes. Even if I'd been willing to hold my nose and put them back on, there was no way they'd let me in to see Bobby, smelling like the Fountain Avenue dump. So I did what any red-blooded American male would've done in my situation—I stole from my brother.

Although he was slimmer than me, we both had monkey arms and I could usually squeeze myself into things like Aaron's sports jackets, coats, and sweaters. We did wear the same shoe size, at least. The thing was, Aaron treated all of his possessions with the same sort of obsessive care with which he treated his car. Whereas my sneakers looked like they'd been robbed off the feet of a Bowery bum, Aaron's looked new out of the box. In fact, he kept them in the box with the tissue paper still stuffed inside. And when it came to his coats, Aaron stored them in his closet in the cleaners' plastic bags. I didn't figure he would kill me for "borrowing" his sneakers. They only cost eight bucks. It was his shearling jacket that worried me. That jacket was his most prized piece of clothing, which, when it came to my brother, was really saying something. There would be no forgiving me if I somehow messed it up. Thank goodness Aaron was still at his girlfriend's house, or I would have had to go to the hospital in a bundle of sweaters and my silly dress shoes. As it was, Miriam nearly sounded the alarm when I snuck out the front door past my mom and dad.

The steely gloom that had hung overhead earlier this morning had lifted or been burned away by the sun. Though the sky above Ocean Parkway had brightened, the weather had turned frigid. Aaron's jacket kept most of me pretty toasty during my short walk to the hospital. I made it up to Bobby's floor without bother. There I saw that most of the cops who'd been guarding Detective Casey's most precious rat had gone. Now only a single uniformed cop, his head buried in a copy of *Sports Illustrated*, sat outside Bobby's room. I tried to just walk past him, but he wasn't having it.

"Where the fuck you think you're goin', son?"

*Son?* "Going to see my friend, officer."

"No, you ain't neither."

"Okay, let's get Detective Casey on the phone and see what he says."

"Listen to me, junior. I don't know no Detective Casey and even if I did, I don't take orders from no little hippie freak."

*Little hippie freak!* That almost made him calling me "son" and "junior" reasonable.

"That's enough!" I growled at him. "What's your name? Okay, your badge number is three—"

That did it. He grabbed me by the arm and marched me toward the elevators, but the thickness of the coat sleeve made it hard for him to get a good grip on my arm. When I felt his hand relax to re-grip, I spun away and ran for Bobby's room. When I burst through the door, I got a big surprise. There, standing over Bobby's bed was Tony Pizza. At the foot of the bed was Tony's muscle, Jimmy Ding Dong. Jimmy did different kinds of magic tricks than his boss. Whereas Tony P made coins disappear, Jimmy Ding Dong made whole people vanish. Only Jimmy displayed no talent for making them reappear. Once they were gone, they stayed gone. Word was that Jimmy was the guy responsible for disappearing Chicky Lazio and Petey Cha Cha, two guys from the Anello family who'd tried to muscle in on Tony P's turf.

I didn't know how Jimmy got the nickname Ding Dong, but it wasn't from eating Hostess cakes. This guy from the neighborhood told me it was because "when Jimmy rang your bell, it stayed rung forever." Who knows? I wasn't going to ask Jimmy. Built like a big cat—lean and sinewy, always ready to pounce—Jimmy's attitude was purely crocodilian. His eyes were cold and devoid of humanity. At least, I thought, cats play with their prey. Jimmy didn't play. Actually, it was Jimmy who saved Tony P and his magic tricks from seeming ridiculous. He was the reason people in the neighborhood gave Tony Pizza as much respect as he got, and why no one called him Tony Pepperoni to his face. There was nothing ridiculous about Jimmy except his nickname.

Funny thing is, Jimmy looked nearly in worse shape than Bobby. His left forearm was in a cast and his face was a roadmap of long, thin scabs. There was a two-by-two-inch gauze bandage taped to his forehead and another one taped to the side of his neck, but it wasn't Ding Dong's face that interested me. Bobby's face was still pretty battered, although all the swelling had gone down and you could see his eyes again. It was the fear I saw in those eyes that caught my attention. That famous smile of his was nowhere to be found.

Before I could make any sense of it, I got tackled from behind. I reacted without thinking, and threw an elbow behind me that connected with something that felt like bone. Whoever it was holding me, let go with a groan. I spun around, up and ready for a fight.

"You little motherfucker." It was the cop from the hallway, nightstick at the ready. He was rubbing his jaw with his other hand. "I'm gonna kick your ass and then I'm gonna—"

"You ain't gonna do shit," Tony P said to the cop. "This kid's with me. You understand what I'm sayin'?" The cop nodded. "Good. Jimmy, take a walk with the officer and give him something green to make his ugly puss feel better."

Jimmy looked at me, his lip twitching up into a reptilian smile. I wanted to believe it was a sign of respect, but there was something else in it—a croc sizing up a future meal perhaps. When the door closed behind Jimmy and the cop, Tony P turned to me.

"Tough old-fashioned Jew, huh?" he said. "I think even with that nightstick in his hand, you woulda kicked the shit outta the cop. I always thought you was just schoolboy material, Moe. Maybe I had you wrong. Maybe I shoulda done business with you. But, hey, you can only play with the cards you get."

I had no idea what he was talking about, but I could tell by the look on Bobby's face he got the message perfectly.

"Listen, Moe, could you do me a favor? I know you went through a lot to see Bobby here, but I sorta bought the time. Maybe you could come back tomorrow, huh?"

Translation: *Get the fuck out of here. Now! I paid the cop off and I got things to discuss with Bobby.*

"Sure, Tony P." I turned toward Bobby. "Take care. I'll be by soon."

Out in the hallway there was no sign of either Jimmy Ding Dong or the cop. I'd had more exposure to cops in the last two weeks than in my previous two decades, and I thought they were an odd breed. There were guys like Nance and this asshole guarding Bobby's door who were either sadistic, corrupt, or inept. Then there were guys like Casey and Malone, and the highway patrol cop who found me sleeping on the side of the road. They seemed to care about people and their job. I guess you get all kinds in every job.

When I got back outside I realized I was hungry, that I'd left the toast I had for breakfast at the Fountain Avenue dump and hadn't eaten anything since. To tell you the truth, after I'd been to the dump, I didn't think I'd ever want to eat again. One thing the cold air and the chemical smell of the hospital had done for me was to get the putrid stench of the dump out of my head. And with it gone, I was rediscovering my appetite. My appetite was even bigger after walking all the way to Brighton Beach.

Late in the afternoon, just as the sun was beginning to fade, was the perfect time to get to DeFelice's Pizzeria. At that time of day, the lines were small and the tables empty. And there was one more perk: Tony P and Jimmy Ding Dong were otherwise engaged. I'd be able to eat in peace. No one was going to pull a quarter out from behind my ear, and no one was going to chop me up and throw the pieces into Sheepshead Bay. Geno was behind the counter, covered in flour, slapping dough out into a circle so he could toss it fully into shape.

"Hey, Moe, how ya doin'?" he asked, barely looking away from the whirling dough.

"Okay, Geno. Yourself?"

"Eh, you know. Same old t'ing."

"Two slices and a large Coke."

"I got fresh for you." He twirled the dough and brought it to a soft landing on the white marble counter next to the oven. He slid over to where a bubbling hot pie sat on a round aluminum tray. With the skill of a surgeon, he carved out two perfectly symmetrical slices, put them on two overlapping paper plates lined with wax paper, and placed them atop the stainless steel counter. He poured my Coke and put it up next to the slices.

I decided to eat at the counter like I'd done when I was a little kid and only the grownups sat at the tables in the back. Besides that, I liked watching Geno make the pies. He was so expert at it, and it seemed so effortless for him. I think one of the things in life I enjoyed most was watching people who were good with their hands. When Geno tossed and twirled the flattened dough in the air, he wasn't showy about it like some pizza makers. He just made it look so easy, the way some outfielders can track down fly balls without seeming to try. I was halfway through my second slice when he finished making the pie and slid it into the oven. Then, just to make conversation, I asked, "What happened to Jimmy, man? He looks like he had a fight with a box of razor blades and lost."

Geno smiled and nodded in agreement. "Yeah, he's no lookin' so good. He smacked his car up real bad. Had a crash wid a big truck."

"Where, on the Gowanus?"

"Nah, someplace in Pennsylvania somewheres."

For the second time that day I got lightheaded, but this time it wasn't from watching a bug crawl out of dead man's nose. "You know where in Pennsylvania?"

"I don't know, somewheres in the mountains someplace. You know, it's a funny t'ing, Moe."

"What?"

"The last time you was in here, that night a few days ago, Tony got a phone call. Remember?"

"Yeah, what about it, Geno?"

"It was some cop in Pennsylvania callin' to tell Tony about Jimmy's accident. He had to go get Jimmy from the hospital. Hey, Moe, whatsamatta? You don't like my pizza no more?"

At first, I didn't say anything at all. But Geno was right: the pizza had turned to sawdust in my mouth. When I realized that it was Jimmy Ding Dong who'd tried to run me off the road that night I was coming home from visiting Samantha's grave, I lost my appetite. Truth was, I was suddenly nauseous and very close to panic. It was one thing to have escaped from Susan Kasten and her band of radical idiots. It was something else to have just missed getting my bell rung by Jimmy Ding Dong. What I was trying to figure out was why Tony P—Jimmy never acted without Tony's say-so—should want me dead? More importantly, I wondered if I was still on his hit list.

"Moe!" Geno shouted.

"No, the pizza's great. It's me. I don't feel so good. I gotta go."

"Hey, Moe," Geno called after me.

"What is it?"

"Not for nothin', but the pizza's not free."

"Right," I said with all the conviction of a zombie and threw a five-dollar bill on the counter. "Listen, Geno, do me a favor, okay? Don't tell Tony or Jimmy we talked about what happened in Pennsylvania."

Geno had been around long enough to understand. "Sure, Moe. Far as I know, you wasn't even here today."

I walked out of the shop without collecting my change. What did the walking dead need with money, anyway?

# CHAPTER THIRTY-FIVE

My brother was at the desk doing his weekly sales reports when I walked into our bedroom. I didn't even try to sneak the shearling jacket past him. I think I would have preferred him killing me and just getting it over with, but he must've seen the look on my face.

"What's wrong with you, little brother? You're white as a ghost."

*Ghost! If you only knew.* "I'm sorry about borrowing the jacket, but—"

"I didn't ask you about the jacket. I asked you what was wrong. Is it Mindy?"

I choked on a laugh. "She's the least of it."

"What's that supposed to mean?"

"If I even tried to explain it, it would blow your mind," I said, brushing off the jacket and placing it back on its hanger. I pulled the plastic bag down over the jacket and hung it back in its place.

"Try me."

"Oh, and I borrowed your Chuck Taylors too." I lifted up my left foot to show him.

He jumped out of his seat and grabbed me by the shoulders. "What's wrong, Moe? You're not making any sense."

"I've gotten myself into something that I can't get out of."

"Drugs?"

"Nothing like that, I swear. I'm not even sure what it is, or how I got into it."

"What?" he asked, relaxing his grip on my shoulders. "Does it have to do with the cop that was here today?"

"He's a detective."

"I don't care if he's Attila the Hun, for chrissakes. Does it have anything to do with him?"

"No, I don't think so, but I can't be sure," I said, my mind racing, the rest of me numb with fear.

Aaron let go of me completely and pulled a suitcase out from under his bed. "Does it have anything to do with this? I found it in the trunk of my car last night."

At first it didn't register. Then I remembered. It was Samantha's suitcase, the one that I'd pulled out of her landlady's attic. I'd put it in the Tempest's trunk the night Susan Kasten and her Halloween-masked friends had snatched me off the street. In the whirl of events that followed, I'd completely forgotten about it.

"I don't know, Aaron. Maybe."

"What the fuck do you know?"

"I know that almost everything I thought I knew, about everyone I thought I knew it about, was wrong."

"Well, that clears it all up," he said, his voice thick with sarcasm.

I grabbed the suitcase and hoisted it onto my bed. "Let's open this up. Maybe you better get a butter knife in case it's locked."

Butter knives are the Brooklyn Jewish take on Swiss Army knives. Between the five of us in my family, we'd used butter knives to do everything short of open heart surgery. It showed. All of our butter knives had blunted or twisted tips from being used as letter openers, screwdrivers, lock picks, or pry bars. Hell, sometimes we even used them to spread butter. Aaron, always the practical one of us, suggested I try the locks before he went to the kitchen. Smart man. *Click. Click.* Both latches snapped open when I pushed the two rectangular tabs to the side with my thumbs. My heart thumping with anticipation, I raised the case's lid.

My heart sank in disappointment when I saw that the case contained nothing more than a cheerleader's skirt and sweater from Koblenz High, a graduation tassel, programs from school plays, a yearbook, and some other odds and ends. But I wasn't going to give up just yet. I removed it all from the case. Nothing. That is, nothing that did more than make me wonder about Samantha as a younger girl.

"Shit!"

"Not so fast, little brother," Aaron said, pushing me aside. "007 would be disappointed in you." He ran the flats of his hands along the faded, satiny interior lining of the suitcase. Then he pulled back the pocket of the same material on the underside of the case's lid. He stopped, his eyes lighting up. He grabbed my hand and placed it inside the pocket. "Feel that?" he asked.

"Yeah, there's something between the lining and the lid."

Aaron curled his right hand around the loosest part of the lining and gave it a sharp yank. The material, old and faded, tore away from the glue without much of a fight. There, taped to the underside of the lid, were two large brown envelopes. I carefully peeled away the tape and held the envelopes in my hands. I was surprised at just how heavy they were.

"Do you think the envelopes are Samantha's?" Aaron asked.

"Probably. Look at the rest of the bag. It's all beat up. The lining is saggy and faded, but the tape is fresh and unyellowed, not brittle like old tape would be."

"One way to find out for sure."

The flaps on the envelopes were held closed by the little spread wings of metal clasps. I knew Aaron was right, that opening the envelopes would tell us about who had concealed them, but I hesitated. I wondered if I shouldn't just put them back inside the suitcase and ship it to Sam's parents.

Aaron shouted, "Open them!"

I suppose if Sam had died under normal circumstances and if my world hadn't been turned upside down just lately, I'd have kept them closed and mailed them to her parents. But Sam hadn't died a normal death, and with me on Jimmy Ding Dong's to-do list, I had to see what was inside the envelopes.

I opened the first one by bending the clasp's spread metal wings together, lifting the flap, and dumping the contents onto my bed. Three white, letter-sized envelopes fell onto the bedspread. One was marked "Last Will and Testament." Another was marked "For Dad." And one "For Mom."

"Is that Samantha's handwriting?" Aaron wanted to know.

"I think so. Wait a second." I scrounged around the bottom of my closet looking for a particular shoebox. After a minute of frantic searching, I found the one I wanted. Pulling off the lid, I reached into the box and came up with a handful of holiday cards, birthday cards, and postcards. I searched through them until I came upon what I was looking for. "Here it is," I said, holding up a postcard with a photo of the Steeplechase on the front. On the back was a note from Sam.

*Dear Moe—*

*Please forgive me. I don't know what got into me the other night. You are a good and loyal friend, which is more than I can say for myself. Getting to know you has been one of my favorite things about moving here. Please don't let a few minutes of stupidity on my part ruin that.*

*Love,*

*Sam*

I held the postcard up to the writing on one of the envelopes. "It's her handwriting, but I'm not going to open these up, Aaron. It's not right."

"I agree. There's nothing in them for us."

I opened the second brown envelope, turned it upside down, and let gravity do the rest. There was another white, letter-sized envelope within. It was marked "To Whom It May Concern," but it was the remainder of the contents that made me go cold inside. Next to the white envelope on the bed lay a NYPD badge and a thick packet of black-and-white photographs. The photographs were of Bobby and Tony P, of Bobby's car—trunk open—at the airport parking lot, of a light-colored van parked behind it. There was a series of photos of a man loading something from the van into the trunk, but the man in the photos wasn't Detective Casey and the things being loaded into the trunk weren't wooden crates of dummy explosives.

"Holy shit!" I thought I heard myself say.

Aaron grabbed the photos out of my hand. "What is it? What are those things in his hands?" he asked, pointing at the plastic- and tape-covered bricks being loaded into Bobby's trunk.

"You're kidding me, right?"

Aaron didn't like it when I got sarcastic. He especially didn't like it when it made him feel dumb or out of touch. "No, I'm not kidding, jerk. Remember whose clothes you've been wearing today and whose car you've been driving lately."

"Sorry, you're right, big brother. Those bricks are bricks of heroin or cocaine. I'm not sure which."

"Get the fuck outta here! Bobby wouldn't do that."

"You're wrong. You wouldn't do that. I wouldn't do that, but I'm not sure there's anything Bobby wouldn't do if a lot of money was part of the equation."

Aaron wasn't believing it. "Big money or not, Bobby's a shrewd guy. He wouldn't risk going away to prison for—" I was already laughing before he could finish. "What's so funny?" he wanted to know.

"I swear I'm not laughing at you," I said. "In fact, even though it looks and sounds like laughter, I'm really crying."

"You're talking crazy, Moe."

"Whatever you say."

"Aren't you going to open the white envelope? It's addressed to Whom It May Concern, not to her mom or dad."

"Not now," I said. "Not here."

"When?"

"I'm not sure," I lied. I knew exactly where and when I was going to open it.

"What about the photographs? Are you—"

"I'll handle it."

"Okay," he said, but his expression was full of worry. Rightfully so.

My brother knew my heart better than I thought he did. What was even more amazing was that in spite of knowing that I was basically an aimless fuck-up, he trusted me. That I hadn't expected, because I wasn't sure that I'd ever done anything to earn his trust. Sometimes, I guess, you just have to trust somebody. I was about to test that theory out.

# CHAPTER THIRTY-SIX

Bobby was sleeping when I walked into his room at Coney Island Hospital, but it wasn't the sleep of angels. His face, his long brown hair were bathed in sweat. His fingers twitched. His head jerked violently from side to side. His lips curled and moved. His arms struck out wildly at an invisible enemy. Maybe it was a nightmare. Or maybe he was being crushed beneath the weight of his deals with various devils. I didn't much care either way, as long as he suffered. I stood there watching him for what might have been an hour, trying to feel something other than anger. I think I could have stood there for days and not felt anything else. Eventually Bobby's night terrors calmed, and he fell into a more restful sleep. I sat down, reading while I waited. He stirred again at around eleven, this time opening his eyes. I got up. I wanted to be standing over him when he woke.

"Hey, Moe." He yawned, stretching his muscles, not without pain. "What time is it? How did you get in here with—"

I might have told him what time it was. I might have told him that I had called Detective Casey to make sure I could get past the relief cop at the door without any hassles. I did neither. What I did instead was to toss something onto Bobby's chest.

He grabbed at it. "What the fuck is this?"

"It's a dead cop's badge."

"What the—"

"Shut up, Bobby. For once, just shut the fuck up. I'm already sorry for saving your life. Don't make it worse."

"About that," he said, "about saving my—"

"Twice, Bobby. I saved your worthless life twice. So please shut up. Shut up!"

He put his hands up in surrender. "Okay."

"We'll talk about the badge later. First, I wanna talk about this." I handed him a photo of the big guy loading up his trunk with drugs. "Are the bricks heroin or cocaine?"

"Where did you get this?"

I ignored him. "Heroin or cocaine?"

He bowed his head. "Heroin."

"What a perfect setup, huh, Bobby? By volunteering to be Detective Casey's rat inside Susan Kasten's bomb plot, you got a pass from the cops that would let you drive all the heroin you could carry through the streets of New York without risking a day in prison. If you got stopped, like we did that day you got a flat tire coming back from the airport, you just told the cop to call the number Casey gave you and the cops would send you on your way. Those weren't dummy explosives in your trunk that day. It was heroin, right?"

"Right."

"You musta gotten a fucking hard-on when Casey explained to you about the number to call if you ever got jammed up. Me, I wouldn't've been able to see a way to turn that into profits, but that's always been the difference between us, Bobby. You could always see all the possibilities in any deal, whether it was trading baseball cards or smuggling heroin."

"Everybody's good at something, Moe."

"Well, I guess that makes it all okay. Hitler was good at killing Jews, and you're good at making money. So, whose idea was it to use your cover to smuggle drugs, yours or Tony P's?"

He looked like he was going to deny Tony Pizza's involvement, but didn't bother. "From when I worked for him a few summers back, I knew Tony was involved in all sorts of smuggling: jewelry, car parts, electronics, fireworks. You know about the fireworks. Everybody in Sheepshead Bay, Brighton Beach, and Coney Island knows about the fireworks, even the cops at the 60th and 61st precincts buy their fireworks from him. At worst I thought Tony would ask me to move some hot jewelry or bottle rockets."

"Bottle rockets. If this wasn't so fucked up, I might even laugh at that. But I guess when you went to him and told him about your sweet setup, he had bigger plans than bottle rockets."

Bobby shrugged his shoulders. "Once I told him, I couldn't take it back, not if I wanted to keep breathing."

"Not if Jimmy Ding Dong knew about it."

"No excuses, but even after Tony mentioned drugs I thought the worst I'd be doing was moving some pot. Not even you could get bent outta shape over a little pot. I swear, I didn't know it was heroin until I moved the first load. I told Tony I didn't like it, but he just told me that was too bad for me, that I should just take the money and keep my mouth shut, so that's what I did."

"I thought you two were old pals, you and Tony P," I said.

"Guys like Tony and Jimmy, they don't have friends. They see you as an asset or a liability."

"Better to be a living asset than a dead liability."

"Especially with drugs. Drugs are big money, Moe. Big as in huge block letters in neon lights. Big as in Times Square on New Year's Eve big."

I was curious. "How much have you made?"

His face lit up in spite of himself. That always happened when he talked money. "A hundred grand, give or take, and that's just from the deal itself."

"What's that supposed to mean?"

"I've invested almost all of it in the stock market. It's already up to almost half a million."

"Such blasphemy," I said with mock scorn. "Karl Marx is spinning in his grave."

"Fuck Karl Marx."

"What about Samantha?"

Bobby didn't like that. "What's Sam got to do with this? Why bring her name up?"

"Because you got her killed, you asshole. That's her badge on your chest. Sam was a cop."

He sat up in bed and swung his legs over the side. "What the fuck are you talking about, Moe?"

I pulled the letter out of my pocket and threw it at him. "Read up, Bobby."

As he did, I explained to him how I'd gone to Koblenz, and about the discrepancy in her age. I told him about Sam's dad being a Pennsylvania state trooper, and how Sam had wanted to follow in his footsteps.

"It all adds up," I said. "She was determined to be a cop, only no one knew about it. See there in the letter, where she explains that she was recruited to be in a special program to infiltrate radical groups using nontraditional means to finance their agendas. And when she hooked up with you, she thought she had hit the daily double. You were connected with every radical group at Brooklyn College and with major heroin trafficking. Just one problem. She fell in love with you. She had enough evidence on you to put you away for a hundred years, but she couldn't bring herself to do it."

Bobby just stared at the letter, open-mouthed, stunned. Then in a whisper, said, "But the bomb, who did—"

"Jimmy Ding Dong is my guess. C'mon, Bobby, think. Tony had to protect his interests. He couldn't afford to let Samantha fuck up your sweet deal. See in the letter where Sam talks about the investigation being compromised, and that she couldn't be sure who to trust anymore. I bet you if you find out who was in her unit, you'll find a crooked line back to Tony P."

"Huh?"

"That apartment she lived in, some guy claiming to be her father rented it for her. Only it wasn't her father. It was another cop. If her landlady hadn't forgotten about the suitcase Sam had stored in her attic, Sam's death would've gone down forever as a screw-up by some half-assed radical group. Don't you see, Bobby? Susan Kasten had nothing to do with Sam's death. For all we know, Sam and Marty just went for a hot dog at Nathan's that night and had no idea the bomb was in the car. The only explosives the Committee had were the dummy explosives you supplied them with, but it wasn't dummy explosives that blew up Sam and Marty all to hell. It was Tony P protecting you, his cash cow. That's why Jimmy Ding Dong tried to run me off the road in Pennsylvania. They thought I was on to something about Sam. The irony is that if Jimmy hadn't tried to kill me, I probably would've put down my trip to Koblenz as a painful waste of time."

"But why didn't the cops do a better investigation if Sam was one of their own? They always go nuts when another cop gets killed."

"Because no one knew she was a cop. That was the whole point. Read the letter again. Her name wasn't on the books, she got paid in cash, and she had only one contact whose real name she didn't even know. It protected her from being exposed, and it protected the cops who could deny any connection to her. I hope that half a million dollars was worth it to you, Bobby."

"Do you want some of it, Moe? I'll cut you in for half. You and your brother can go into business, take care of your folks, never have to worry about anything again."

I felt myself squinting at him in disbelief. I couldn't quite believe I'd heard what Bobby had just offered. "Are you outta your fucking mind? I don't want your blood money, Bobby. Forget all the junkies whose lives you and Tony are ruining. You can probably rationalize that away, but you can't rationalize away what happened to Sam. You'll be repaying that debt the rest of your miserable fucking life."

"You're right," he said, swallowing his words. "I'll never stop repaying it. I promise."

"Well, it's over now. I won't turn you in, Bobby. I should, but I won't. Tony P would have you killed the second you got inside because he could never trust that you wouldn't rat him out. I don't want that on my conscience too. I figure you'll have to run anyway because without your magic get-out-of-jail number, you've become a liability to Tony. Either way, you're fucked." I turned to go.

"There's one problem," Bobby called after me.

"Yeah, what's that?"

"It's not over. I have one more run to do. That's what Tony and Jimmy were doing here before, letting me know."

"But you're not protected anymore."

He laughed. "You think they give a shit about that now? Besides, Moe, it's not like I have a choice."

"Yes, you do. You have to run anyway. Why not run now, before this last shipment? I'll help you get out of here tonight and you can be on a flight to Mexico before they know you're gone. With all your money, you can get to Europe and make a nice life for yourself. You'll even have your guilt to keep you company."

He shook his head no. "Can't do it."

"Why the hell not?"

"For one thing, even if I get away, you'll still be here. And . . ."

"And what?"

"Tony and Jimmy have Lids."

"How?"

Bobby shouted, "Hey, you told me to find Lids, right? Wasn't it you who said I had all the connections? So I used my best connection, and Tony had the number you gave me traced. Tony said he would keep Lids safe. I had no reason not to believe him. How the fuck was I supposed to know you'd gotten yourself tangled up in all this shit?"

He was right. When I asked Larry to help me find Lids, I hadn't thought anything through. Now I'd helped deliver Lids into the hands of the man he feared most. After a moment of quiet came the revelation: Whether he did the one last drug run or not, Bobby, Lids, and I were all on the roster of the soon-to-be deceased. Bobby and I seemed to hit on that realization at about the same moment. We were both looking off into space and then, as it came to us both, we turned toward one another, our eyes locking together in mutual understanding and fear. If this was what seeing the future was like, I wanted no part of it. We are all born into this world under penalty of death, but we don't walk around with destiny on our shoulders. Now I felt like I would snap in half under its weight. Bobby too, from the look of him.

I said it first. "We're all dead, you know that, right?"

"I know. Tony P may be a fat *gavone* and a buffoon with his stupid magic tricks, but he's not stupid. Believe me, the guy's smarter than you think. He makes all kinda money."

"That's why we're dead. He knew your deal with the cops was gonna come to an end sooner or later. What, did you think he was just gonna give up the drug trade and happily go back to car parts and fireworks?"

"I never thought about that. All I could see was the money," he said, his face turning red with shame. In all the time I'd known Bobby, I'd never seen him red-faced. "Besides, I haven't been doing a lot of clear thinking since Sam got killed."

"Well, think about it now. The whole time you've been doing these runs, Tony and Jimmy have probably been looking for another way to transport the heroin and to cut you out of the deal. My guess is the only reason you're not dead yet is because all the pieces of their new system of getting the heroin out of the airport aren't in place yet."

Bobby seemed surprised. "Get outta here."

"Christ, Bobby, use your brain. If you've made a hundred grand, that means he musta cut you in for what, half?"

"Forty percent."

"Did you really think he was gonna keep giving up almost half of the profits?"

"Like I said, Moe, I haven't been thinking."

"The most fucked-up part of this, Bobby, is that I've admired you my whole life. I wanted to be like you. Shit, I wanted to *be* you. You always seemed to know where you were going and how to get there, and I've always felt lost."

Bobby didn't say anything to that and then he mumbled, "I can't die yet."

"Do you know where they have Lids?"

"Tony said they'll have him at the drop and that when I deliver the last shipment, they'll let him go."

"Yeah, and Santa will come down the chimney holding the Tooth Fairy's wing and the Easter Bunny's paw."

"What can I tell you? That's what he said, that he'd let Lids go if I did this last thing for him."

"Is this drug run the same as the others? You park in the lot outside the Eastern terminal at JFK, they load your trunk, and you deliver it?"

"That's how it's always works."

"Okay, I think maybe there's a way to keep us alive."

"You can't go to the cops. Like you said, if I go away, Tony P will have a hit put on me. I won't last five minutes inside."

"For once in your life, Bobby, you don't get a say in things. You do what I tell you or you won't live to see the inside of a prison. When's the drop set for?"

"Monday. I'm supposed to get released tomorrow."

"In a few hours, you call Tony P and tell him I ran, tell him I figured out that Jimmy was trying to kill me. He'll ask where, so tell him you think I caught a bus to Texas at the Port Authority. Tony will believe you."

"But—"

"Just do it. I'll call you in the morning with the rest of the details."

# CHAPTER THIRTY-SEVEN

There are months I love and months I hate. March, for instance. I have always loved March. October too. I love October because its still-warm days beg you to play basketball in the park: no sweat-shirts, no gloves, no shovels necessary to scrape away the snow and ice. I love it because while its waning heat invites you to play ball, October throws leaves on the court, leaves so much more beauti-ful in death than in life; leaves to remind you to savor those last moments, to savor what you have and what you have left. I hate January for its endless cold and sense of hopelessness, New Year's notwithstanding. I'd never given much thought to February, not until that February.

On that Monday in that February, late in the afternoon, the sky was already darkening, but not quite as quickly as it had darkened the week before nor as slowly as it would the week after. That day, the sky had reneged on its promise of snow, delivering only panic in its stead. I remember that the stores were overrun by shoppers buying out milk and bread and eggs. To this day, I wonder why it is that snow makes people hungry for just those three things. That day, not all promises of white delivery were reneged on. At 4:35 P.M., in the parking lot closest to the Eastern Airlines terminal at Kennedy airport, a van pulled up behind Bobby Friedman's Olds 88. A big guy got out of the van, keyed the lock, and popped the trunk lid. He moved three two-kilo bricks of heroin into the trunk. According to Bobby, the bricks, like the ones he'd moved before, were covered in blue plastic and brown packing tape. The big man shut the trunk, got back into the van, and drove away. Ten minutes later, Bobby made a call from the Eastern Airlines terminal.

"It's done," he said. "I hope you know what the fuck you're doing."

"For the first time in my life, I think I do."

"I hope it's not the only time in your life."

"If you can come up with a better option that doesn't end up with the three of us dead, Bobby, let me know. Get moving, I'm going to make the call."

*Click.*

✦

There were few benefits from my father's litany of failures. More often than not, my dad's going in the tank did not happen with a resounding clap of thunder but with a meek, pitiable sigh. His failures tended to play out like long, sad songs with only tears and debt collectors at the end. Although there was the occasional perk, like the time he thought he would capture the market on the next kid's fad and bought a thousand star-shaped Hula Hoops from a Japanese importer. They were about as popular as square eggs and kosher bacon, but Aaron, Miriam, and I had a lot of fun with them. It took him about five years to sell them off, and the loss was minimal. Then there was the time he invested some money in a scheme hatched by the sons of two guys he worked with. They were going to build household computers smaller than a TV set. Sure they were.

But one of his ridiculous investments was hopefully going to pay off for me if not for him. About two years ago, he had put money into a personal storage warehouse out in Suffolk County on Long

Island in someplace called Lake Ronkonkoma. Only my dad could invest in a business in a place he couldn't even pronounce. The idea was to compete with the big cold storage warehouses by renting small lockers and garage-sized compartments to people who could come and go as they pleased. Aaron and I went with my dad for the grand opening. We knew it would fail when we saw that almost no one lived in Suffolk County, and that those who did all had big private houses with garages, backyards, and sheds. If it had been built in the city, it might've had a chance. *If*, now there's a dangerous word. The building had sat empty for a year now. Technically, my dad didn't own any part of it anymore, but I still had a set of keys. And while it might not have been the perfect place for storage, it seemed like the perfect venue for our showdown with Tony Pizza and Jimmy Ding Dong.

Among the first things I learned about sports was that there were advantages, both obvious and subtle, to playing home games. Knowing which way a ball bounces when it hits a dead spot on the court, or at what time of day the wind comes up, or at what hour the sun drops beneath the bottom ledge of the backboard to shine in your opponents' eyes, can mean the difference between winning and losing. And since playing ball was the only thing in the world I really knew anything about, I let it guide me. Another thing I knew was that we couldn't afford to play this game on Tony Pizza's home court. Bobby explained that he was supposed to drop the heroin off at a body shop Tony Pizza owned on Flatlands Avenue in Canarsie, as he had previously. Scared, inexperienced, and outgunned, we were already at too much of a disadvantage. Flatlands Avenue at night was deserted, and Tony and Jimmy probably knew every inch of the place and the surrounding area. There was no way we could walk in there and have any hope of walking back out. That's why I dropped the money down the slot of the pay phone across the street from the warehouse and dialed the number Bobby had given me.

"Body shop," someone said at the other end.

"Let me talk to Tony or Jimmy."

"Who's calling?"

"Tell him it's the delivery man. He'll understand."

"Hold on."

"Yeah, Bobby, what?" Tony barked into the phone. "Get over here. I don't have time for your bullshit."

"For one thing, Tony, this isn't Bobby. For another, you're gonna have to make time."

"Moe? Moe, I thought you split to Mexico or—"

"I guess Bobby musta got that wrong, Tony."

"Listen, kid, don't let that tough Jew thing I said about you the other day go to your head. I'm not some shithead cop."

"Don't worry, Tony, I'm plenty scared. Me and Bobby, we both are. But we're smarter than we are scared and we've gotta use the only leverage we got."

"Leverage, huh? It's harder to use than you think."

"I guess we'll find out. Meantime, Tony, write this down."

"You know, Moe, that sounded a lot like an order. I never liked orders much."

"Okay, sorry, Tony. Let me put it to you like this: If you want your three bricks of heroin, I would politely suggest you write this down."

There was a second or two of confused silence, then, "Put Bobby on the phone."

"Can't do that, Tony. He's not here. As a matter of fact, you won't know where he is until we talk. I'm gonna give you a number to call and a place to call it from. When you let Lids go at that phone booth, I'll give you an address where I'm at. I just want to have a conversation. You get your drugs, and Bobby, Lids, and me, we get to keep breathing. After we talk and reach an agreement, I'll give you the location of the bricks. Someone will be watching you and Jimmy when you show up at the phone booth. If you don't have Lids with you, or if you don't let him go after we talk on the phone, or if you bring anyone with you other than Jimmy, I'll know it. And don't bother looking for the spotter. You won't see him."

"You're takin' big chances here, kid," he said, trying to sound calm.

I didn't take the bait. I was barely holding it together as it was, and I didn't want to give him the chance to shake me any more than I already was. "Write this down," I said, and dictated to him. "Got it?"

"Yeah."

I hung up the phone almost before I heard it.

Almost forty-five minutes passed before the phone rang again. I'd spent the time getting the warehouse ready and trying not to freeze to death. It was Tony on the line.

"Gimme the address, kid."

"Put Lids on the phone."

"Okay, but I'm also gonna teach you a little lesson about usin' leverage. You ready, Moe?" Before I could answer, I heard Tony say, "Jimmy, break the little prick's arm."

I shouted into the phone, but it was no good. I heard a snap and Lids screamed like he was on fire. I was sick to my stomach. The only thing that prevented me from totally losing it was the fear of what they might do next.

Tony got back on the line. "Listen to me, kid. Jimmy's cast has some nice benefits. You don't gimme that address right now, I'm gonna have Jimmy break every bone in this asshole's body and then he'll start gettin' really nasty. Understand?"

"I'll dump your drugs out into a sewer or I'll call the cops."

"You sound scared there, kid. You dump my drugs and you have no leverage, and Jimmy will kill you as slow and painful as he's gonna kill your little piece a shit friend here. And you won't call the cops, because I will see your friend Bobby fries with me. How long you think he'll stay alive inside? That's if he stays alive long enough to get inside. See, kid, leverage ain't always what you thought it was. Now gimme the fuckin' address and let's talk."

"Not until you agree to let Lids go."

"Gimme the address and I'll think about it."

"No. I may not be able to make your heroin scream, but I do have matches here and I'll make a nice toasty fire using your six kilos for kindling."

"Fuck you. Here's the deal. We're taking this little prick with us, but I promise I won't hurt him no more. Take it or leave it."

"Here's the address."

I knew Tony and Jimmy were now no more than half an hour away, and I could see that my plan was going to shit.

# CHAPTER THIRTY-EIGHT

The next twenty-eight minutes passed more slowly than the previous twenty years of my life. I tried to convince myself that that was a good thing, because they were bound to be among my last. Problem was, I was too scared to focus enough to see any value in the passage of those long, excruciating moments. And then I heard a car pull up. Two doors slammed—*bang, bang*—and then, a moment later, a third. Feet shuffled. Grit crunched and scraped beneath hard soles of men's shoes. A metal gate swung open with a squeal like the cry of a gull. Faint voices echoed in the hallways of the vacant warehouse. As fiercely as my heart was already thumping, it thumped harder still when I noticed that there were only two sets of footfalls and that there were other sounds: the soft steady *shhhhh* of something being dragged along a dusty concrete floor, and a hushed, ghostly moaning. The roll-up steel gate that was the last solid thing standing between me and my fate was pulled up.

"The kid's fuckin' us around," Jimmy said, staring into the blackness of the unit. Something crashed to the floor with a sickening thud. "Lemme go look for—"

I switched on the Coleman lantern, shredding the veil of darkness that hid me from their view. I was seated in the far left corner of the unit, maybe thirty feet from them. As soon as I switched on the lantern, I saw exactly what I was afraid I was going to see. Lids was sprawled out on the floor before Tony P and Jimmy. He was groaning in pain. The groan was feeble and constant. His face was a pulpy, bloodied, barely human mess, his limbs bent and twisted. If I wasn't already in knots and sick, one look at what was left of Lids would have had the same effect. At that moment, I wished the body I'd seen in the Fountain Avenue dump *had* been Lids, because that guy's pain was over. But seeing Lids that way did something to me. It hardened me, turned me cold inside. It made me realize that I couldn't surrender to my better instincts, that these guys meant deadly business.

I heard myself say, "You said you weren't gonna—"

"I kept my word, Moe. I didn't hurt the little prick after we talked, but I didn't say nothin' about what Jimmy would do to him." And he had the nerve to laugh after he said it.

Jimmy smiled his crocodile smile.

"You guys think it's funny, huh? I'll show you funny."

I shined the flashlight in my left hand at the front right and front left corners of the storage unit so they could clearly see what was there: a brick of plastic explosive in each corner. Once I was sure they had gotten a good look at the plastique on either side of them, I moved the beam of the flashlight so they could see the wires running from the blasting caps to two large batteries at my feet. I turned the flash along the wires leading from the batteries to my right hand. Then I showed them what was in my hand.

"You know what this is, don't you, Jimmy?"

"A detonator."

"Correct. And why don't you tell your boss what those silvery things are sticking out of the plastique."

"Blasting caps."

"Again, correct. You know a lot about explosives, don't you, Jimmy Double D?"

He didn't say anything, but smiled his chilly smile.

Then I talked directly to Tony, keeping an eye on Jimmy. "See how my thumb is pressing the button down, Tony? Anything that releases the pressure of my thumb from the switch and *baboom*! You, Jimmy, Lids, and me will get blown all to hell. See, I'd rather go this way than have Jimmy work his kinda magic on me."

Tony said, "You're bluffin'. Anyways, the shit Bobby was deliverin' to those asshole bombers was fake stuff."

I could tell by the look on Jimmy's face that he wasn't as sure as his boss.

"Not all of it, Tony. Remember, Bobby had to prove to them that he could deliver the goods. So the detective who was running the show gave him a few bricks to prove he was the real deal."

Tony P pumped up his chest and smirked. "Bullshit!"

"Come on, Tony, this is Bobby Friedman we're talking about here. Bobby, who sees all the angles in things. Wasn't it Bobby who saw that he could use his police cover to smuggle shit for you? Detective Casey gave him three bricks for demonstration purposes, but Bobby used only one. He kept the other two just in case. And I'd have to say, this would rate as a 'just in case.'"

"Bullshit!" he repeated. Only this time, there were cracks in the façade.

"Ask Jimmy if he thinks I'm full of shit."

Tony P didn't ask, but he did take a sideways glance at Jimmy. Somehow, Tony saw something in Jimmy's reptilian face and turned back to me. The thing was, Tony P, as ridiculous as his Santa Claus physique and magic tricks had always made him seem, proved himself even more cruel than Jimmy.

"Okay, kid, you're serious. I give you that, but what's the deal? If my merchandise ain't here, what's with all the drama?"

"I needed to buy some time, so that you wouldn't just walk in here and blow us all away. I wanna talk, to work something out.

And don't even bullshit me, Tony P. If Bobby was here with the drugs right now, only you and Jimmy would be walking outta here alive, no?"

"Bobby, he's smart, he knows money, but you, kid, you understand people. That's more dangerous, and it's worth more. So you wanna talk, talk."

"Here's the deal: we just wanna keep on breathing."

"I kinda figured that out already. I'm smart that way. But what's my reason for lettin' you?"

"Well," I said, looking at my watch, "if I don't call Bobby up in ten minutes from now, you'll never see your six kilos and you'll be out for all the money you owe the supplier. My guess is you don't wanna be dipping into your cash to pay him for drugs you'll never sell. You take a double hit that way. Second, Bobby will give you back the money he made off the original deal between you two, plus a little something on top as a sign of good faith."

"How much good faith?" Tony P wanted to know.

"Twenty-five grand worth."

"I'm still listenin'."

"Once Bobby drops the drugs off in a safe place for you to collect them, we're all through. There's nothing to tie you to Bobby. He's got nothing to tie you to anything. Me, I never had any real connection to you except the quarters you used to pull outta my ears. I don't know anything about your operation. And even though I know it was Jimmy that killed Samantha Hope, I can't hurt you. I got no proof."

"Here's the problem with that, Moe," Tony said, holding his palms up to the ceiling. "You, I trust. I swear." His expression was as sincere as a first kiss. "I'm sure you mean what you say and I could sleep safe at night knowing you would keep your word. Problem is, I don't trust Bobby as far as I could t'row him, not where money's involved. And what I'm thinkin' is maybe you shouldn't've trusted him neither. What makes you so sure he's even gonna be on the other end of that phone when you call him up? He's probably got the stuff stashed somewhere and he's halfway to California by now, or maybe he's already got a buyer for it and they're making the swap as we speak. See, the thing is here that I know Bobby like you don't. Bobby would never pay me back the money he made and there's no way he'd put extra on top. Sorry, kid, I think your pal fucked you and left you holdin' the bag."

"But—"

"And you know what else I think, kid? I think those explosives really are bullshit."

"You wanna find out?"

Tony P's face turned hard. "Maybe I do. Yeah, in fact, I'm sure I do. Jimmy," Tony said without looking at his muscle, "this little weasel's moanin' and groanin' is annoyin' the shit outta me. Do me a favor, shut him up."

With that, Jimmy reached underneath his coat and pulled out a .45.

"Wait a second," I shouted, thrusting my detonator hand forward. "You're forgetting something."

"No, Moe, I ain't forgettin' nothin'. I just wanna see how serious you really are. Are you gonna blow us all up to save this drug-pushin' piece a shit? You realize he works for me, right? Who do you think supplies him with his product, the welfare office?" Tony P smiled. "Fact is, Moe, seems like all your friends work for me."

"Wait! Wait!" I shouted again. "I'll let go of the—"

Then the world changed speeds. Instead of things happening in a smooth flow of actions, one second spilling into the next, space fractured. Movement is a series of rapid still photos, a series of blackness and bright strobing flashes; sound lags sadly behind.

Jimmy Ding Dong racks the slide of the automatic, a chambered bullet ejects into space. I swear I can see each individual tumble as the shell spins in midair and arcs to the ground, bouncing as it hits. Jimmy turns to look at me, his face coming in and out of focus. Then, in an eternal second, his face frozen in that cruel, icy smile of the crocodile, he has placed the muzzle of the .45 behind Lids's left ear.

I shout again, "Wait!" but there seems to be no sound. I release my thumb from the detonator switch. Tony P is only half right. The plastic explosives are fake. The blasting caps are not. There are two bright flashes. Smoke, lightning, but no thunder. Shocked faces, panicked faces lit by the flashes emerge out of the dark background. Jimmy jerks his gun arm away from Lids and raises it at me. Another figure strobes into the frame. Bobby! Something's in his hand. Something metal. Something I've seen before.

Sound returns to the world in a dizzying rush. I hear everything all at once: the racking of the .45's slide, the pinging of the ejected bullet shell against the concrete floor, my scream, Lids moaning, the blasting caps exploding, Bobby's footfalls. Then there is a distinct sound, a new sound: *cha-ching*. And suddenly I know what it is in Bobby's hand. This time when lightning comes, it comes with thunder. Jimmy Ding Dong's neck and shoulder explode in a spray of flesh and blood and bits of bone, some of it splashing onto the skin of my face. It's warm, I think, almost like human blood. Jimmy falls forward, his .45 skittering along the cement floor to my feet. *Cha-ching!* Thunder and lightning again. Tony P goes down in a heap, his abdomen and groin a bloody red mess.

"You fuckin' bastard!" he's screaming in anger and agony, but paradoxical tears stream down his swollen cheeks. "You fuckin' little bastard. I'm gonna kill you."

Bobby, his permanent smile gone forever, puts the sole of his boot against Tony's face, pressing it against the floor. He pumps the shotgun one last time—*cha-ching*—and places the muzzle against the soft flesh of Tony's fat neck.

"What's the matter, Tony Pepperoni, you fat, ugly fuck, nothing to say to me now? No fucking threats? Beg and maybe I won't kill you slow."

"Stop it, Bobby," I said, voice cool.

"No, this asshole's gonna pay for having Sam killed."

"Put the shotgun down, Bobby," I said, realizing that I had Jimmy's .45 in my hand and that it was pointed at Bobby Friedman's chest.

"Look what he did to Lids. He was gonna kill us all. He—"

"Put it down, Bobby. C'mon, just leave him for the cops. He's probably gonna just die here anyway."

Then, as if what he'd just done hit him in the gut, the air and fight went out of Bobby. He laid the shotgun, the one he'd stolen from Detective Casey's white van, on the floor behind Tony. Bobby dropped to his knees and began sobbing uncontrollably. Killing, I guess, isn't as easy as it seems, even if the victim deserves it. What happened next is not what I thought would happen, because I found myself kneeling not over Lids but over Tony P. I was kneeling over him and pushing the barrel of Jimmy's .45 against Tony's cheek.

"You wanna live, Tony? Gimme the name of the cop who ratted out Samantha," I heard myself say.

"Fuck you!"

I pressed the muzzle harder to Tony's cheek and counted, "One . . . two . . . thr—"

"Fitzhugh!" he shouted, his eyes getting big. "Detective Patrick Fitzhugh. He's on the Luchese family pad. We share info sometimes and they get a taste of my profits. Now get me some fuckin' help. Jeez, this fuckin' hurts, man. It hurts bad."

"Okay, when we get outta here, I'll call you an ambulance." I turned to Bobby. "Get Lids into the car. I'll clean up in here."

But almost as soon as I got those last words out of my mouth, Tony P's body started jerking like crazy. He gasped for air, clawing at his throat. Then he stiffened. His body just kind of shook like a jolt of electricity was shot through it. And suddenly it was over. This was no sleight of hand, no illusion. Tony Pizza, or Pepperoni, or whoever the fuck he had been, was no more. There was no rabbit, no hat to pull it out of, no quarter, no ear from which to make it appear. There was nothing left of him but his fat carcass and his beloved car. I looked away from Tony to Bobby, and away from Bobby to Lids, and wondered just how different they really were from one another. It struck me that I was glad there was no mirror in the room, and I stopped wondering.

*From Long Island Newsday*
**Bodies Found in Storage Warehouse**
Kathleen Eull

Last evening Suffolk County Police discovered the bodies of two men in an abandoned storage warehouse in Lake Ronkonkoma. The victims, identified as Anthony Pistone, a.k.a. Tony Pizza, and James DiLaurio, a.k.a. Jimmy Ding Dong, both of the Brighton Beach section of Brooklyn, were known to police and were suspected of having ties to organized crime in New York City. Both Pistone and DiLaurio died of shotgun wounds.

"The bodies had been there for a minimum of a week, or as long as two," said a spokesman for the Suffolk County Police. "An investigation is underway."

Sources within the New York City Police Department speculate that the murders of Pistone and DiLaurio are the result of an ongoing border clash between the Anello crime family and rogue members of the Luchese and Gambino families.

"In the name of peace, the Anellos had tolerated a certain amount of rival family activity on their turf," said Salvatore Barone, author and expert on New York's organized crime families. "But it was only a matter of time after two of Anello's most trusted soldiers, Chicky Lazio and Peter 'Cha Cha' Gooch, disappeared off the streets of Brighton Beach. Neither has been heard from in months, and both are presumed dead. Then when word began circulating of large shipments of heroin being moved within his territory, Tio Anello had to put his foot down." It has long been rumored that Tio Anello, the presumed head of the Anello crime family, has a strict policy forbidding his people from selling drugs.

"It's not out of the goodness of his heart," said Barone about Anello's alleged no-drug rule. "He just doesn't think the money he'd make is worth the risk. And with these two guys, Tio had to act or he'd appear weak to his enemies."

Speculation was fueled by the discovery of a huge cache of heroin in Queens by NYPD Detective Wallace Casey. The nearly pure heroin had an estimated street value of well over four million dollars. Casey got an anonymous tip about the stash of drugs. Most sources believe the tip came in courtesy of the Anellos. Detective Casey and the NYPD have refused to comment.

# CHAPTER THIRTY-NINE

On a Friday night two weeks after the events at the warehouse, Detective Casey picked me up at my folks' apartment and we went drinking at the Onion Street Pub. Although I didn't know it then, the Onion Street Pub was a cop hangout. The place was crowded and loud and full of cigarette smoke. The jukebox was blasting, and the atmosphere was much friendlier than I'd found it during my first visit. Even Angie, my dance partner, was there, but she'd let her blonde hair down. Of course, I didn't realize until later that she was a cop groupie. A lot of bar patrons stopped by our spot at the bar to pat Casey on the back. He had, after all, just made one of the biggest heroin finds in New York City history.

"Six fucking kilos," one drunk cop said, hugging Casey around the shoulders. "How the hell did you do it, man? I didn't even know you were working narcotics."

"Clean living," Casey said, "and luck."

"There'll be a bump in it for sure, you lucky son of a bitch. Let me buy you and your buddy here a shot to celebrate."

It was apparently bad form to turn it down, so Casey agreed and the bartender lined up three shots of Scotch. We clinked glasses and gunned the shots in single gulps, slamming the overturned glasses down on the bar when we finished. After another round, this one on Casey, the drunk guy faded back into the crowd.

The good cheer vanished from Casey's face. He turned, staring straight ahead. "Pretty amazing."

"What, the Scotch? I never really drank it before, but it's not bad. What kind is it?

"Cutty Sark. Smooth as razor blades," he said. "But that's not what I'm talking about, Moe."

"Then what?"

"The anonymous phone tip I got telling me where to find all that heroin."

"Like you said, Detective Casey—"

"Just call me Casey," he said. "Everyone calls me Casey."

"Like you said, Casey, it's luck. Maybe it's like they said in the papers."

He curled up his lips into a joyless smile. "That it was the Anellos. I don't buy it. Those guys would rather eat their young than rat out even their worst enemies."

I shrugged my shoulders. "Who knows?"

"You're right, and besides, not all my luck has been good. The garage where I keep the van I used to deliver the dummy explosives was broken into."

"Can't be a good thing to steal a police car. I hope the moron who did that got outta town quick."

"I didn't say the van was stolen, Moe. Only its window was busted, and the guy took my shotgun and the shells I kept in there for protection."

"Hope it turns up."

"I doubt it will," he said. "My bet is the shotgun's at the bottom of a lake somewhere."

Before Casey could see me turn pale, two more well-wishers stopped by and bought a few more rounds. By the time they left, I couldn't see straight.

Casey said, "I hear your buddy turned up, but that he was in rough shape."

"Huh? Oh, Lids, yeah. I heard that too." I wasn't sure if it was my head or the room that was spinning, nor was I sure it was all a product of the Scotch. Casey was scaring the shit out of me with his talk of the shotgun and the drugs. I needed some fresh air, and I bolted.

Outside, the cool early March air was giving me some relief. Relief or not, I found it difficult to stand, so I sat down on the sidewalk, my back to a cold brick wall. Above my head, lazy jet after lazy jet, engines whining, followed the end of the glide path to the runways at JFK. I was so drunk that I swear I thought I could make out the faces of individual passengers. Some of them seemed to be staring right at me, pointing down at me. Why I should matter to them was beyond me. I wasn't a circus freak. I wasn't feeling guilty about things. I hadn't killed anyone. I hadn't gotten anyone killed.

Mostly, besides feeling woozy, I was feeling profoundly lost. Before all this happened, what I thought of as being lost was really just aimlessness; I was adrift. School was then at least an anchor, if not a sturdy one. Now even that was gone to me forever. I had tried going back to class, but it was no good. I just couldn't force myself to care after seeing so much death, and the capacity for darkness inside people's hearts. There had to be something in the world for me to keep me out of the dark. I was watching another jet when the silhouette of a man blocked my view.

"Having fun out here?" It was Casey. He stepped out of my way and sat down beside me.

"Just thinking," I said.

"I've been thinking too, Moe."

"Yeah, about what?"

"About you."

"What about me?"

"Look, I may seem like just a big dumb schmuck, but I didn't get my gold shield by being one. The Suffolk County PD, they've got no reason to connect you or Bobby to those two dead assholes in the warehouse. On the other hand, it didn't take me long to find that Irving Prager was one of the original investors in that warehouse. Frankly, the world's a better place without guys like Tony P and Jimmy Ding Dong, so you got nothing to worry about from me."

"I agree," I said. "The world's a better place."

"You know, you've got all the makings of a great cop."

"Pardon my manners, Casey, but get the fuck outta here."

"No, I'm serious. Whether you're gonna admit to anything or not, you got to the bottom of two huge cases. You busted up a major heroin ring, and you saved your friends' lives. You did all that without an ounce of knowledge about how to do it. You're tough. You're smart and you give a shit. You're already a better goddamned detective than I am. You do a few years in uniform, and you're a lock for a gold shield. And there's something else; you're comfortable in there," he said, pointing back at the bar. "It's all cops in there, and you fit in."

"Maybe because there aren't any asshole cops in there like Nance."

"You want things to change, make 'em change. Be a cop, set an example instead of whining about it. And it'll get you outta the war."

We laughed about that last part there. It got quiet between us for a minute after that. Casey didn't realize at the time, but he'd given me the chance I'd been looking for since that night at the warehouse. I'd struggled with how to let someone inside the NYPD know that Sam and Marty had been murdered as a direct result of a dirty cop.

"Three cases," I said, "not two."

"What are you talking about?"

I didn't answer directly. "You know a detective named Patrick Fitzhugh?"

"He's a real prick. A face on him not even his mother loved. Why?"

Again, I didn't answer directly. Instead I took Sam's badge out of my pocket and handed it to him. "You found out about my dad owning part of the warehouse without too much trouble. Look into who that badge belonged to and see what you come up with."

Feeling a little better, I got up and went back into the bar. I turned around to see Casey palming the badge and starting to put two and two together.

# EPILOGUE –
# DECEMBER 2012

Through the front windows of my condo on Emmons Avenue, the sun was hinting at its rebirth. The oily sheen had returned to the surface of Sheepshead Bay, and the cold rain that had ravaged those same waters only a few hours before were now barely a memory. That is one of the glories of water: it has no memory. As I stared out at it, I imagined myself as water, as having no memory. Then, in the next instant, the images of that long-ago night in the warehouse came back into my head as fresh as the new day would come. I could feel Jimmy Ding Dong's warm blood on my face and smell the acrid smoke from the blasting caps and from the shotgun blasts. I could almost taste the iron on my tongue from the spray of blood in the air. No, I was nothing like water.

Sarah, yawning, came and stood beside me. "What happened after Tony died?"

"Bobby got Lids out to his car while I tried to clean up any hints of our having been there, but I didn't know how successful I was at it. We rode over to Lake Ronkonkoma and threw in Jimmy's .45 and the shotgun. Strange thing is that years later, when I was working a case as a PI, I wound up by that lake again. I'd blocked it out of my mind that I'd been there before."

"What case, Dad?"

"I don't wanna talk about it."

"Oh," Sarah said, "that case."

"That's right, kiddo. The one I fucked up that eventually got your mother killed."

Sarah put her arms around me and squeezed. "Forget it, Dad. I forgave you for that. We can't hold onto those things, not now. Did the police ever find the guns?"

"You know, there's a legend about Lake Ronkonkoma that the restless soul of an Indian princess lives in the lake. They say she drowned in the lake centuries ago and is forever searching for her lover. Whenever a man drowns in the lake, the locals blame it on the princess. They say she pulled the victim in to see if he is her lover. I guess the princess took the guns and buried them as gifts for her lover's return."

"What happened to Lids?"

"We dropped him off by the ER entrance to a hospital in Smithtown. Jimmy had broken him up really bad. He was barely more alive than Tony or Jimmy. He spent almost a year in the hospital and in rehab centers."

"But what happened to him after he got out?"

"I don't know," I said. "I was already on the job by then and living out on my own. I heard he came back to his parents' apartment for a little while, but he was still so broken. They fixed Lids's bones, but his mind was never right after MIT, and what Jimmy did to him only made it worse. He just left one day and never came back. My friend Eddie Lane said he thought he once saw a guy who looked like Lids panhandling on Telegraph Avenue in Berkley. That was the last I heard of him."

Sarah went and sat back down on the couch. I made some French press coffee for us. Me, as an old cop and PI, I could drink swill and deal with it, but Sarah loved French press coffee.

"You want some eggs, kiddo?"

"No, Dad, I'm not hungry."

I didn't like the look of her. The mention of eggs kind of made her turn green around the gills and she hadn't slept all night. "You okay? You wanna lay down?"

"Just tired, Dad, really. So what happened between you and Bobby?"

"Nothing. Bobby moved out of New York in the middle of March and I didn't hear anything about him for five years. I got a call from Uncle Aaron one day. He told me to go buy a copy of the latest *Forbes* magazine. There was Bobby on the cover. Apparently he'd turned his drug profits and other investments into such a fortune that he was rich enough to lend money to God at low interest. The article called him 'The Boy Wonder of Wall Street.' But he kept his promise to atone for his sins. While he was away, he found his way back to Judaism, something his parents always fiercely rejected. He made it a habit to give away almost forty percent of his yearly income to all sorts of causes. Everything from a fund for the families of cops killed in the line of duty, to groups against gun violence, to drug treatment centers. My guess is that he left most of his money to charity."

"Is that when you guys hooked up again, after the article?" Sarah asked, sipping her coffee and making a face.

"Isn't the coffee okay?"

"No, it's fine, Dad. So, you and Bobby . . ."

"One day in 1987 I'm in my office in Bordeaux in Brooklyn and I get a call on the intercom to come upstairs immediately. And when I get upstairs, there's Bobby in all his glory, a gigantic smile on his face. Twenty years had passed, but there was the same smile he'd had on the night I bailed him out of the Brooklyn Tombs. He was dressed in a suit that cost more than two months of most people's mortgage payments. He came down to the office and we talked. We worked it out. Our friendship from then on was more of a truce or understanding than anything else."

"But you invited him to my bat mitzvah, and he was at my wedding."

"Of course he was, and he no doubt gave you the biggest gifts for both," I said, shaking my head, looking again into the past. "We were locked together forever, kiddo. I'd saved his life and he'd saved mine. But Tony P had a point about Bobby. I could never quite trust him again. I had some sleepless nights in the years following what happened to us. Bobby wasn't supposed to show up at the warehouse that night. He was just so furious at Tony and Jimmy and at himself for what happened to Samantha that he couldn't control his rage. To this day I wonder that if he hadn't been so overcome with rage, whether Bobby would have been on the other end of the phone when I called. Part of me thinks Tony P was right, that Bobby would never have given up his money, and that he would have left me and Lids to die there."

Sarah shuddered. "My God, Dad. I don't want to think about it."

"Neither do I, honey, but you asked. I guess what's always plagued me is that I thought I knew the answer. The phone would've just kept on ringing."

"Whatever happened to Susan Kasten?" Sarah changed the subject.

"She went underground, but not in the Mideast or Latin America. She was arrested in 1992 or '93 in Waukesha, Wisconsin, the most Republican county in the state. She was a housewife with three kids, a dog, two cats, a minivan, and a husband who was an executive for a firm that made missile guidance systems. I think she's out of prison now and back home. Weird, huh?"

Sarah laughed. "A long way from Manhattan Beach and bombing the 61st Precinct."

"A long way, yeah."

"What happened to you and Mindy?"

"We got married and lived happily ever after."

"Don't be a jerk, Dad."

"She pretty much made a full recovery, but I stopped visiting her once I knew it was her who'd tried to kill Bobby. I couldn't live with that. Any feelings I had for her ran right out of me. Besides, by the time she got out of rehab, I was in the academy. I was the enemy."

Sarah said, "I guess I understand that." She sipped at her coffee again, her face belying her previous assessment of my French press technique. "Did Casey put two and two together?"

"I don't know. What I do know is that about six months later, they found Fitzhugh beaten to death at Bear Mountain. Every bone in his body was broken. A few weeks after that, about ten guys from the Luchese family were arrested on drug and corruption charges. Who knows? A month or two after that, it came out that Sam had been a cop. She was reburied with full police honors. I shipped her suitcase and documents to her folks, but I couldn't bring myself to go up there for the reburial. I'd already said my goodbyes. And poor Marty Lavitz just moldered in his grave because he was in the wrong place at the wrong time."

"Did you ever figure out why Samantha put the moves on you that night?"

"I'd like to think it was for all the reasons she said, but I think the truth is much colder than that. My guess is she was trying to turn me into a spy for her. If I had slept with her, she could threaten to tell Bobby unless I kept tabs on him. We'll never know."

"Dad, you still haven't answered my original question: how did you become a cop?"

"Okay, okay, already. Like I said, I left Casey on the sidewalk with Sam's badge in his hand. He came back into the pub a few minutes later and some more guys came over and bought rounds of drinks. Around three in the morning, we were both blind drunk and—"

Before I could finish the sentence, Sarah got up and ran to the bathroom. She ran so quickly, I didn't even have time to ask her if she was all right. Ten minutes later, she was back. She looked much better and color had returned to her cheeks. Before I could ask, she told me that she was fine.

"You were blind drunk and . . ."

"And I turned to Casey and asked him to tell me why the place was called the Onion Street Pub. He said he wasn't supposed to tell, but he said he would tell me under one condition. If I agreed to take the entrance exam for the police academy, he would explain the name to me. I told him I wouldn't. So he goaded me, saying I was afraid I wasn't smart enough to pass the test. That did the trick. You know how I hate that. I said I'd show him I could pass, but that he had to tell me why they'd given the bar the name Onion Street. He held out his hand, we shook on it, and the rest is history."

"You became a cop on a drunken dare?"

"I did, and it was the best drunken thing I ever agreed to. Being a cop was the only job I ever loved."

"So . . ."

"What?"

"Why was the bar named the Onion Street Pub?"

"Weren't you listening?" I asked. "I can't tell you that."

"Dad!"

"Maybe if you tell me what's going on. Why you volunteered to come down here so fast, why all the questions. Then maybe I'll think about it."

Sarah bowed her head. When she looked up at me, mascara-stained tears were pouring down her cheeks. I opened my mouth to speak, but she held her hands up to stop me and collected herself. "You've been so sick, Dad, and I had questions I needed answered."

I went to her and wrapped my arms around her like I had when she was a little girl. It had been a very long time since we had been like this together. Although she had forgiven me for the events leading up to Katy's murder, it wasn't ever the same between us. I guess she couldn't quite trust me, the way I could never quite trust Bobby again. Doubt, even a tiny shard of it, is a powerful thing.

"But why this question, kiddo? Why now?"

"Because I needed to know what to tell your grandson if your cancer comes back and you can't tell him yourself."

I was lightheaded, but for all the right reasons. God had finally answered with a yes. I looked up at the ceiling, and thought of Mr. Roth. "You're preg—"

"Almost five months, now."

Later that day, after Sarah had headed back to Vermont, I went to the liquor store and bought a bottle of Cutty Sark. I had moved up to Dewar's decades ago, but remembering all those long-past events had made me sentimental for the taste of Cutty Sark. My oncologist wouldn't have approved, so I toasted him, and I toasted Bobby Friedman, and I wondered about where Lids and Mindy had gotten to. I toasted the coming birth of my grandson. I toasted fulfilling my promise to my daughter. When the baby was born, I had vowed, I'd tell her why it was called the Onion Street Pub. We shook on it.

## The End

MYS
FIC          Coleman, Reed Farrel,
Coleman       1956-

             Onion street.

$24.95

| DATE | | | |
|---|---|---|---|
| | | | |
| | | | |
| | | | |
| | | | |
| | | | |
| | | | |
| | | | |
| | | | |
| | | | |
| | | | |
| | | | |
| | | | |